Laura Marshall is the bestselling author of four psychological thrillers. Her debut novel, *Friend Request*, was a Kindle No.1 and *Sunday Times* bestseller, with over half a million copies sold in the UK. Laura's books have sold in twenty-four territories around the globe. She grew up in Wiltshire, studied English at the University of Sussex and currently lives in Kent with her family. For more information visit Laura's website www.lauramarshall.co.uk or find her at www.facebook.com/lauramarshallauthor or on Twitter @laurajm8.

My Husband's Killer

Laura Marshall

SPHERE

SPHERE

First published in Great Britain in 2022 by Sphere

1 3 5 7 9 10 8 6 4 2

A CIP catalogue record for this book
is available from the British Library.

Hardback ISBN 978-0-7515-7506-4
Trade Paperback ISBN 978-0-7515-7507-1

Typeset in Caslon by M Rules
Printed and bound in Great Britain by
Clays Ltd, Elcograf S.p.A.

MIX
Paper from
responsible sources
FSC® C104740

Papers used by Sphere are from well- managed forests
and other responsible sources.

Sphere
An imprint of
Little, Brown Book Group
Carmelite House
50 Victoria Embankment
London EC4Y 0DZ

An Hachette UK Company
www.hachette.co.uk

www.littlebrown.co.uk

For Hattie, who always believed in me

Chapter 1

Liz

Today is my husband's funeral, but my grief has been stolen from me by what I've just found in the pocket of his shorts. Instead of crying, I am burning with rage. I kneel on the floor, his weekend bag still open at my side, swallowing down nausea. I don't have time for this now. My children, Ethan and Josh, are downstairs looking younger than their eleven and nine years, upright and silent in their formal clothes. They are waiting for me to go down and make it OK for them. That's what I have to do every day for the rest of their lives – try and make it OK that their daddy has died. Andrew has gone. There's no one else who can help me.

I close my eyes and shove the shorts back into the bag. It will have to wait. I paint on a smile and try to make my footsteps sounds light and breezy as I run downstairs.

'Right, boys! Time to go.'

In the church, the boys sit either side of me, huddling in as close as they can possibly get, my arms enfolding them in the vain hope of providing some comfort. The vicar's voice echoes up to the rafters, sonorously reading out the eulogy I wrote, the eulogy I put my whole heart into. I sat up at the kitchen table late into the night, crafting every word, retrieving every memory I could, contacting his family and old friends to ensure I didn't leave out any vital facet. I don't hear a word. All I can think of is my hand meeting that small packet. When she has finished, my husband's best friend Owen stands and makes his way from the pew behind me to the lectern, a couple of sheets of A4 paper in his hand. He stands for a moment looking at the papers, clears his throat and begins.

'I knew Andrew for over thirty years, since our school days at Winchester College. I was a scholarship boy, out of my depth and petrified. The other boys were either indifferent to my plight, or minded to laugh at me. Andrew was different. He took me under his wing, and that was where I stayed. Until now.' His voice cracks and he takes a moment to compose himself. He tells a couple of anecdotes about their school days that raise a few gentle laughs, and then moves on to talk about Andrew meeting me.

'Liz and Andrew were a great match, and I watched as first love, and then fatherhood, transformed him.'

Ethan and Josh huddle in even tighter. I screw my eyes shut, unable to feel the way I want, and ought, to feel. What I found this morning prevents the uncomplicated tears of grief that should be falling. Fury rises in me, hot and uncontrollable. My anger is partly directed at Andrew, because it has thrown everything I thought I knew about him into total disarray. He wasn't perfect, sure, but who is? But I never once suspected this. My ire is mostly reserved, however, for someone else, because what I found indicates there must have been a someone else. I don't know who she is, but what I do know is that she is sitting here in this church.

We finish with a hymn to which I hardly bother to mouth along, having let the vicar choose it, and a final prayer committing Andrew's body, wherever it may be, to a God he had little belief in. Originally I had mooted a non-religious ceremony but Andrew's parents had objected, and as I didn't have any strong feelings either way a church service seemed the right thing to do.

The boys and I are the first to leave with Andrew's parents following behind, his mother wailing and clinging to her husband who has aged ten years in the last three months. Mourners – family, friends, colleagues, red-eyed but offering supportive smiles – reach out from the end of almost every row. There are three serious men and a woman who I think are work associates. A dark-haired young woman I don't recognise sits in the final row, stifling tears, rummaging in her bag for a tissue.

The air in the churchyard is humid and oppressive, the sky a peculiar dark grey tinged with orange. Water droplets cling to the leaves in the trees, occasionally giving up and splashing to the ground. His mother wanted him to be buried here, but the Tyrrhenian Sea has so far refused to give him up. Behind me, she begins to cry, her raw unfettered pain echoing around the churchyard. I am dry-eyed, consumed with jealousy at her straight-forward misery. My friends Poppy, Saffie and Trina form a phalanx of support around me, a guard of honour as we walk to the car.

Afterwards, we gather in the village hall. The weather is still unpleasantly oppressive, but inside the hall the atmosphere is lighter now the worst bit is out of the way – or the worst bit for everybody else at least. For me, it's only the beginning.

I smell patchouli and herbal shampoo and before I know it, my best and oldest friend Poppy has enveloped me in a massive hug.

'I know I've said it a million times, Liz, but I am so sorry.'

I allow her to hold me, limp like a ragdoll in her arms, but I can't be comforted by her today. She releases me and steps back. She's dressed conservatively (for her) in a deep purple maxi dress and tan suede boots, her pink-streaked chestnut brown curls tamed into submission in a knot at the nape of her neck, a hammered silver pendant hanging almost to her waist.

'Thanks.' I'm aware I sound stilted but I hope she'll put it down to grief. 'Who are those lot, do you know?' I indicate a small group of men in mostly ill-fitting suits chatting quietly amongst themselves.

'They're the GreenEc lot,' Poppy says. 'God, I suppose I ought to go and schmooze them – sorry not schmooze . . . I didn't mean to make this sound like some sort of grim *networking* event.'

I smile despite myself. Andrew had had his doubts about going into business with Poppy, but when he'd been looking for a partner to set up a PR agency with fifteen years ago, she'd been the obvious candidate. Her personal life might be chaotic but at work she was dedicated and professional, an ideal fit to support his vision for a PR firm serving ecologically, ethically sound businesses. For him it was a gap in the market he was keen to fill, but for her it not only chimed with her green instincts but was a natural next step from working as an in-house PR for various eco-charities.

'It's fine,' I say now. 'Go and talk to them.'

'OK, I'll have a quick word. Back soon.' She gives me another hug, a brief one this time, and heads over to the group. The men's faces light up. They are the earnest types – all natural fibres and vegan shoes – for whom Poppy's alternative style and natural beauty are catnip.

When Andrew and I were first together we would lie entwined in bed, discussing which of each other's friends we found attractive. It sounds like a dangerous game (and probably would be at a later stage of a relationship) but back then we were so secure in our love and attraction for each other that it felt perfectly safe. Poppy never featured very high on Andrew's list, although in retrospect that may have been political on his part. Is it ever a good idea to tell your partner you fancy their best friend? But I believed him, and have never experienced a speck of mistrust over all the time they've been working together. Mind you, how many times have I heard that over the years? By the time you get to your mid-forties, you've witnessed a lot of relationship break-ups. For every one of my friends who saw it coming, there's another that was blindsided by a partner who behaved in a totally unexpected way, as if they'd been a different person to the one they seemed to be all along.

As Poppy passes Trina and Saffie, she gives them an almost imperceptible signal that indicates I've been left alone. As one, they descend on me like well-schooled dancers in a ballet, getting every step right. Saffie is as glamorous and elegant as ever. Her dark blonde hair falls in neat waves over the shoulders of the unfeasibly expensive navy trouser suit she's wearing over a cream silk blouse, demurely buttoned almost to the neck as befits a funeral. Trina's wearing a classic black shift dress that used to be fitted but is now loose around her hips and gapes under the arms. Her always-sharp cheekbones are more pronounced than ever under the wings of her pale blonde bob.

'All right, darling?' Saffie presses her cheek to mine and I breathe in a waft of her perfume, heady with jasmine. Trina gives me a brief hug, all angles and bones – she's definitely lost weight.

'Have you seen the boys?' I ask, aware that they've slipped from the orbit I've held them in so carefully all day.

'They're playing outside with Milo and Ben,' Saffie

says. 'Owen's watching them, don't worry.' I can sense how hard she's working to say her ex-husband's name in a neutral fashion, to not let their animosity spill into my husband's funeral. Of the two of them, it's Owen who has more right to be angry. Nine months ago, Saffie left him for Todd. Todd is an improbably good-looking, rich American with whom it transpired she'd been having an affair for some time, a betrayal of his best friend that Andrew – and I, if I'm honest – struggled to come to terms with.

'Julian's out there too,' Trina adds. 'He's setting up a cricket game with a stick and an old tennis ball they found in the bushes. Do you need wine? Food? Anything?'

'Nothing, thanks.'

A silence descends in which they regard me anxiously. They'll put it down to grief, but I know I'm being short with them and until this morning I would have said they don't deserve it. Along with Poppy, these women dropped everything to support me today, and over these last terrible three months. They came to the registrar with me when, having finally received confirmation of presumption of death, I went to register Andrew's death, unable to deal with it alone. They sat with me at the meeting with the vicar, helping me plan the service, knowing what I wanted without having to ask. They set up the projector for the montage of photos of Andrew I spent hours putting together as I wept uncontrollably at his innocent childhood face. But one of them has ruined everything.

'I could do with some fresh air,' I say, unable to stand here with them any longer. 'I'll go and check on the boys.'

I leave, not having to look back to know their faces are creased with concern.

Outside, Trina's husband Julian has set up a small suitcase as makeshift cricket stumps. He's calling out encouragement to my eldest, Ethan, who is preparing to bowl at his younger brother, Josh. Saffie and Owen's boys, Milo and Seb, crouch in the field, concentrating furiously. Owen is surveying the scene, his back to me, and I feel a throb of gratitude towards him. He's not only Andrew's friend, he's mine, too, and I'll be forever thankful for the energy he's putting in to make this an OK day for my children, a day which is so difficult for him personally. I give myself a mental pat on the back for encouraging my friends to bring their children today. It's so much better for the boys to be out here playing than sitting inside enduring a stream of well-meaning sympathy.

'Hey.' I touch Owen's elbow gently.

'Liz. Hi. Was it OK? My speech?'

'Yes, it was lovely. Thanks for doing it.'

'God, you're welcome. It was the least I could do. How have you been coping?'

That bloody question. I must have been asked it hundreds of times over the last three months and each time I've been at a loss as to how to answer. I usually fall back on clichés like 'as well as can be expected', which I think is what they want to hear. They certainly don't want the truth. They don't want to hear about the gaping hole that has opened up in my life, the shock and trauma of my husband being by my side for almost twenty-five years and now suddenly gone. Disappeared. They don't want to know how I sit on the sofa night after night, when the kids have gone to bed, staring in horror at the empty space at the other end where he used to sit. They don't want to know what a monumental effort it is to get up every morning, exhausted from a tormented night lying awake, and put on a mask of happiness for my grieving children who mustn't be allowed for a second to think that their mum is not OK. They don't want to hear about how telling my boys their daddy was dead was the worst thing I have ever had to do, or ever hope to do, in my life. How when I opened my mouth, I wished I could suspend time and let them have a few more moments of innocence before I shattered their lives and took it away for ever. How I can't bear that they have had to learn this lesson so young – that life is cruel and unpredictable, that things change and people can be taken from you in the blink of an eye.

Since my discovery this morning, I'm even more poorly equipped to answer the question.

'I'm OK,' I say, unable to muster anything more detailed.

'Of course you're not,' Owen says. 'How could you be? None of us are. But it's a million times worse for you.'

For the first time today, a sob almost escapes my lips.

'Hey.' Owen takes me in his arms, and for a second I allow myself to relax, my face in his shoulder.

'Do you think we knew him?' I say indistinctly into his shirt.

'What?' Owen draws back, hands on my shoulders.

'Do you think we really knew him? That's what I keep going over and over.'

He hesitates for a second before replying.

'Yes, I do.'

'You don't sound very sure.'

'I mean … to the extent that we know anybody. There's always a part of everyone that's hidden, that they keep for themselves, I think. Don't you?'

'I suppose so.'

'And that's OK. Just because you didn't know every single little thing about Andrew doesn't invalidate your relationship with him, doesn't mean it wasn't real.'

'Mm hmm.' I press my lips together to keep the words inside. I want so badly to share with someone what I found this morning. Would it be wrong to do it here, now? Owen was Andrew's best friend. If there was something going on, there's a chance he knows about it. Andrew let his guard down around Owen. Once, years ago, drunk and uncertain of Andrew following an argument at a party, I'd asked Owen if he thought Andrew really loved me. Owen said he knew he did, and then asked me if I loved him. When I said yes, Owen said, *There's your answer. You're meant to be together.* I take a breath, unsure whether I'm going to tell him what I found or not, and then Julian comes jogging over, and the moment is gone.

'So sorry, old girl.' Julian leans down, hair flopping over his forehead, to give me a kiss on the cheek. I didn't know people in real life said 'old girl' until I met him. I once heard him say – unironically – 'tally ho'. I loathed him on instinct when I first met him, assuming he would look down on me for my background, but actually he's never been anything but kind and rather sweet. 'Anything I can do, you only have to shout. Boys seem to bearing up OK.'

'Yes.' I watch Josh racing up the pitch as Milo runs for the ball. 'I worry they're coping too well on the outside – that they're not telling me how they really feel.'

'They'll be OK,' says Owen. 'But don't feel you're alone – let us support you.'

'Thanks.' I bite back tears again. 'I'd better go back in – let me know if the boys want me.'

I just about make it through to the end of the afternoon. Trina, Poppy and Saffie come back to my house, not wanting to leave me alone for the evening. Not 'our' house any more, unless you count the children who are in bed, exhausted after a day of seeing adults who are normally in full control of their emotions weeping and embracing. Enduring hugs and kisses from people they barely know. Coming to terms with their new lives, the one where they will always be those kids whose dad died.

We've all been drinking this afternoon, but the empty Prosecco bottles continue to accumulate on the kitchen worktop. A casual observer would think it a touching scene. A woman, widowed far too young at forty-five, surrounded by three other women, old friends, a group supremely at ease in each other's company. The kind of friends who can conjure up a shared joke with a single word, who can go for months without speaking and pick up exactly where they left off without drawing breath; who can count on the others to be there when the chips are down, to catch them when they fall. We all lived in London in our early twenties, and then one by one moved out to the same family-friendly commuter town of Haverbridge. Andrew and I were the first to go, twelve years ago when I was pregnant with Ethan, in search of green spaces and extra bedrooms. Owen and Saffie, also expecting their first child, followed shortly after. A couple of years later, Poppy was left homeless after yet another disastrous relationship and with Scarlet due to start secondary school, moving here was a no-brainer. Trina and Julian were the last to tire of London but eventually they did.

There were tears earlier, of course, but now there is laughter and shared reminiscences and stories. The conversation around the kitchen table ebbs and flows like the tide that washed Andrew away. I'm not saying much, but my friends understand. They give space to my grief, allow me to just be, present but apart from them. The very best of friends. They think they know everything about me, but they don't. None of them would guess in a million years what's going on inside my head, eating away at me – chewing me up and spitting me out.

They are my three oldest, dearest friends, and I would have been lost without them these past three months. They helped with the logistics of my husband disappearing abroad, presumed drowned. They liaised on my behalf with the Landell Trust, a charity that helps people whose loved ones have died overseas. They brought lasagnes and flowers and books and chocolate in those slow, quick, hazy days after we got home from Italy, days I can now scarcely remember. They took my boys – shell-shocked and dazed but still needing company and entertainment – on outings, giving me time to deal with the endless admin, or to do nothing at all but stare into space or cry on the sofa. They sat beside me today, holding my hand, in the church. They walked down the aisle with me so I didn't have to do it by myself. They tell me, over and over, that I am not alone. That although we're not related by blood, they are my family, and I theirs.

Part of me wishes I had never opened my husband's bag this morning, the one he took to Villa Rosa, the Italian villa where we spent his final weekend with these three women and their families. The place where he died. I hadn't been able to bring myself to touch it before, but this morning I was looking for his watch. I wanted to wear something of his at the funeral, and I couldn't wear his wedding ring because he was wearing it when he drowned. I forced myself to rummage through the bag, a brand new one he'd bought for the weekend away. The smell of him – washing powder and cologne and something indefinably him threatened to overwhelm me as I ran my shaking hands through the contents. His toothbrush was in there, and the things from the bedside table – his glasses, the book he was reading. Clean underwear he never got to wear. Someone must have packed this up in the aftermath. Or perhaps it was me and I've blocked it out. No watch, though. I felt something in the pocket of a pair of shorts that he'd worn on the last day of his life, before he changed into his evening wear. I slid my fingers in and they met a small slippery square packet. I thought perhaps it was a sweet, although Andrew didn't eat them. I certainly didn't feel any trepidation as I drew it out into the light. It was like a kick to the stomach. I was already hollowed out by grief and exhaustion and the overhanging dread of the day ahead, but this was something else entirely. Something that snatched the breath from my lungs, made me tremble all over and press my hand to my mouth, stifling the urge to vomit. I had a contraceptive coil fitted after Josh was born. Andrew and I hadn't used condoms since we were first together. So why did he have one in his pocket? In sick fascination, I turned the shiny wrapper over and over, as if that would make it into something other than the betrayal it represented.

I look from one to the other of the dear faces of my oldest friends, seated around my kitchen table. They are more careworn and lined than when we first met, but as familiar to me as my own. All I can think is: which one of you bitches was sleeping with my husband?

PART ONE

Villa Rosa, Italy

Three months earlier

Chapter 2

Andrew

SATURDAY NIGHT, VILLA ROSA

What an absolute disaster of an evening that had been. Andrew knew he hadn't covered himself in glory but it wasn't purely his fault. Todd was an arrogant arsehole, there were no two ways about it. Even if Todd hadn't stolen his best friend's wife, Andrew wouldn't like him. He wished he hadn't allowed Liz to persuade him to come on this stupid weekend away. Watching Todd and Saffie swanning around like the lord and lady of the manor had been grinding his gears since he arrived, and it made it worse to know that Todd had paid for every morsel of food and every drop of expensive wine. Liz and Andrew had offered to pay their share, but Saffie had said Todd wanted to pay. Liz had thought it a nice gesture, but Andrew had known all along that Todd wanted to be in control, and paying for everything was the best way to achieve that. He wouldn't be so smug when Andrew told everyone what sort of a man he really was.

He was still reeling from the weekend's revelations. His life was going to change beyond recognition. He couldn't bear the thought of explaining it to Liz. It was one thing to upend his own life, but doing the same to hers was a different matter. He would do anything to avoid hurting her – although, thinking of Trina's anguished face, he knew he already had. He wondered whether Trina and Julian's relationship would survive.

Underneath the sharp pain of tonight's events was a low-level, nagging worry about the business that had been dogging him for months. It was becoming harder and harder to work alongside Poppy, and he couldn't see any prospect of that improving. He should never have gone into business with his wife's best friend.

The evening had already become a blur thanks to the copious amounts of alcohol he had consumed. Initially he'd been drinking in an attempt to appease Liz by being sociable and pleasant, but by the end it had been the only way to block out the noise. He sat at the very far end of the garden, near the top of the steps that led down to the beach, watching as the lights slowly went off in the house. First the downstairs windows switched from yellow to black as everyone took themselves off to bed, and then one by one the bedroom lamps clicked off, leaving the house in darkness.

Andrew swigged from the bottle of whisky he'd snaffled as he left the drawing room. Usually, he'd wince at the strength of it, but tonight he guzzled it down like water.

A twig snapped and he turned, tension leaching from his body as he saw the figure he'd been expecting.

'Thank God,' Andrew said. 'I've been dying to talk to you all night.'

Chapter 3

Liz

Saffie smooths an imaginary hair back from her forehead and readjusts the studded leather belt artfully slung around her cream linen shirt dress. If you didn't know her as well as I do, you'd think she was sublimely relaxed and happy. What does she have to be nervous about, after all? She and her gorgeous, rich boyfriend are playing host to her oldest and dearest friends in a luxurious villa on the Amalfi coast to celebrate said boyfriend's fiftieth birthday. There's enough champagne in the capacious wine fridge to sink a fleet of ships. The food for tomorrow night's party will be delivered by the caterers in the morning. Tonight, Trina's husband Julian is going to a nearby trattoria that does amazing pizzas to take away. Saffie, like Andrew and I, has sensibly left her young children with their grandparents, allowing her to have a real break – although what she needs a break from is unclear.

She and the boys have moved into Todd's amazing seven-bedroom house with swimming pool, where she spends most of her time instructing the interior decorator and posting the results on her wildly successful Instagram account. It started when she was doing up her and Owen's former home, posting helpful tips about home improvements on a budget along with astonishing before and after shots of their fixer-upper. Since she moved in with Todd, things have stepped up a gear and she and her immaculate home – with its butler's pantry, its his and hers marble countertop basins – are now the envy of every middle-class yummy mummy on Instagram. And it's not as if we haven't met Todd before – we don't know him well, but she's hosted dinners at his house for us all – the odd barbecue, a couple of parties. And yet she is nervous.

Trina and I sit at the artistically battered oak kitchen table, enjoying our first glasses of champagne. We're decanting olives and ricotta-stuffed cherry peppers into earthenware bowls hand-painted in jewel colours and studded with turquoise. Saffie flits around us, doing unnecessary job after job. She arranged a food delivery from an outlandishly expensive website that the rich use when they go on holiday, which arrived shortly after we did. We unpacked it all straight away, but now she's rearranging it, crossing the kitchen with armfuls of a fancy Italian Kettle Chip equivalent and honey-roasted cashews.

'What on earth are you doing, Saff?' Trina throws back

the last of her champagne and reaches for the bottle that we didn't bother to return to the fridge.

'I think it'd be better if all the snacky stuff was in one cupboard. Otherwise we won't know what we've got left, and it'll make it harder to know if we need to go out for more supplies.'

'More?' I say. 'Jesus, we've got enough salty snacks to last us a lifetime, haven't we? We're only here for three nights.'

'You know what it's like,' Saffie says. 'You always need more than you think.' She stoops to retrieve a dropped bag of root vegetable crisps and stuffs them into a low cupboard in the marble-topped island. 'So all that stuff is in here now. I'm going to put the breakfast cereals where the nuts were, because some of them are too tall for that cupboard you put them in, Liz.'

'OK.' I bite my tongue and shake my head at Trina who's about to take the piss out of Saffie. 'Why don't you take these out to the terrace, Trina? There's a tray on the side there.'

Trina loads up the tray with snacks and moves towards the door.

'Hold on,' Saffie says. 'Can you take a few beers as well?' She nips to the utility room and comes back with a handful of bottled lagers. 'Todd might want one. Or someone else.' She adds a bottle opener to the tray.

'No problem, mein Herr,' Trina says, leaving the room.

'Do you think there's enough booze?' Saffie opens the wine fridge that's set into the end of the island and surveys row upon row of Veuve Clicquot and Laurent Perrier champagne. The top shelf of a wooden butcher's block to the left of the larder groans with Cabernet Sauvignon and Merlot and the shelf below it houses several different gins, vodkas and a variety of spirits earmarked for specific cocktails. There's another enormous fridge in the utility room stuffed with beer, white wine and mixers.

'Enough? If we get through the weekend without one of us being hospitalised with alcohol poisoning, it'll be a miracle.'

'Oh God, is it too much?'

'Saffie, it's fine. Come and sit down a minute.'

'But there's so much to do.'

'There isn't! You're inventing tasks. Grab a glass and sit here with me. Tell me what's going on.'

She sighs and her shoulders drop. She takes a champagne flute from the cupboard, slumps down opposite me, and picks up the bottle.

'It's ... organising this weekend, for one thing. It's been quite stressful.'

I swallow down what I want to say. Aside from updating her Instagram, Saffie doesn't work and now she's with Todd has endless cash at her disposal. How stressful can it be?

'I want Todd to have a good time,' she goes on. 'And Kitty.'

'I'm sure they will.'

She takes a swig of champagne.

'Kitty won't. She'll have a terrible time to spite me.'

'Is that still not going well?' I know Todd's twenty-four-year-old daughter had trouble accepting Saffie when they got together six months ago, but I thought things had improved. When I think about it, though, Saffie has never actually said so. She just stopped talking about it.

'Worse than ever, if anything.'

'What does Todd do about it?'

'Sod all,' she says, uncharacteristically unguarded, although almost as soon as the words are out of her mouth, she's taken them back, taking refuge in her usual 'everything's fine' mode. 'No, that's not fair. It's hard for him. Kitty's his daughter, he loves her.'

'Yes, but he's with you now. He needs to back you up a bit more.'

'He does, he does,' she protests. 'I dare say it'll get better in time. Todd always gets what he wants in the end. The problem is he's always been so keen on her making her own way, didn't want her to be one of those entitled rich kids who had everything handed to them on a silver platter. She gets resentful when she sees me . . . you know . . . spending his money, as she sees it. But I'm his partner. We live together. It's our money. And it's not like I don't contribute anything – the advertising revenue from my Instagram is going up all the time.'

That's undoubtedly true, but it must be a drop in the ocean compared to Todd's income as a hedge fund manager.

'What does Kitty do for money?'

'Events organising,' she says. 'Parties, launches, that kind of thing, I think.'

'That must be fun. Nice job to have at her age.' It's similar to what I used to do, although mine were boring business events. I imagine hers are a lot more glamorous. 'I suppose she gets to meet lots of interesting people.'

'Yes, I suppose that's one good thing about it. So . . . I was going to ask you . . . ' Saffie says, uncharacteristically uncertain. 'Have you seen Owen?'

Saffie's ex-husband Owen and Andrew are best friends, the longest-standing of the group, having known each other since boarding-school days and gone on to university together. Owen and I have always been close, too, and both Andrew and I have done our utmost since the split to make sure he doesn't feel betrayed by us, or that we've abandoned him in favour of Saffie and Todd. The others in the group haven't made any significant efforts in this regard. It's not been easy for Owen, being shut out from a group of friends he thought of as his, who have turned out to be on Saffie's side.

'Of course we've seen him. He's Andrew's best friend.' I take a mouthful of my champagne, stifling a cough as it burns my throat. Although I like the fuzziness it bestows, and I've learned to ooh and aah over it, all wine tastes sour and vinegary to me. I often wonder if anyone genuinely likes it or whether it's a big conspiracy – the Emperor's new pinot. My mum and dad used to drink cheap wines that I've since learned to sneer at – Blue Nun and Liebfraumilch – but I don't think they're discernibly different to what I'm downing now, especially after a couple of glasses. What I don't tell Saffie is the extent of Andrew's issue with her and Todd's relationship. I know he feels he's betraying Owen when we spend time with Saffie and Todd. I had to work hard to persuade him to come on this trip at all.

'How are things with you and Andrew?'

I put my glass down in surprise. I can't remember the last time anyone asked me that. When you've been with your husband for almost twenty-five years, it's not a question you get asked. Everyone is hungry for the details of a new relationship – the passionate embraces, the first declarations of love – but nobody ever wants to know how a long-married couple are doing, even though it's more pertinent. Naturally 'things' between new lovers are good, otherwise they wouldn't be together. What's the point of a new relationship, if it's not full of long afternoons in bed exploring each other's bodies and lives, leaving only to top up wine glasses or fetch a decadent snack from the fridge? In long-term relationships, you had all those meaningful conversations in those long-ago afternoons in bed and now all you have left is mundanities. There are peaks and troughs, but the light is not always distinguishable from the shade and there are periods of grey nothingness. I don't say any of this to Saffie.

'Good,' is all I manage. It's not a lie. Things are fine. Andrew is stressed at work, but that's nothing new, and between our jobs and the children there is little time for 'us', but that's every working parent, isn't it? We're not remarkable. Nothing to report. Hopefully this weekend will give us a chance to unwind and spend some proper time together.

'Just good?' Saffie says with a touch of pity.

'I mean . . . ' I'm fumbling my way towards expressing these thoughts when Trina's husband Julian bursts in wearing the classic ex-public-schoolboy-abroad uniform of chino shorts, a striped shirt rolled to the elbow and deck shoes, holding a pad of paper and a pen.

'Here you are, girls! What pizza are you having? Have you looked at the menu?'

'Why don't you get a variety and we can share?' Saffie says. 'Don't get an individual one for everyone, though. How big are they? Would a large one be enough for three? Or even four? Because everyone's been snacking, so they might not be that hungry.'

'Yes, yes, don't worry your head,' he says. 'Better to have too much than not enough, though. What about you, Trina?' he says to his wife as she comes in with the empty tray. 'Happy with anything?'

'Yes, whatever you like.'

She stands at the sink, wiping invisible marks from the tray's surface and drying it elaborately with a tea towel.

'Good girl,' he says. 'I'll see you in a bit.'

'Will that be enough, d'you think?' Saffie says when he's gone. 'If he gets one pizza between four?'

'It'll be fine, Saff. Don't stress. Is everything OK, Trina?'

'Yes, why?' she says, but doesn't wait for an answer. 'I'd

better get back out there and check on the drinks.' She gives the tray one final wipe and leaves the room.

'Sorry, Liz.' Saffie turns her attention to me. 'What were you going to say before all that?'

She looks at me enquiringly, but the moment has gone.

'Nothing!' I say brightly. 'Let's take our drinks outside.'

'Can you bring some more crisps?'

I grab a bag of hand-cut, skin-on slices of organic potato fried in extra virgin olive oil, assailed by an unaccountable longing for the neon orange dust and claggy maize of the cheesy puffs of my childhood, and follow Saffie out to the terrace.

Todd's daughter Kitty has taken up residence at one end, sipping moodily on a glass of champagne. She's intimidatingly attractive, all endless brown legs and sleek honey-blonde hair. It's the first time the rest of us have met her, but she's not troubled herself to engage with us. Todd himself is sitting with Poppy, on the steps that lead down to the lawn, drinks in hand. Andrew is at the far end of the terrace, deep in conversation with Trina. I see him as a stranger would – tall, dark and broad, not classically handsome, but ruggedly attractive – and experience a twinge of a long-buried jealousy that I thought was ancient history. Andrew and Trina went out together at university for a year or so, and had broken up not long before I met him. At first I had found it difficult that he had such a friendly relationship with his ex, although in retrospect it reflects well on both of them that they were able to stay friends. Not long after he and I got together

Trina had gone off travelling the world, at which I was secretly relieved. When she got back he and I were so happy and secure that it had never been a problem, and she's ended up being one of my closest friends.

When she spots me and Saffie, she comes bustling over.

'Let's sit and have a drink. You've been on your feet since you got here, Saff.'

The two women cross the terrace to a wooden bench and sink down onto it. I stand for a few seconds, surveying the scene. It's a beautiful early summer evening, the air still warm, the scent of elderflower drifting across the lawn from nearby woodland. Champagne fizzes in my glass, crisp and cold. The prospect of a weekend spent in the company of my dearest friends stretches ahead of me. I want more than anything to be able to loosen up and enjoy it, but something is stopping me. I tell myself I'm being silly, give myself a mental shake and go and join Saffie and Trina on the bench.

Chapter 4

Poppy

Todd stands up to go and get more champagne. Poppy surveys the garden which is just on the right side of wild – manicured would be too vulgar for this house. The grass is neatly cut, but around the edges brightly coloured flowers and feathery grasses riot, artfully clashing. The lawn stretches down to a low stone wall, beyond which a path leads to the house's own private cove, a picture-perfect confluence of white sand and azure sea framed by a dramatic, craggy rockscape that plunges seawards from the cliffs above. She's never stayed anywhere like it, and is unlikely to ever again so she might as well make the most of it.

How is it that Saffie has ended up with all this at her disposal, and Poppy always seems to be scraping by? Her daughter Scarlet (the result of a brief fling in her twenties, the father long gone from both their lives) is at university, but when she was younger Poppy was always the one who forgot to pay for school trips and sent her PE kit in on the wrong days. On several occasions she'd forgotten to pick Scarlet up and had to endure the humiliation of being phoned by the school secretary who colluded in the fantasy that Poppy had been merely held up, ostentatiously calling her *Mrs* McAdams, when she knew she was nothing of the sort.

Saffie's heart doesn't sink like Poppy's as the end of the month approaches and next month's bills loom large. She probably doesn't have a clue when the direct debits go out, if rich people even pay their bills that way. Poppy hasn't told anyone how bad things have got. They wouldn't understand – she gets a decent salary as a partner in her and Andrew's PR business, after all, although there haven't been any bonuses to speak of for a long time. What they don't know is how many times she's re-mortgaged the house to get herself out of trouble – there's barely a square inch of it that doesn't belong to the mortgage company and the last time she called them they point blank refused to lend her any more. Just as well because the mortgage payments take up an unsustainably large chunk of her salary as it is.

She tries to force what she has done to the back of her mind, as if not thinking about it will make it go away. She knows it's a mistake and she's going to rectify it. She just needs a little more time. Or a miracle.

She slips her phone out of her pocket to check there

hasn't been another text from Scarlet. She'd sounded wretched on the phone last night. Poppy had begged her to confide in one of her friends about how unhappy she was, but Scarlet said she hadn't got any friends, and she refused to access the mental health services available on campus. She'd barely left her room for days. When she started at university last October, she'd appeared to settle in quickly, but how much of that was a charade for Poppy's benefit? She could see which way this was heading. Scarlet had already missed most of the last month's seminars, and the more she missed, the harder it would be to catch up. The best thing for her would be to leave and apply again next year to a different university. To come home. A shiver runs down Poppy's spine. What if there is no home?

She watches Saffie taking a selfie with the honeyed stone of the house in the background, the latest in an endless stream of carefully curated photos for her Instagram. She's been playing the dutiful hostess but Poppy has seen how tired and drawn she is in the odd moment when she thinks no one is observing her. If anyone asks, Poppy knows Saffie would blame the stress of organising this weekend – ha! As if Saffie has any idea what stress means. She wouldn't last a single day living Poppy's life, dealing with what she has to deal with. She pushes that thought down as firmly as she can. She's promised herself she won't think about it this weekend, that she'll allow herself a couple of days off from the coruscating worry that has been consuming her. She will not think about Scarlet, crying alone in her room, or about the bills piling up at home – the final demands, and the threats of further action. She will force out any thoughts about Andrew, and about how Liz will feel if she ever finds out what Poppy has done.

Todd returns bearing an unopened bottle of champagne and gives Poppy a wolfish grin as he sits down beside her on the top step. He's movie-star handsome, the kind of handsome you never see in real life. The movie-star thing is exacerbated by his American accent, still strong despite twenty years living in the UK. No wonder Saffie had an affair with him. Poor old Owen didn't stand a chance. This weekend must be costing him tens of thousands of pounds. They haven't even had to chip in for food or drink. Todd is an extremely wealthy man. She sits up a little straighter and sucks in her stomach. She doesn't know what she hopes to achieve, driven only by the fact that Todd has the one thing she wants. The thing she needs. She's appalled by her train of thought, as if it belongs to someone else, someone who would do things Poppy herself never would. But Poppy is desperate, and desperate people will do things they never thought possible.

Todd pops the cork expertly and pours them both a glass.

'What shall we drink to?' he says, holding out his glass to clink.

'New friends?' She smiles and taps her glass lightly

against his, looking directly into his eyes. He holds her gaze. Maybe Saffie's life isn't quite as perfect as she would have the rest of them, and her Instagram followers, believe.

Chapter 5

Trina

Beside her on the bench, Trina can see the streaks in Saffie's foundation and the places where her eyeshadow has bled into the faint lines around her eyes. Her Instagram followers hang off her every word, but if Trina only 'knew' her online and not in real life, she'd hate her. She knows it's the way of things now – documenting everything on social media, not being able to have a single thought or experience without sharing it with thousands of your closest total strangers – but she can't stand it. She's always been naturally reserved – in her family they weren't encouraged to talk about their feelings – and with everything that's happened to her over the years, holding her tongue has become second nature.

She almost blurted something out to Andrew earlier, the thing she's been wanting to say to him for six long months, but she stopped herself. She does need to say

35

it – wants to say it – but now's not the time or the place. It wouldn't be fair to Todd and Saffie as hosts – or more pertinently, to Liz. Trina loves Liz dearly. Liz has been an amazing friend to her. Trina knows it wasn't easy for her when they first met, knowing Andrew and Trina had been in a relationship, but when Trina got back from her time away travelling, things had shifted and she knew it was going to be OK. She's petrified of what Julian's reaction will be if he finds out, but she's dreading telling Liz almost as much. The last thing on earth Trina wants to do is hurt Liz. She wishes there was a way to keep the truth from both of them.

'I'm so glad to have you all here,' Saffie says. 'It means a lot to me. Todd too.'

Trina's not sure it means that much to him, although he's paying for it so he must be on board to a certain extent.

'Thanks again for treating us,' Liz says. 'It's so beautiful here and it's great to have the chance to get to know Todd a bit better.'

She sounds sincere, but Trina knows it hasn't been easy for her seeing Saffie with someone new, especially because she and Andrew are so close to Saffie's ex, Owen. It's been strange for all of them, after all these years as a gang – her and Julian, Liz and Andrew, Saffie and Owen. And Poppy, of course. Her boyfriends never fitted with the rest of them, with their long hair and weekends spent on protest marches, and they never lasted long enough to become enmeshed in the group.

'Thanks, darling,' Saffie says, throwing an arm around Liz's shoulder and giving her a squeeze. 'It's our pleasure. It was Todd's idea, actually. I thought he'd want us to go away with his friends, but he said he'd like to get to know you guys better. He's got a golf weekend in Spain with his pals coming up, but I think he was looking forward to this one more.' She regards him fondly, sitting with Poppy on the steps down to the lawn, both of them laughing as he tops up Poppy's champagne. They look to be getting on well, although on the surface they have little in common – the hedge fund manager and the Greenpeace supporter with pink streaks in her hair.

'How're things going with Kitty?' Trina asks quietly, peering down to the end of the terrace, where Kitty sits alone. 'Why did she come, anyway? I wouldn't have thought there'd be much to interest her, coming away with a load of oldies?'

'God knows,' Saffie says. 'To annoy me, probably. Or top up her tan for free. To be honest, it's no better. Worse, if anything. She loves to tell me how amazing her mother is, how happy she and Todd were – which I *know* is all lies, Todd and Maddison have been divorced for years – but it's still not nice to hear.'

'Have you met her – the ex?' Liz asks.

'No, thank God. She went back to the States when she and Todd separated and she hasn't been over since we got together. It was a pretty acrimonious split by the sounds of it.'

'Does Todd talk about her much?' Liz says.

'No, not at all. It's ancient history, which is why it riles me so much that Kitty's always bringing her up.'

'It's her mum, isn't it? It's only natural she should talk about her,' says Liz, ever the peacemaker. She's always so ready to see both sides of the story. Trina prays she's able to do the same when she breaks the news to her.

'Yes, I get that,' says Saffie. 'But it's always so clearly designed as a dig at me. She'll mention how naturally beautiful Maddison is as I'm putting a load of make-up on, or talk about how damaging Maddison thinks social media is when I'm uploading an Insta video. It's so calculated.'

'That must be hard, but she'll come round eventually,' Liz says. 'It's only been six months.'

'Yes, and things have moved pretty fast,' Trina adds.

'Not that fast,' Saffie bristles. 'And anyway, what's the point in waiting? When you know, you know.'

If Trina had a pound for every time a female friend has said that to her, only to find herself consoling that same woman a few months down the line when the love of her life has left, she'd be paying for this villa herself. However, now is not the time for cynicism, especially when Saffie and Todd are paying for everything.

'Cheers to that,' Trina says instead, raising her glass to Saffie, to Liz, to the tranquil garden bathed in evening light and even to Todd himself who – unless she's imagining it – is sitting much closer to Poppy than he was a few moments ago.

Trina takes a large gulp of her drink, hoping alcohol

will dampen down the secret that rages inside her, squashing it, allowing her to at least have this weekend with her friends. She knows it will have to be unleashed, but not here in this beautiful place. Not now.

Chapter 6
Kitty

FRIDAY NIGHT, VILLA ROSA

Kitty put everything she had into not letting her expression betray her shock at seeing him here at the villa. She could tell he was fighting a similar battle when he clocked her. Luckily, he's been staying away from her. God, she hopes he can keep his mouth shut.

She wishes she'd followed her instinct and stayed at home, but the lure of a free weekend in the sun was too much to resist. You'd think she'd be holidaying all the time, but her dad has these fucking tiresome rules about making sure she understands the value of money. He'll pay for her to come on holiday with him because he wants her there, but when it comes to giving her her own money so she can go away with friends, no chance. He insists she has to earn her own money, like he did. He doesn't even help her pay the mortgage. Just her luck to have a self-made man for a dad instead of a chinless wonder like her friend Xanthe's dad who inherited half of Gloucestershire when he turned eighteen. He bought Xanthe a house outright for her twenty-first birthday and she has unlimited access to his endless pots of cash.

Of course, Saffie doesn't have to earn her own money. Oh, she'll have everyone believe she's making a fortune from Instagram, but she's not. Kitty knows real influencers who've got tons more followers than Saffie has, and they're barely scraping a living. Whatever Saffie gets is pin money. Kitty doubts it even covers her gym membership. It definitely isn't paying for her Botox. Kitty saw the bill hidden in the top drawer in Saffie's dressing room, presumably so Todd wouldn't know about it. You might think Kitty shouldn't be snooping, but it's her inheritance Saffie's pissing away, she needs to keep an eye on things. Thank God Saffie and Owen are not divorced yet, otherwise Kitty can see Saffie marching her dad straight down the aisle while he's still blinded by lust. Hopefully by the time she is divorced, her dad'll have seen sense.

She's only got to make it one more year, until her twenty-fifth birthday. That's when the trust fund kicks in and she'll be free and clear. But if her dad finds out the truth about her before then, he could cancel the whole thing. He won't give her a penny.

She's been lucky so far, never having come close to being exposed – until now. She never thought it would happen here. She needs to find a way of getting him on his own sooner rather than later, although surely he won't say anything. He's got just as much to lose as she has.

41

Chapter 7

Liz

FRIDAY NIGHT, VILLA ROSA

Saffie has decided it's a good idea to sit round the enormous mahogany dining table to eat our pizza, so I find myself laying out solid silver cutlery and heavy, gold-rimmed plates from the cabinet in the dining room. I start at one end of the table, but pause when I feel a pair of eyes on me.

'Umm . . .'

'OK, what is it, Saffie? What have I done?' Jesus, she's such a perfectionist.

'Well . . . they're fish knives, darling. Normal ones would be better. Or even steak knives in case the pizza crust is tough.'

I redden, my complete ignorance of fish knives yet another of the tiny yet significant ways in which I don't fit in, still can't pass for middle class.

'Right, sorry.' I begin collecting the knives in.

'Also . . .'

'What? Do they put their knife and fork the other way round in Italy? Do we have to have our pizza on tiny plates?'

'No, sorry, sorry. I was just thinking it'd be better to put everyone in the middle section of the table. If you start at the end, we're only going to be half to two-thirds of the way down and it'll feel . . .'

'Unsymmetrical?' That would never do for the Instagram story.

'Yes,' she admits. 'And a bit unsociable.'

I don't know why we couldn't have eaten on the terrace. It's still beautifully warm, there's plenty of seating and everyone was beginning to ease their way into the week-end. Now we're going to have to reset, recalibrate into this much more formal environment. The little groups that had formed naturally outside are going to split and re-form. Conversations will come to an end. In here, people might end up sitting next to those they don't want to. I take heavy crystal wine glasses from the sideboard and put one by each plate. We're going to need them.

Outside, the crunch of tyres on gravel indicates that Julian's back with the pizza.

'I'll go and call everyone in,' says Saffie, hurrying out of the room.

I'm bending down to get the last wine glass out when a hand caresses my waist. I jump and the glass almost slips from my grasp. Andrew grabs for it, but ends up gripping my wrist.

'Jesus! Don't sneak up on me like that!'

I pull my wrist away roughly and set the last glass in its place.

'Sorry. I was trying to be ... romantic, I guess. Spontaneous. My mistake, obviously. Won't do it again.' He walks round to the other side of the table and looks moodily out of the window.

'Sorry,' I say. 'I didn't mean to sound harsh, you just made me jump.' I go and stand beside him, slipping my arms around his waist, my head on his shoulder. At almost a foot taller than me, solid and broad-shouldered, I've always loved how small and protected he makes me feel. 'Please do it again.'

His body relaxes against mine and a puff of laughter escapes his lips.

'You should be so lucky. Sorry I snapped. I'm a bit on edge, being around Todd and Saffie.'

Saffie cheating on Andrew's best friend hit us both hard. We'd known other couples who'd divorced over the years, but this was the first close one that was due to infidelity, a subject Andrew has always been very censorious about. Both Andrew and I assumed it would be Owen, as the injured party, who got to keep the gang of friends, but somehow it hasn't worked out that way. We still see Owen, but on his own. Saffie and Todd, with their massive house and garden, tend to be the hosts of the group get-togethers – the parties, the kitchen suppers, the impromptu barbecues – which naturally excludes Owen.

'I know,' I say, anxious to be placatory. 'Thanks for

coming. I know it's not easy for you.' I lift my face and he puts his lips on mine, a warm, comforting kiss with a hint of something more, prompting a faint stirring of unfamiliar desire in my belly.

'Oh!' Saffie bursts through the door, grappling two bottles of wine in each hand. She appears discomfited for a nanosecond but she paints her famous smile on so quickly I wonder if I imagined it. 'Look at you two love-birds!' She distributes the wine at equal intervals along the table. Andrew steps back and I drop my arms to my sides, the tiny flame inside me extinguished.

'Grub's up, everyone!' she calls, and the others troop in. Julian is carrying a tower of pizza boxes, having clearly ignored Saffie's instructions to get one pizza between four. Andrew and I sit opposite each other at one end. Poppy flops down next to me and everyone else arranges themselves along the table. I'm glad to see Todd take a seat at the far end, away from Andrew. Julian is reaching to open the pizza box nearest him, when Saffie tings her glass with a fork. He snatches his hand away as if it's been slapped.

'I just want to say a quick word before we eat. Thank you all so much for coming. I know everyone's busy, and I – well, we,' she smiles at Todd, 'really appreciate you taking the time to come and celebrate Todd's birthday. It's been a difficult year in many ways.' Andrew drains his glass and reaches for the bottle to pour another. I know he's thinking of Owen, at home in the poky flat that was all he could afford once their worldly goods had been divided minus lawyers' fees. With Saffie playing hostess in a luxury villa paid for by Todd, the man who cuckolded him, I know who Andrew thinks has had the more difficult year.

'But I can't tell you how much it means to both of us to have your support and your company. Love you guys. Cheers!'

We all raise our glasses with varying degrees of enthusiasm, and Julian leans forward to open one of the pizza boxes.

'One more thing!' Todd's on his feet, his arm around Saffie, pulling her tightly to him. Her smile falters.

'We were going to wait to tell you all, but it feels right to do it now, so we can properly celebrate – don't you think, Saff?'

Saffie's eyes widen and sweep the table, taking us all in, then she looks up at him. 'Yes, OK.'

'I'm delighted to say that I've asked Saffie if she'll marry me, and she's said yes!'

Andrew swears quietly. I daren't look at him. Nobody else has reacted at all, all of us stunned into silence. They've only been together six months. Saffie's not even divorced yet. Colour stains Saffie's cheeks and I suspect she's on the verge of crying, despite her rictus grin. I can't bear it.

'Congratulations!' I manage to get the word out into the silence, and it breaks the spell.

'Oh my goodness, yes, congratulations!' Trina, who is next to Saffie, gives her an enormous hug, and kisses Todd on the cheek. 'What wonderful news.'

'That's lovely news, chaps,' Julian says, reaching across the table to shake Todd's hand and blowing Saffie a kiss.

I nudge Andrew's foot with mine under the table, willing him not to make a scene.

'Congratulations,' he says dully, raising his glass and knocking the contents back in one.

'That's great,' Poppy says. 'Congrats to you both.' To everyone else she probably sounds genuine, but I know her well enough to be positive she's faking it.

The only one who hasn't yet reacted is Kitty. She is sitting very still, her glass on the table in front of her. All day she's been coated in a veneer of sophistication and supercilious boredom, but in this moment she's like a lost little girl. Todd turns to her expectantly. I can't believe he's chosen to tell her along with the rest of us, virtual strangers.

'What do you say, Kit?' he says triumphantly.

'Congratulations,' she says in a monotone, picking up her glass.

'We know it's quick,' Saffie puts in hurriedly, 'but it just feels right. And of course it won't happen for a while – I'm still technically married, after all.' She laughs nervously and risks a glance at Andrew, who is gazing studiously at his plate.

'Right,' says Julian, 'I'm starving. Let's eat. Can I tempt you with a slice of this one, girls?' He offers Poppy and me a pizza oozing with soft cheese and topped with rings of vivid scarlet chilli and ribbons of salty cured ham.

We each take a slice and he turns towards the other end of the table.

'That was a bit of a shocker, wasn't it?' I say under my breath to Poppy.

Poppy is my best friend, the first person I met at university. She had the room next to me in halls, and on the first day she knocked on my door and confidently introduced herself, like an adult. I'd been sitting on my bed since my parents left, trying not to cry. I'd been waiting for this day for years, the day I finally spread my wings and got away from my parents. Having used an inheritance to send me to private school, they weren't like the parents of the other girls who called tea 'supper' and went skiing at October half-term. But when they'd gone, I could only remember Mum bringing in tea and biscuits as we sat and watched telly together, or Dad patiently sitting in the car outside parties until I emerged, blatantly hammered, then driving me home and helping me get to bed without alerting Mum to the fact that I was drunk. Poppy had taken one look at me and declared that I needed a drink. We were inseparable for the following three years.

'Just a bit,' she says. 'What do you think?'

I notice Saffie eyeing us up and realise what matters now is showing our support.

'Later, yeah?'

Poppy clocks Saffie too and nods in agreement.

'How are you?' she says. 'I've hardly seen you since we arrived.'

'I'm fine,' I say automatically.

'Really?' she regards me sternly, her bullshit detector kicking in.

'What? Oh no, honestly, I'm OK. Andrew's been a bit preoccupied recently, but I think that's work stress ... you'd know more about that than me.'

Andrew never talks much about his and Poppy's PR agency. I suppose I don't talk about work either, not that's there much to say about my admin job in the admissions department of the local college. The best I can say about it is it's part-time and fits in with the kids. I don't know how it got decided that Andrew's career would be the one we would prioritise. When we met, we were both on course for interesting, fulfilling careers, and when we had Ethan eleven years ago, I was determined that motherhood wouldn't change that. That feels very naïve now. I did go back to work after maternity leave, but I'd underestimated how draining it would be trying to do everything else my life now demanded of me around a full-time career. Andrew was very supportive of me seeking a less full-on job and at the time I was grateful. But sometimes I question why it was me and not Andrew who had to make the choice between parenthood and career, and why – when it was clear something had to give – that something had to be me.

'What has he said about work?' Poppy says.

'Nothing, but I can tell he's worried. He goes quiet.'

'Everything's ticking over OK,' Poppy says vaguely. 'I don't think there's anything too much for him to stress about there.'

'Maybe he's having a mid-life crisis then,' I say, as if I'm joking. 'What about you? You and the birthday boy looked very cosy out there on the step.'

'Todd? We were just talking.'

'Poppy! You've gone red!' I laugh delightedly. 'I wouldn't have thought he was your type!'

'Don't be ridiculous,' she says. 'He isn't, and anyway, I'd never do that to Saffie.'

'I know,' I say, taken aback. Despite her alternative lifestyle, Poppy's always been very critical of anyone cheating on their partner. 'I was only joking.'

'Oh God, sorry, love. I'm a bit jittery myself.'

'Why, what's up?'

'Work stress, you know . . . and . . . '

'But you said everything was all right at the agency.'

'Yeah. It is, it is,' she says. 'It's . . . ' she lowers her voice, 'I'm worried about Scarlet.'

'Oh no, why?' Guilt pricks me. Scarlet is my unofficial goddaughter (Poppy would never have done anything as traditional as having her christened). When she was little, I used to take her for days out and have her round for sleepovers to give Poppy a break. Since I had the boys, and Scarlet became a teenager more interested in getting drunk with her friends than popcorn and a movie with a middle-aged woman, I've seen her less and less.

'She's miserable at university.'

'Poor thing. Still, she'll be home for the summer holidays soon. Things will look brighter when she goes back for her second year.'

'I'm not sure she will be going back at this rate. She's not going to lectures, she says she's got no friends. She doesn't leave her room.' She inhales sharply to calm the wobble in her voice.

'Oh Pops, I'm sorry. Would she see a counsellor? They must have them on campus.'

'They do but she won't make an appointment, and I'm not there. I can't make her.'

'That's such a worry. But as I said, at least she'll be home for the summer soon, and you can try and get her some help while she's with you.'

'Yes, that's true.'

'In the meantime, we must try and enjoy all this. It might be the only chance we ever get to stay somewhere like this.'

'Yes.' She doesn't sound convinced.

'What is it?' I know her too well not to sense the doubt.

'This makes me sound awful, so don't hate me.'

'Promise.' I could never hate Poppy. She's seen me through thick and thin.

'I'm finding it difficult – being here, in this house, with you guys all in couples. I'm happy on my own, but it's not easy being the lone adult in the family, and – you know, I'm just about scraping by, what with Scarlet at uni and everything. And here's Saffie waltzing straight from one relationship into another with a man who's not only gorgeous but a bloody millionaire. And now they're getting married.'

'That doesn't make you sound awful. We wouldn't be

51

human if we weren't dying of jealousy at all this.' I wave around at the elaborately corniced ceiling, the crystal chandelier that hangs over our heads, the furniture that definitely didn't come from Ikea. 'But money isn't everything. Saffie's got her troubles.'

'Like what?' Poppy leans in.

'The split from Owen, obviously, and all that hooha over custody of the boys. Plus ... ' I lower my voice further, 'Kitty's no happier than she was about Saffie waltzing in, as you put it, and I don't think for a moment tonight's news is going to improve that.'

'What are you two whispering about?' Trina says from across the table, a momentary lull having fallen in her conversation with Andrew.

I check the others out. Todd, Saffie and Julian are engrossed in a conversation about the vineyard we're going to tomorrow. Kitty is ostensibly involved in the discussion, but she's silent, staring blankly ahead of her. I lean in to fill Trina in when Poppy butts in.

'I was just moaning about Scarlet, and how I don't know what's going on in her life any more.'

I look at her in surprise but she stays focused on Trina.

'That's teenagers for you, though, right?' says Trina. 'Especially now she's left home.'

'I know. I'm being silly. But it's so much harder being a teenager than it was when we were kids. Social media and all that crap. It feeds their insecurities.'

Saffie swings round.

'What about social media?' she says, hackles rising.

'It's OK, I wasn't talking about you,' Poppy says. 'I was saying how it's trickier for teenagers these days with all the pressure from social media.'

'It does a lot of good too,' Saffie says pompously. 'Teenagers don't have to wait to leave home to find their tribe – online communities can be a great source of support and companionship for all sorts of reasons.'

'Sure, I totally agree,' Poppy says.

'I'm dreading it,' I say glumly, thinking of Josh and Ethan. 'Even at their age they're obsessed with watching people play computer games on YouTube, and I fear it's only going to get worse.'

'Tell me about it,' Saffie says. 'Milo and Ben are the same.'

The moment passes and the conversation moves on, but I'm left with a sour taste in my mouth. Poppy's unhappy. Trina seems uptight and anxious. I can hear Julian making polite enquiries of Todd about when and where they're hoping to get married, but neither Trina, Poppy or I have asked Saffie anything. For a group of women who are meant to be each other's closest friends, there's an awful lot we're not talking about.

Chapter 8

Kitty

It's taking everything Kitty's got to keep a neutral expression as Saffie blethers on about wedding venues to that awful overgrown public schoolboy, Julian – a type Kitty comes across at work all the time. She's not only reeling from the news itself which is bad enough, but how *dare* her father tell her along with these ... nobodies that he barely knows and what's worse, are Saffie's friends? Is that really how little he thinks of her? She thought at least he was proud of her for making her own way like he wants – although he doesn't know exactly how she does it. She stupidly thought that the one good thing about him not supporting her financially was that he saw her as an equal. She thought she was finally good enough, but she is to him what she's always been – an inconvenience, a disappointment, a reminder of her mother.

She takes a bite of pizza, forcing herself to chew and

swallow methodically although she tastes nothing. She washes it down with champagne so it doesn't stick in her gullet along with this new and unwanted information about her father and Saffie. She'd foolishly assumed Saffie would eventually go the way of Todd's previous girlfriends, a series of glamorous gold diggers each a little younger than the last. She should have realised Saffie was a different proposition – a mere five years younger than Todd for a start and with a career of her own, however vapid. And Saffie has two children. Once they are married, she won't be content with Todd treating them like stepchildren, like the cuckoos they are. She'll insist that Milo and Ben are treated as if they are his own – right down to what they inherit. Indeed, if Kitty isn't careful, Saffie and her children could end up with everything.

She has seen how her father is in business – ruthless, never giving anyone a second chance. She mustn't give him any ammunition that could be used against her. If she can make it through the next year without him finding out the truth about her, she'll have her trust fund and he won't be able to take it away from her. But there's someone here who could ruin everything. Kitty needs to find a way of making sure he keeps his mouth shut.

Chapter 9

Liz

No sooner has a bottle of wine been placed on the table than it's been emptied and another called for. I'm aware of the need to pace myself – it's Todd's birthday bash proper tomorrow night. I ought to save myself for that. No one else seems to have got the memo, though. Aside from Julian asking polite questions about wedding plans, no one's talking about Todd and Saffie's announcement. There's a sense that everyone's waiting until they're not there to discuss it.

Andrew hasn't spoken for a while.

'Are you OK?' I mouth across the table at him.

He nods briefly, frowning, not wanting me to draw attention to him, but it's too late. Trina turns to him.

'You're very quiet,' she says, slurring her words. 'How do you think your mate Owen's going to take the news?'

'My mate? He's all of our mate, surely,' Andrew says tightly.

56

'Not now, Trina,' Julian hisses at her, before turning back to Saffie.

'All right, sorry, sorry. How's the PR game, Andrew?'

'Not bad,' he says, 'all things considered. It's not the greatest climate for a small business at the moment.'

Unfortunately, a lull has fallen at the other end of the table, and Todd hears him.

'Ah, it's like that workman with his tools,' he says. 'A bad business always blames the climate.'

'Todd!' Saffie remonstrates, but her tone is that of an indulgent mother to her child, not someone who's genuinely offended.

Andrew says nothing but there's a tell-tale twitch in his eyelid. As he reaches to take another slice of pizza, his sleeve catches a glass of red wine and it spills. I mop at it ineffectually with a serviette, but it's soaking into the tablecloth, bleeding unstoppably into the fibres.

'Don't worry, Liz, the cleaner can sort that,' Saffie says. 'I'll text her when we've finished and she'll come in and clear everything up.'

'You met with that new client recently, though, didn't you?' I say to Andrew, wanting to defend him, to show Todd that Andrew might not be a high-flying financial whizz like him, but he's hardly stacking shelves in the supermarket – he owns and runs a successful business.

'What client?' Poppy says.

'You know, the financial company – DOSH, isn't it?' I say to Andrew.

'DOSH?' Poppy sounds horrified. 'You said you weren't going to pursue that!'

'For God's sake, Liz, let's not talk about this now,' Andrew mutters, shooting daggers at me. It's not my fault, though – if he didn't want me to talk about it, he should have told me so.

'We're supposed to represent ethically conscious companies!' Poppy splutters. 'DOSH is the opposite of that! They're practically criminal!'

'Criminal?' says Andrew. 'For God's sake, Poppy, they're a financial services company.'

'They're little more than a payday loan outfit. I am *not* doing their PR.'

'Beggars can't be choosers, eh, Poppy?' Todd says unpleasantly.

She reddens. Andrew eyeballs him with undisguised dislike.

'Like I said, we can talk about this another time,' he says to Poppy. 'Maybe when we sit down next week to go through the accounts.'

'Fine,' she says, her former bravado evaporated. 'Just going to the loo.' She pushes her chair back and stumbles from the room.

I saw at the crust of my pizza, trying to blink back hot tears of humiliation. Trina drains the last of a bottle of wine into her glass.

'Pace yourself, my darling?' Julian suggests mildly.

'We're on holiday, for Christ's sake!' she says. 'Is there any more of this one, it's delicious?'

'I think so,' says Saffie. 'Let me go and see.'

'I'll go, sweetheart,' Todd says, standing up.

'Thank you.' She looks up at him adoringly and he bends and gives her a lingering kiss on the lips before leaving the room. Opposite, Kitty radiates pure revulsion.

'Give it a rest, you two,' Trina giggles. 'You'll make us old marrieds jealous. I can't remember the last time you kissed me like that, can you, Julian? As for anything else, forget it! Julian's got this mask for his sleep apnoea, haven't you, Ju? Makes him look like the elephant man. Once he puts it on, I know that's it for the night, nothing doing.'

'Yes, you pick up your book with a sigh of relief, don't you?' Julian's trying to sound jokey and unconcerned, but his jaw is clenched. I've never seen Trina like this before. She'll have a few drinks but only to get merry. She's usually reserved to the point of secretive. Tonight, she's out of control, teetering on the edge of something unpredictable and dangerous.

'Do you want my advice, Kitty?' Trina waves her glass down the table, wine slopping out unnoticed onto her hand, and goes on, not waiting for an answer. 'Don't get married.'

Julian's head goes down, waiting for it to be over. He's given up trying to stop her.

'Nothing against you, Julian. I love you. Or you, Saff, I'm sure you and Todd'll be deliriously happy. But you're a beautiful girl, Kitty. The world's your oyster. Don't rush into anything.'

'I wasn't intending to,' Kitty drawls, horrified by this drunken, middle-aged display.

'Sensible girl,' Trina says, plonking her glass down on the table, spilling yet more wine. 'Here's another word of advice – don't have kids. You'll be much happier.'

'I think that's something Kitty can decide for herself, don't you?' Julian says, every word stretched taut. Trina has always said that her and Julian's decision not to have children was entirely mutual, but I've sometimes thought, watching Julian playing with my own kids, that perhaps it was driven more by her.

'Did you mention you'd picked up some ice cream at the trattoria, Julian?' I say with false cheeriness.

'Yes,' he says gratefully. 'It's in the freezer.'

'I'll get it,' I say. 'Has everyone finished with the pizza?' I don't wait for an answer and start collecting in the plates.

Poppy re-enters the room and sits down, not clocking the atmosphere – or perhaps assuming it's left over from her exchange with Andrew. She's flushed and I wonder if she's had too much to drink too.

'I'll give you a hand,' Andrew says, clearly grateful for the opportunity to escape for a short while. As we leave the room, Todd is coming back in. He stands aside to let us through with an exaggerated bow.

In the kitchen, we load the plates into the dishwasher.

'I'm sorry if I was short with you,' he says. 'I didn't tell Poppy about DOSH because it never came to anything, and I knew she wouldn't be comfortable with it. It was only a preliminary meeting, and as it didn't work out, I thought I might as well avoid the confrontation with her. I should have told you not to mention it.'

'That's OK, although I wish you had.'

'I didn't think you'd remember – I didn't know you were actually listening when I talk about work.' He grins and pulls me towards him, kissing me on the forehead.

'I suppose we'd better go back in,' I say after a moment.

'Do we have to?' he groans. 'Can't we go to bed? I'd love to spend a bit of time just the two of us this weekend.'

'No, you can't,' says Julian, coming in and opening the freezer. 'It's only nine-thirty and everyone else is a nightmare, including my own wife. Come and have ice cream.'

He gets three big square tubs out and we follow him into the dining room, where he dumps them on the table and takes off the lids, revealing creamy gelato swirled with streaks of candy pink, vibrant orange and deep blackberry purple. He dollops some into a bowl for me and I spoon it mindlessly into my mouth. I exclaim loudly at its deliciousness although I hardly taste it, the sweetness dissolving on my tongue like smoke into a summer sky. Andrew is silent again, shovelling in ice cream automatically, all trace of the closeness we shared in the kitchen gone.

'So, how did you guys meet?' Todd asks Julian and Trina.

'It was way back in the mists of time, wasn't it, Ju? At university – with Saff, and Andrew and Owen. I actually went out with Andrew before Julian, but that never would have worked, would it?' She nudges him with her elbow. He gives a tight smile. My left leg jiggles of its own accord until I make a conscious attempt to still it.

'Really?' Todd looks delighted. 'I didn't know that. So you weren't at uni with these guys, Liz?'

'No, Poppy and I were at Manchester. I met Andrew at his twenty-first birthday party in Exeter where these guys were all at university, not long before finals. I was there with a friend of mine.'

'I see. So Andrew, were you and Trina dating when you met Liz?' He makes the question sound innocuous, but there's an unpleasant undertone. He knows Andrew is uneasy around him and Saffie because of Owen, and he's playing on it.

'No,' Andrew says shortly. 'We'd broken up. Trina got together with Julian at the same party.'

He doesn't say it had only been a month since Trina and Andrew had split up, or that as soon as we'd all finished our final exams, Trina took off travelling round the world on her own, despite her new relationship with Julian. She never said it was because she couldn't bear to see Andrew with someone else, but I did wonder at the time. Mind you, she and Julian have stayed together, so I was probably being paranoid.

'On the rebound were you, Trina?' Todd says.

'That's enough.' Julian puts his spoon down with a clatter.

'No,' Trina says, putting her hand on Julian's arm. 'Of course not. Julian was the one I was always meant to be with.'

Julian keeps his eyes firmly fixed on the half-eaten bowl of melting ice cream in front of him.

'Why don't we have more drinks on the terrace?' Saffie says, standing up.

'I'll clear the table,' I say. 'You guys go.'

'Darling, the cleaners can do it,' Saffie says. 'God knows we're paying them enough.'

'I'll take the dishes through to the kitchen and put them in the dishwasher,' I say. 'I'll leave everything else.'

Everyone files out after Saffie and Todd. Alone in the dining room, I sink into my chair and down a glass of water. The pizzas that had been so appetising a short time ago lie abandoned, cold and slimy. Grease spots, smears of tomato sauce and blobs of melting ice cream litter the tablecloth. There's a large stain, deep crimson in the centre fading to rose pink at the edges, where Andrew spilled his red wine. I try to banish the fanciful thought that it looks like blood.

A movement at the window catches the corner of my eye. When I turn there's no one there, but the feeling of being watched remains.

Chapter 10

Liz

I take a tiny sip of my whisky. I've never liked it, but Trina forced it on me the moment I came out onto the terrace after stacking the dishwasher. As I was finishing up, a wrinkled, snow-haired woman and a much younger dark-haired woman in her twenties had arrived as Saffie had promised. They'd seemed upset that I was clearing up, worried they'd get into trouble. The older woman reminded me a little of my mum. When I was small she was a cleaner, and in the school holidays she'd take me with her, along with a book or toys and strict instructions to be quiet and unobtrusive. Some of the women she cleaned for were nice, but others regarded my mum as a different species rather than a fellow human being doing a job of work. I couldn't articulate it at the time, but it hurt to see my mum making herself small for those women. I think of Saffie's dismissive comment that 'the cleaner' would deal with our mess but try to squash down the comparison. I'm only here thanks to Saffie and Todd's generosity. I mustn't slag her off, even mentally, when I'm eating and drinking at her table.

Sitting on the bench with Trina and Poppy, I watch Saffie and Andrew engrossed in conversation, huddled together at the far end of the terrace. Then Trina speaks and I wrench my attention back to her.

'God, this place is amazing!' The golden stone of the building is clad in fragrant wisteria and subtly uplit by lamps hidden in the flower bed. 'Saffie's fallen on her feet with old Todd, hasn't she? No wonder she's so keen to put a ring on it. He must be bloody loaded. And did you see that kiss at dinner? They can't keep their hands off each other. Poor old Owen never stood a chance. Can't blame her for upgrading from Owen, can you? Todd's hot. Lucky old her.'

Poppy stiffens next to me. We're all drunk, but Trina is out of control. I've always been wary of allowing Saffie's affair to become a topic of gossip amongst us. Owen leaned heavily on Andrew and I in the wake of the separation. I think sometimes he found it easier to confide in me even than in Andrew, and I spent many nights sitting up with him talking things over. I was extremely torn – Owen and I have always been close but Saffie and I are very good friends too. I tried so hard not to judge her, to understand what had driven her to do what she did, but I've never been able to fully reconcile myself to her behaviour, having seen what it did to Owen.

65

It sounds melodramatic, but Saffie's affair didn't just affect Owen, or even me and Andrew – it sent shockwaves all around our friendship group. Poppy has been through various break-ups over the years with different partners, but none of those had anywhere near the impact. She wasn't married to any of them and none lasted more than a couple of years. Her boyfriends had always had their own friends who remained separate from us – they weren't an intrinsic part of our lives the way Owen was. Most of the time I hadn't missed them, or noticed their absence at all. And it was what we'd come to expect from Poppy. That was her role in the group – the ditzy, alternative one who flipped from one relationship to the next, leaving a trail of havoc in her wake. If I'm brutally honest, Poppy's unruly love life makes me feel better about my own relationship and life choices.

But when Saffie left Owen for another man, a man she'd been having an affair with, I was shocked, yes, but it was more than that. I felt, ridiculously, betrayed. Not only on Owen's behalf, but on my own. We'd got married around the same time, and this represented the end of innocence. It was as if she'd taken off her blindfold and could see clearly, leaving the rest of us still blindly wandering in the dark. I wasn't unhappy with Andrew, but neither was I delirious with happiness. We were just plodding along, like most couples. Why did Saffie get to do whatever she wanted? How come she could break the rules the rest of us were obeying? I'd chosen my life – a safe, known life where I could predict what I'd be doing on any given day for the next forty years. Saffie tore up the book, and it left the rest of us feeling foolish for assuming everyone was playing by the same rules. I know Saffie was unhappy with Owen, and I know it wasn't fair of me to expect her to stay with him out of a misguided loyalty to the group as a whole, or the ideals we had when we got married. But I can't deny that something fundamentally changed. Is Trina's assessment of the situation accurate after all? Maybe we're all a bit jealous.

'Although I'm not sure I could be bothered,' Trina goes on, oblivious. 'All that hair removal and squeezing into sexy underwear. What about you, Liz? You're very quiet. Is it nightgown up to the neck or are you and Andrew still at it like knives?'

'Oh, somewhere in between.'

I try to laugh but my heart's not in it. The truth is I can't remember what it's like, that lick of desire as a brief kiss on the lips becomes longer and more urgent, a hand slides around a waist, or up a thigh, heat rises, an involuntary sigh escapes lips. Any sex Andrew and I have these days is infrequent and perfunctory, a task to be ticked off the list so that neither of us can accuse the other of withholding it. We're so familiar with each other we could do it with our eyes closed, and we usually do. I don't know how you recapture that magic with someone you've been with for almost twenty-five years. I don't know if that's even a realistic option. I fear the stark choice is between admitting you'll never get that feeling again, or starting over with someone new, like Saffie has.

'And you, Poppy?' I'm grateful that Trina has turned her attention away from me. 'You'd know more about this than us old marrieds – got your eye on anyone?'

'God, no!' she says. 'Happy on my own!'

'Good for you,' Trina says. 'You've got the right idea.'

Poppy is overly bright, desperately trying to sound happy, but Trina's too drunk to notice. She gets up and stumbles over to a small ornate metalwork table which houses a makeshift cocktail cabinet. She glugs vodka into her glass and wanders over to Andrew and Saffie. Todd and Kitty are by the drinks table engaged in serious-looking conversation. Julian is nowhere to be seen. Trina clutches Andrew's arm to steady herself.

Poppy shifts and sighs beside me.

'Are you really OK, Pops?' I say, taking advantage of a moment alone with her. 'You seem a bit distracted. Are you thinking about Scarlet?'

'It's not that.' She fiddles with the stem of her glass. 'Have you ever done something you know is wrong, but done it anyway because the end justified the means, sort of thing?'

'I don't really know what you mean. I don't think so. Is something going on? What is it?'

'No, it's ... not me, just a conversation I had with a friend. It doesn't matter.'

Saffie leaves Andrew and Trina and comes across to

sink down in Trina's recently vacated spot. 'God, I'm exhausted.'

I can't see Poppy's face, but I can sense her scepticism. She doesn't have much sympathy for Saffie's first-world woes at the best of times.

'Congratulations again, it's so exciting,' I say, suspecting Saffie's low mood is due to her announcement not garnering the response she was hoping for.

'Thanks,' she says. 'I know you all think I'm insane and it's too soon, but I've never felt like this. Todd makes me feel like a woman. With Owen, I was just the mother of his children and the ... co-captain of our family life. He didn't *see* me.'

That's life, I want to say. That's what happens when you've been with someone for a long time, especially if you've got children. Does that mean it's OK to throw in the towel and start again? Of course Todd makes you feel like that now. You've only been together for six months – it'd be weird if you weren't still in the honeymoon phase. Let's see what he's like when both your kids are throwing up and want you to cuddle them and you ask him to deal with the vomit-soaked sheets. Let's see what he's like when you make him go away to Bognor Regis with your parents for the weekend. Let's see what he's like when you're ill or tired or simply fed up and you can't be bothered to shave your legs and slip into silk lingerie to please him. Maybe then you'll yearn for the familiar steadiness of a good man like Owen. I don't say any of this.

'Is Todd having a good time?'

'Oh yes. They're simple creatures, aren't they, men? Give them good food, drink, sex and they're happy as Larry.'

'And the feeling of being superior to everyone else,' Poppy chips in.

'Poppy!' I dare say she's going through one of her life crises – there have been so many we've all become immune – but that was unforgivably rude.

'Sorry, Saff,' she says, sounding unrepentant. 'I didn't mean Todd specifically – I meant men in general like to feel that way.'

'Right. OK.' Saffie is lost for words for a few seconds. 'You do . . . like Todd, don't you?'

'Of course!' I say. 'He's great. And you're clearly deliriously happy, which is all that matters to us, isn't it, Poppy?' I nudge her thigh with mine.

'Right. Yes. Sorry, Saff, had too much to drink.'

'That's OK. Me too. In fact, I think I'm going to go to bed. 'Night.'

She drifts over to Todd and presses herself up close to him, whispering in his ear. He smiles smugly, cupping her bottom. Kitty grimaces. Julian's appeared and is staring out into the darkness of the garden.

The evening is finally winding to a welcome close. Andrew is nowhere to be seen, so I assume he's gone to bed. Trina is sitting at the top of the steps that lead down to the lawn, tapping at her phone, the light of it casting a ghostly hue up onto her face. I'd better make sure she comes in before I go to bed otherwise she'll fall asleep

70

there. I'm longing for sleep myself, but I should see if Poppy's going to unburden herself of whatever it is that's bothering her, so I sit a little longer beside her. Neither of us speaks. The silence lengthens.

Chapter 11

Saffie

Saffie sits at the ornate dressing table, smoothing on the first of the array of potions she applies nightly to keep herself looking like someone her Instagram followers would want to be. Someone worthy of being Mrs Todd Blake. She's always taken care of her appearance, but being with Todd has ramped it up several notches because now she has something she is afraid of losing. Todd is the best-looking man she's ever been with – she sees the way other women relate to him, even her friends. She'll do everything in her power to keep him.

It started, this nightly ritual, before she met Todd, when things between her and Owen had got particularly bad. She'd always had a need for control, for whatever she was doing to be flawless. First it was her schoolwork, where she deemed anything less than an A grade a failure. As she got older, it was her attractiveness to men that defined her.

72

She'd always secretly pitied those women who seemed not to understand what it was men wanted, or how to provide it. Look at poor Poppy, lurching from one romantic disaster to another. Saffie has always relished walking into a party and knowing that every man in the room wants her. Nothing compares to the sweet victory of setting her sights on a man and making him fall in love with her.

It had always been easy until Owen. He was a tougher nut to crack. He'd never admitted it but she suspected that when they got together, which wasn't until after they'd all left university, he was still harbouring feelings for someone else. Never one to admit defeat, Saffie had got there in the end, and had been so relieved she hadn't lost her powers she'd ended up marrying him.

When they had the boys, that became her focus, determined to win at motherhood as she had at everything else. She read all the books, enrolled them in a wealth of middle-class extra-curricular activities, sent them (against Owen's wishes) to the best private prep school and was available for them night and day. It was as they were growing older, forming their own interests and wanting to spend less time with her, that the cracks in her and Owen's relationship began to show. Rudderless, she returned to the thing that had never failed her – her attractiveness to men. She'd nearly made a fool of herself on one occasion. She hopes Andrew will have the sense to keep quiet about that.

Her cream silk nightdress and matching gown slither coolly against her skin. For a second, she sees herself from the outside, and has the sense that she's playing a part. She's watched this scene many times in movies – a woman dressed as she is, performing her nightly skin rituals. Any moment now, her gorgeous fiancé will come up behind her and lift her thick rope of her hair, and she'll give a secret smile as she tilts her head, allowing him to kiss the nape of her slender neck.

What actually happens is that Todd comes stomping out of the bathroom dressed in a T-shirt and boxers and flings himself onto the four-poster bed like a toddler who's had his favourite toy taken away from him. He picks up his phone and starts scrolling, then sighs.

'The fucking WiFi in this house is shit. Unbelievable. We should get our money back.'

'What do you need WiFi for?' Saffie refrains from commenting that no one else has had a problem with it. 'Surely Arrow can do without you for a couple of days?'

'I need to check something. I'm not a bank clerk, I'm a hedge fund manager. I can't just switch off. That's why I make the big bucks – why I can afford to spring for all this for you and your friends.'

'And we're very grateful, darling.' What she really wants to do is remind him that it had been his idea in the first place, but she learned in the early days of their relationship that when he was like this, it was better if she kept her mouth shut.

But it had been his idea. When he first suggested it, Saffie thought he meant it for his friends, and her heart sank. There was nothing wrong with them per se, but they weren't her kind of people – mostly financiers like Todd and their trophy wives, faces stretched and pulled to their absolute limits. Saffie wasn't averse to a bit of Botox, but these women had been nipped and tucked to a ridiculous degree. She'd have thought Todd was cut from the same cloth if they'd met in any other way than they did. But the fact that it was in a therapist's waiting room gave her a clue that there was more to him than met the eye. She'd wanted Owen to go with her for couples therapy but he wouldn't do it, so she'd gone alone, hoping it would fix her, knowing her constant drive for perfection wasn't healthy. It had helped when she'd had that moment of madness with Andrew.

Todd had the appointment before her, and a weekly smile became a hello, became waiting for her outside her session, turned into going for coffee. Before she knew it, she was in the throes of an affair unlike anything she'd ever known. Todd was intoxicatingly different to Owen – not only handsome and rich and charming, but sophisticated, a man of the world. This was the type of man she should have been with all along, if only Owen's perceived indifference hadn't been so attractive to her. Being with Todd was like diving into warm water, and she never wanted to get out.

'I'm not sure all your friends agree.' He puts his phone down on the bedside table.

'What do you mean?' A chill runs down Saffie's spine. If one of her friends ruins this for her, she'll never forgive them.

'You haven't told them how we met, have you?'

'They know we met in the therapist's waiting room.'

'Yes, but they don't know why I was there?'

'No, darling. I said I wouldn't tell.' She summons up every ounce of self-control she possesses and channels it into keeping her voice level. 'Of course I understand why you want to keep that quiet.'

'OK. Good. Poppy's a strange one. I can't quite get to grips with her.'

'Oh, Poppy. Don't worry about her. She'll be wary of you at first – you're not her type, she's kind of an eco-warrior, but you'll charm her no problem.'

'Plus, Andrew was shooting daggers from the other end of the table.'

'Andrew's OK. He's just protective of Owen. They've been friends since school. You can't blame him. He'll come round.'

'When? It's been six months.'

'Eventually.' She stands and crosses to the bed, sitting down next to him and taking his large hand in both of hers. 'You know how hurt Owen was. Still is. How much we hurt him.'

'Are you sure it's not more than that?' Todd says, snaking his other hand under the hem of her nightdress. 'I've seen the way Andrew looks at you.'

'Don't be ridiculous. He's sticking up for his friend. Like I said, he'll come round. No one can resist you.'

She puts everything she has into giving him a long, lazy look, all lust and invitation, and he draws her closer, his hands roaming over slippery silk. He slides the spaghetti straps down and grazes his lips across her bare shoulder. She can't fully give in to the sensation. She has to remain watchful, on the alert for any mistakes she might make, anything she could do that he would consider wrong. Crucially, he mustn't suspect for a second that someone here knows why he was at the therapist's office. She slips out of her nightdress and presses her body to Todd's. All she needs to do is to take this weekend hour by hour, and for the next hour at least, Todd's not going to be thinking about anything else.

Chapter 12

Liz

I come inside for a glass of water, but as I wait for the tap to run cold, I realise I've got an opportunity to escape. If I go back outside to say goodnight, I'll be badgered to stay up. No, better to sneak up to bed without telling anyone. They're all so drunk they won't remember who went to bed when.

I'm oddly tearful as I tiptoe up the stairs, not wanting to wake anyone who's asleep. I was so excited about this weekend when it was first mooted. A free mini-break in a beautiful setting, no kids to worry about, a chance to reconnect with my husband and catch up with my oldest friends. Before I met Andrew I'd never been abroad, and although I've now been on countless foreign trips I still get a thrill from being somewhere where everything – landscape, shops, the air itself – is different. But now I'm here, it doesn't feel right.

Andrew's been distant and my friends seem unable to relax. Maybe that's just life – but I'd hoped this weekend offered a brief escape from it, if only for a few days. A chance to feel young again, like our old selves before everything got so complicated.

I push the bedroom door open and step softly in case Andrew's asleep. At first I think he is. He's lying on his side facing away from the door. The main light is off but both bedside lamps are on. I'm preparing to creep into the bathroom when I hear a sniff.

'Are you awake?'

He starts.

'Jesus, what are you doing sneaking around like that?'

'I was trying not to wake you. Are you ... OK?' His eyes are pink. 'You haven't been crying, have you?' In all our years together, I have never seen him cry. Is that normal when you've known someone as long as we've known each other?

'No,' he says. 'It's the bloody dried flowers they left on the pillow, I had an allergic reaction. I've chucked them and taken the pillowcase off but my eyes are still sore.'

I have to admit I'm relieved. 'Are you OK? Things seemed a bit tense between you and Poppy earlier.'

'To be honest, there are a few problems at the agency – nothing for you to worry about,' he says quickly, sensing my alarm. 'But it's not fair to involve you. Poppy's your friend, it's complicated. Don't worry, I'll sort it out.'

'OK.' I know from experience that when Andrew shuts a topic down like that, there's no point trying to push it, but the prospect of problems between Poppy and Andrew is going to niggle away at me like toothache. 'What about this engagement thing? I know it's not easy for you, because of Owen.'

'I'm all right. Obviously, I wasn't predisposed to like the guy because of Owen, and to be honest I'm not the biggest fan of him. Frankly, I think he's a dick. But I'm willing to be civil for the sake of the group.'

'Thanks. I know it's especially hard for you.'

Andrew has talked about the problems Owen, a scholarship boy from an ordinary family, had in adjusting to life at a prestigious public school where everyone else had come up through prep school together, bound by a shared code of privilege and wealth. It was one of the things Owen and I first bonded over, as I'd had a similar experience at a less exalted private school. I too knew how it felt to use the wrong words for everyday items or meals, and to spend a great portion of each day on internal alert for situations in which you could accidentally reveal yourself. The fact that Andrew, sporty and popular, had taken Owen under his wing was one of the things I loved most about him.

'I find it all so tiring, the way Saffie and Todd are orchestrating everything, wanting everything on their terms. Sending Julian out for pizza, making this big announcement, having a go at you for clearing up because the servants can do it.'

'Saffie wants everything to be perfect. You know what she's like.'

'Yeah, that's her problem. No, that's not right. Her problem is she wants everything to *look* perfect, no matter what's going on beneath the surface.'

'That's harsh. I know she's got her Instagram and all that, but this weekend I think she really wants everyone to have a good time. And what do you mean, what's going on beneath the surface?'

'Who knows? That's the whole point. But I'm fairly certain not everything is as good as it seems. In fact, I know it isn't. I need to get some kip.' He turns off his bedside lamp and rolls over. 'Don't fall asleep with your light on.'

I stare at myself in the mirror as I brush my teeth. I haven't put the big light on, just the uplighter under the mirror, and my face is full of shadows. I think of the days when Andrew and I would get home from a night out and snuggle up in bed together to dissect everything that had happened – who was flirting with who, who was being off with their partner, what we thought of a new girlfriend or boyfriend. He could make me laugh until I thought I'd be sick. I'd never been with anyone so funny, so on my wavelength, and now I can't remember the last time we laughed till we cried.

Is the distance between Andrew and me merely middle age, exhaustion and being too caught up in family life to make time for each other, as a women's magazine would put it? They would suggest surprising each other with thoughtful gifts and scheduling in a regular date night, no doubt. But I don't think that would be enough to fix this. There's something else at play here. I just wish I knew what it was.

Chapter 13
Trina

Trina stiffens as Julian strokes the outside of her thigh in an exploratory fashion. He only ever touches her like this when he's trying to initiate sex. Last night both of them were far too drunk for it to have been in any way on the table, but this morning is a different story. It's warm and sweaty under the covers and her head is fuzzy with last night's vodka – conditions that would usually lead to sex for them. They've never had to deal with the seismic change of going overnight from being a couple to becoming parents that a lot of her friends have, and the consequent impact on the frequency of (and desire for, if her friends are to be believed) sex. It was one of the reasons she'd been so against having children. She'd seen the way parenthood overshadowed everything else once it began, seen the frustration and resentment it had bred in her friends' relationships. She never wanted to become like them. Julian had agreed, although in her secret heart she suspected if he'd been with a woman who had wanted children, he would have been happy to be a father. He'd been unsure of Trina from the start, worried that she was on the rebound from Andrew, that he wasn't exciting enough for her. When he asked her to marry him, he'd wanted so badly for her to say yes, to finally make her his, he would have agreed to having anything from zero to fifteen children if that was what she wanted.

She stays very still, pretending to be asleep, her jaw tight and her stomach a knot of tension. The stroking becomes more insistent, his hand straying down towards her inner thigh. This teasing, feather-light touch usually drives her crazy but today it makes her feel nauseous, almost as if she's being sexually assaulted. Her head is full of her conversation with Andrew last night, the look on his face when she told him. It was a mistake to do it here. She hadn't planned it – the opposite, in fact. She was deliberately waiting until they got home, away from everyone. She curses herself for drinking so much – she should have known it would loosen her tongue. Julian's hand moves up, sliding under her vest top into the curve of her waist and upwards towards her breast. Instinctively she grabs it, holding it still, preventing him from going any further.

'What's wrong with you?' Julian says, thick with sleep. She knows it's an accusation as opposed to an enquiry after her welfare. He may come across as mild-mannered, but his privileged upbringing means he is used to getting what he wants.

'I'm dying for the loo.' She slips out of bed away from him, tugging her vest top down, before he has a chance to reply. In the bathroom she takes off her pyjama bottoms and vest and steps into the shower, staying in there for as long as is feasible. Luckily each bathroom in the villa is equipped with large fluffy bathrobes, so she won't have to go back into the bedroom wrapped in a towel, risking the possibility of Julian undoing it. When she finally emerges, he's sitting up in bed scrolling through his phone. Her guilt is no match for the relief she feels that he's given up.

'I think I'll go out for an early walk, before it gets too hot,' she says, grabbing underwear from the drawer and wriggling into it under the robe. She needs time to order her thoughts. Should she try and speak to Andrew again today, or would it be better to leave it till they're home and do it in private?

'That's a marvellous idea. Shall we go down to the beach? It looks amazing.'

Trina tries to pretend that a joint outing was what she had intended. 'Great. Saffie said something about the tide, though, we'd better check with her first.'

'I already did. Apparently, the cove gets completely submerged when the tide comes in, but it's on the way out now, so we've got hours before we'd have to worry.'

'Great.' She tries to inject a note of enthusiasm, knowing it's unreasonable to be annoyed when he's trying to do a nice thing.

The house is silent and the grass still damp as they pick their way through the garden towards the path that leads to the cove. There are narrow steps carved out of rock that lead down to the beach. Halfway down, Trina has to take her sandals off.

'I did say wear something sturdier.'

'I don't have anything sturdier with me. It's meant to be a luxury weekend. I didn't know I'd need *sturdy* shoes.' She knows how she sounds. Like a bitch. She can't help herself.

'Here.' To make her feel even worse, Julian takes her shoes from her and offers her his other hand.

'It's OK,' she says, holding onto the cliff face next to her instead. He shrugs and continues on down the steps. Trina inwardly curses. Why didn't she take his hand, his olive branch?

'God, it's beautiful,' Julian says, when they finally reach the bottom. 'And there's no one here. If this was in Cornwall it'd be overrun with Hooray Henrys and Henriettas all dressed in Boden.'

Trina refrains from saying this is a bit rich coming from Julian, a product of public school who grew up assuming everyone skis at Verbier twice a year.

'Saffie said it belongs to the owners of the villa – it's part of the estate. The public aren't allowed onto it. There's no access to it other than from the grounds, even when the tide's right out.'

The cove is small and narrows as it goes inland, plunging into the coastline like an arrowhead, overhung on either side by sharp, flinty rock that glints in the morning sunshine. Julian inhales deeply, the early morning air pleasantly warm, and walks away from her towards the water. He's wearing long beige chino shorts, almost to the knee. His legs below the hem are pasty and thickly covered in downy blond hairs. His feet are encased in sensible brown leather sandals, from which protrude his peculiarly bulbous big toes, topped by yellowing toenails. She follows slowly behind, the soft sand, still cool, oozing pleasantly between her own toes, nails buffed and neatly painted the colour of dried blood.

At the water's edge, they stand side by side, eyes on the horizon.

'What's wrong, Trina?' Julian says, without looking at her.

'What do you mean?' Instantly she's on the defensive, fight-or-flight mode activated.

'You know. With us.'

'Nothing. I'm tired from work.' It sounds hollow to her own ears, so God knows what he'll make of it. She knows she'll have to tell him but she wants to delay the moment, wants as much time as possible before her world implodes.

'What were you talking about to Andrew last night?' He thinks a change of tack will prompt her to open up. 'On the terrace. You looked upset.'

'I can't remember.' She wills her face to remain impassive. 'I don't think I was upset about anything.'

'I thought there might be something you wanted to

talk to me about . . . to tell me. If there is, it would be better if I heard it from you.'

'I've no idea what you're on about.' She concentrates firmly on the sparkling sea and the endless sky. She cannot look at him or he will know straight away.

'You know how I feel about lying. And cheating. It's the one thing I won't have.'

'Yes, you've made yourself very clear about that over the years. There's nothing to tell.'

'Good.'

He bends to undo the buckles on his sandals, slips them off and steps into the shallows, the waves lapping around his ankles.

'Water's lovely and warm. We should go in.'

'I didn't bring my swimsuit.'

'There's no one about. You said yourself it's a private beach.'

'Someone from the house might come.'

'I don't think anyone's awake yet. And who cares?'

Trina dips one foot in.

'It's freezing!'

'It's lovely. Don't be so feeble.'

'I'll go later, with the others. You go in if you want.'

'Fine.'

He strips off his polo shirt and shorts, revealing the blue-and-white-striped pure cotton boxers that he insists on ordering from a gentlemen's outfitter on Jermyn Street.

'I'll keep these on just in case. Don't want to frighten the horses.'

He strides in and within seconds has dived beneath the rollers. She sits down on the sand as he pulls away from her, an energetic front crawl begun at private swimming lessons and cultivated on multiple holidays abroad as a child.

The morning sun caresses her skin and a light breeze ripples the shrubs that dot the cliffs on either side. She can taste the salt in the air, and there's no sound other than the breaking of sea on sand. It should be wonderful, but she can't enjoy it. Can't shake the feeling that this could be the last weekend like this with Julian. She's been pretending for months now that everything's OK, that everything isn't teetering on a knife edge, but her conversation last night with Andrew has put an end to that. She can't pretend any longer that she isn't about to watch her life crashing down around her.

Julian, fifty metres or more from the shore, flips onto his back and waves at her.

'For God's sake, Trina, it's gorgeous. Come in!'

Suddenly, she finds she is stripping off, down to her bra and pants, striding in, ignoring the needle-sharp lick of the waves. She plunges into the clear blue water and paddles towards him, but he hasn't noticed and is swimming away with strong, clean strokes that scissor through the water – out, out and away, further and further from her. She tries to call to him, to let him know she's changed her mind. She imagines him swimming back to her, wrapping her arms and legs around him, weightless in the salt water, clinging to him as if her life depends on it, painfully aware that it could be her last chance. But he doesn't hear, or is pretending not to, so she lets him swim on. Once he finds out, even if he is able to forgive her, things will never be the same.

Chapter 14

Poppy

Poppy sits alone at the kitchen table. The morning sun streams through a stained-glass window over the sink, reflecting jewelled light onto the wall. Dust motes dance in the shafts. It's warm outside even at this hour, and the flagstones are deliciously cool beneath her bare feet. She sips gingerly on a black coffee, attempting to piece together the events of last night. She shouldn't have drunk so much. Fragments keep coming back to her. Clinking glasses with Todd on the terrace. A vague memory of another conversation later – a churning in her stomach – but she can't bring to mind what was said. A lingering sensation of awkwardness from the dinner table and afterwards, of things being on the brink of tipping over into an argument. The one thing she can be absolutely sure of is that she didn't tell anyone about what she's done. Nobody must ever find out – especially

Liz. She couldn't bear to see the look in her eyes. And Scarlet – the consequences of her finding out what her mother has done could be catastrophic. Her mental health is precarious enough as it is. This could tip her over.

'Morning, darling.' Saffie floats into the kitchen, a vision in a satin kimono with a bold flamingo print over a cream silk nightdress. Her hair is smooth and glossy and she's applied a face full of 'natural' make-up. Even though Saffie's constantly glamorous appearance isn't one Poppy aspires to, she nonetheless tugs the frayed hem of her old cotton dressing gown out of view and rummages in the pocket for a hairband to tie back her sleep-matted curls.

'Are you hungry?' Saffie opens the fridge and loads the table with punnets of ripe, glistening berries, tubs of Greek yoghurt, fresh orange juice, a wicker basket of eggs, primrose-yellow butter studded with rock salt crystals. From the cupboard she takes out unfamiliar cereals, bags of glossy brioche rolls and a jar of golden honey.

'Not madly.'

'Did you overdo it last night? Oh, Poppy.'

How many times has she heard that said, in that precise way? By her parents, her partners, her friends. Affectionate, a touch despairing, but always with an undertone of self-satisfaction. Was that destined to be her main function in life, making her friends feel better about themselves? They might have messed up, but they could never be as chaotic as poor Poppy.

'I don't think I was the only one. Trina was putting it away.'

'I hope you're going to be OK for Todd's birthday dinner tonight. It's going to be amazing. I got the caterers George and Amal Clooney use when they're in Italy. Todd better be grateful!'

'Lovely.' Poppy refrains from saying that presumably he's paying for it, so it's Saffie that should be grateful. It's too early for an argument, plus her brain is busy reaching for a memory that has been nudged into life.

'Morning, ladies!' Julian breezes through the door followed by Trina, their hair wet and clothes clinging to them. The thought evaporates.

'Have you two been out already?' says Saffie.

'Yes, we walked down to the cove. It's spectacular. We swam – you girls must try it.'

'Oh.' Saffie's tone is disapproving. 'I'd thought we could all go together mid-morning before we head off to the wine tasting.'

Poppy suppresses a groan. If she'd known how much enforced activity there would be, she would have thought twice about coming this weekend.

'Not to worry, I'll happily swim again,' Julian says. 'You will, too, won't you, Trina?'

'I might,' she says.

'It is Todd's birthday weekend,' Saffie goes on. 'He'd like us all to go to the beach together.'

'I'll go,' Poppy volunteers, although it's the last thing she feels like doing. She doubts if Todd gives a rat's arse

93

who does what, but she knows Saffie must be stressed because this is what she does when she feels out of control – attempts to organise everyone else to within an inch of their lives.

'Thanks. Hopefully Kitty'll come too – I know he wants to spend some quality time with her.'

'I'm going to go and get showered,' Trina says. 'My skin's all salty.'

'Me too,' Julian says. Poppy doesn't think she imagines Trina's wince.

As they open the door to leave, Kitty is standing right outside. She saunters past Julian, who tries not to look flustered. Her skin is fresh and dewy without the need for make-up, her hair casually twisted into a messy top knot. She's wearing tiny grey marl shorts and a shoestring strap vest revealing endless tanned legs and enviably toned arms. It renders Saffie's glamorous morning look absurd and wildly over the top, like an ageing movie star trying to recapture her lost youth.

'Morning. Wow, Saffie, that's quite a dressing gown,' she remarks as she pours herself a coffee from the cafetière. 'Is there any sugar?'

'Thanks,' Saffie says, although Poppy senses she knows it wasn't a compliment. She ties the belt a little tighter. 'Sugar's in the bowl on the side there. Breakfast?'

Kitty spoons two heaped teaspoons into her mug. 'No thanks. I never eat breakfast.' She somehow manages to convey her disdain for those mere mortals who do choose to eat first thing.

'Most important meal of the day.' Poppy breaks one end off a brioche roll and pops it in her mouth, feeling protective of Saffie.

'If you say so.' Kitty walks out cradling her coffee mug.

'God, she's even worse now she knows I'm here for the long haul. She's never going to come round, is she?' Saffie sinks down at the table and puts her face in her hands. 'Why do I bother?'

'Then don't,' Poppy suggests. 'She's going to keep making digs at you whatever you do. I say ignore her. She's like a toddler, she wants the attention.'

'What she wants is me out of her father's life.'

'That's ridiculous. She's an adult, she needs to get over it. And she will eventually. In the meantime, sod her.'

'Thanks, Poppy.' She squeezes her hand and stands up. 'Right, help yourself to breakfast if you do want anything. I'm going to take a coffee up to Todd.' She pours a mug and adds milk. As she's going out of the door she turns back to Poppy and smirks. 'I might give him something else as well, make sure his daughter is as far from his thoughts as possible.'

Poppy grins and reaches out to take a raspberry. It's halfway to her mouth when she stops, her smile fading abruptly. Her encounter in the corridor last night has come rushing back with total clarity like a tidal wave, taking her breath away. She can't believe she could have forgotten it, even temporarily. She can see the pores in his skin, smell the mix of sharp cologne and alcohol and fresh sweat. She can remember his exact words. She mustn't think about it, consider it. It's repulsive, disloyal, unforgiveable.

It could be the answer to all her prayers.

Chapter 15

Liz

Saturday morning, Villa Rosa

I lie back and close my eyes, making a conscious effort to make my limbs heavy, to allow them to sink into the sand. I try to focus mindfully on the lulling, repetitive crash of the waves, the wild call of the seagulls wheeling in the sapphire sky – but it's no good. I can only feel the scratch of the sand that has worked its way inside my swimming costume and the too-hot sun that I fear is turning my English-rose skin lobster-pink. I can't block out the sound of Trina moaning at Julian for applying her sun cream too violently, or my worries about how withdrawn Andrew has been this morning.

Before we came to Italy, I'd been hoping we'd indulge in lazy morning sex, something we used to love before we had kids but which has been off the table for years due to the boys' propensity for wandering into our room at all hours. It seems there's no chance of that. By the time I woke this morning, Andrew was already in the shower. He dressed in near silence and went downstairs without so much as asking me if I wanted a coffee.

He sits stiffly beside me now. He's never been a fan of the beach in summer. Too many people (although he can hardly accuse this private cove of that), no shade and crucially, he can't swim – or not well enough to enjoy it. There had been an incident in his early childhood when, on holiday with his parents, he'd got out of his depth and into trouble and ever since he's avoided the water where possible. Tension emanates from him. Everyone except Kitty is here, and preparing to swim. We don't go on holiday with others – Andrew prefers it to be just the four of us so we can spend time together as a family.

'Come on, you two!' Trina stands in front of me, blocking the sunlight. She's wearing a black bikini held together with two thick rose gold hoops at each hip and one between her breasts. Her weight's been up and down over the years and she has a few faint, silvery stretch marks but her body is toned and smooth, a result of all that Pilates and what I assume is a punishing moisturising regime.

'I think I'm just going to enjoy the sun,' I say, although the thought of immersing myself in cool water is madly appealing. I know Andrew won't want to go in and I hope to save him embarrassment by joining him.

'Don't be ridiculous!' she says. 'It's gorgeous in there. Even early this morning it was bliss. You'll love it.'

Reluctantly I get to my feet. Saffie, equally toned but

curvy in a tropical-print bikini, is rubbing waterproof sun cream into Todd's neck. Andrew's still wearing shorts and a T-shirt and Julian is in plain, loose swimming trunks but Todd's gone for skin-tight jockey shorts that leave nothing to the imagination.

'Right, guys,' he says when Saffie has finished her ministrations. 'Up you get, Andrew.'

'I'm not coming in, thanks,' he says. 'I'm happy here with my book.'

'Oh no, no, no,' Todd says firmly. 'You cannot come all the way here, to the most beautiful beach on earth, and not swim.'

'I think you'll find I can,' says Andrew, trying to make it sound like a joke.

'It's my birthday!' says Todd. 'You have to do as I say!' His delivery is light, but there's a hint of steel not far beneath the surface.

'We're on holiday,' Poppy says tightly, unwrapping her paisley print sarong. 'No one has to do anything they don't want to do.'

'Now you know that's not true, Poppy,' Todd says, playfully swiping at her with his towel. 'Andrew, I won't take no for an answer.'

'I'm afraid you're going to have to. Not what you're used to, I dare say.' Andrew is simmering. I need to get Todd off his case before he comes to the boil.

'Andrew's not a keen swimmer,' I say. 'Let's leave him to it.'

'Oh . . . ' I think Todd is trying to sound sympathetic

but there's an unmistakeable note of suppressed glee. 'Can you . . . not swim?'

'Yes, I can swim,' Andrew snaps. 'I just don't want to.' He takes a breath. 'Seriously, you guys go and have fun. I'll watch from here.'

'OK. Your funeral,' Todd says. 'Let's go.'

The sand is hot beneath our feet so we half run, half dance our way down to the water. Julian and Todd dive straight in, immediately engaged in an unspoken male competition.

Trina, Poppy, Saffie and I walk in to mid-thigh level and stand for a moment taking in the spectacular vista. Sunlight glistens on the water, which stretches away, deeper and deeper blue until it meets the sky.

'Can Andrew really not swim?' Trina says. 'I never knew.'

'He can,' I say. 'He's not the strongest, but it's not like he can't swim at all. Honestly, it's not that big a deal.'

'Let's go in,' Poppy says, sensing my unease. I give her a grateful smile.

I bend my knees and slide slowly in, doing a few strokes of breaststroke, the cool, salty water caressing my skin. I dip my head under and enjoy a few seconds of peace in the murk before emerging and flipping onto my back, floating, weightless, intensely alive in a way I haven't been for a while. The other three tread water around me.

'God, this is amazing,' Poppy says. 'I wish we could stay here for ever, and . . . I dunno . . . start again.'

'Me too,' says Trina. 'Everything's so simple here.'

'It's heaven.' Saffie, floating, lifts one foot skywards, toenails painted neon pink.

The four of us settle into a comfortable silence. Despite the tension, I feel a surge of affection for these three women. It's good to be here with my oldest friends. Maybe everything's going to be OK.

Chapter 16

Liz

I offer to drive to the wine tasting, as I can think of
nothing less appealing than an afternoon spent drinking. I know in theory it's about tasting it, not throwing
it down your neck, but I've been on too many of these
not to know that despite best intentions, it always
ends in the latter. Tonight's going to be a big drinking
evening so I don't want to peak too soon – and anyway
it's wasted on me as all wine tastes more or less the same
to my palate.

Trina, sitting next to me in the front, grips her seat as
we drive along an impossibly picturesque – and impossibly narrow and windy – road that hugs the cliff, the ocean
sparkling and dancing far into the distance.

'God, this road,' she says. 'I can't bear to look.'

'Come off it, Trina,' Andrew says from the back seat.
'Don't be so pathetic.' He'd offered to drive there, but

I wanted the practice before driving a car full of pissed people later.

'I'm just being cautious,' I say through gritted teeth. 'I'm not used to the car.'

'You're doing really well,' Julian says reassuringly.

Todd's driving the other car, although Saffie has offered to drive back as she wants to be fresh for the evening's festivities, and it was natural Kitty would go with them. Poppy hadn't been keen, wanting to come in our car, but we had divided into couple lines, so she didn't have much choice. At first, I was following him, but he soon sped away, his driving style predictably Alpha.

Andrew's phone pings with a message. The next time I tear my eyes away from the terrifying road to check the rear-view mirror he's texting away furiously. There are a couple more pings to which he replies and then tucks his phone into his shorts pocket.

'There it is.' Trina points to an artisanal sign with a bottle and bunch of grapes on it. I signal and swing left, away from the sea, and bump down a stony track trying to avoid the worst of the dips to save the underside of the hire car. Todd and Saffie's car is parked under a tree with dark green, shiny leaves and the four of them are standing in the small sliver of shade it provides. We pull up next to them and unfold ourselves from the car. A wall of heat hits us, the car's air con already a distant memory. On one side there's a high stone wall, and on the other, rows of vines stretch away to a stripe of blue sea, a few shades darker than the brilliant sky above it. A small, elderly bald man appears through a door in the wall.

'Are you the Blake party?'

'Yes.' Todd holds out his hand. 'Good to see you.'

'Are you Antonio? We spoke on the phone. I'm Saffie.'

'Welcome, welcome.' He shakes them both effusively by the hand. 'Welcome to all of you. Is this everybody? Please come through.'

We follow him through the door and along a path into a neatly tended courtyard garden. From there, he leads us into a blissfully cool stone-built outbuilding. Antonio tells us about the history of the vineyard and talks about the grapes they grow and the kinds of wines they produce, but I barely hear him, dizzy from the heat outside and the concentration required to navigate the vertiginous roads.

'Would you like a glass of water, signora?' I must have swayed slightly.

'Yes please.'

Antonio clicks his fingers and a young dark-haired girl in a black shirt and trousers with a crisp white apron hands me a frosted glass clinking with ice cubes and filled to the brim.

When he's finished his spiel about the vineyard, he directs the girl to bring out the first wine. A boy dressed identically (and so similar he must be her brother) follows her with a tray of tiny, delicate canapés – slivers of wafer-thin Italian ham wrapped around hard, salty cheese that makes the roof of my mouth tingle, juicy sun-dried tomatoes doused in olive oil, crisp rectangles of fried polenta topped with tender, garlicky mushrooms flecked with herbs.

'Not for me, thanks,' I say when the girl gets to me and offers the tray of wine. 'I'm driving.'

'Don't be a killjoy, Liz,' Todd says. 'It's only a taste. You can't come here and not try any.'

'She can do what she likes,' Andrew says, all sharp edges.

'Try a couple, darling,' Saffie says. 'They're meant to be amazing.' She's trying to sound casual but there's a pleading note. She's so desperate for this weekend to go without a hitch.

'OK, I'll have a taste,' I say.

Saffie looks relieved. I don't look at Andrew but I can sense him glowering beside me.

We all sniff self-consciously at our glasses as Antonio encourages us to say what we can smell.

'Er . . . flowers?' Poppy ventures.

'Yes! Very good! This is floral!'

Poppy is delighted. Julian asks Antonio a question about the wine and he goes over to him to answer in more detail.

'Teacher's pet,' I say to Poppy. 'Remember when we used to add orange squash to our wine?'

'God, that sounds disgusting.' Kitty says, horrified.

'Ah, but we were young,' Poppy says, ignoring the fact that we were around Kitty's age. 'We just wanted to get hammered. Obviously, these days I'm quite the expert.'

'Still all tastes the same to me,' I say.

'Jesus.' Kitty rolls her eyes.

'You provide me with a challenge!' Antonio pops up at my elbow.

'Sorry, I didn't mean your wines . . .'

'No, no, I often hear this, but I am sure I can make you think differently. Stefania!' The girl comes over. 'Can you bring out the next one, please?'

She returns with a tray of tiny goblets of a glowing, deep red wine.

'This one is very special. Please, try.'

I take a glass and sniff it.

'Now, what can you smell?' he says, having seemingly decided to make me his project.

'Um . . .' It reminds me of Ribena that's gone off. 'Blackcurrant?'

Behind me, Todd snorts.

Andrew swings to face him.

'Something funny, Todd?'

'No, no, but . . . *blackcurrant*. That's what everyone says they can smell in every red wine.'

'No, she is right,' Antonio puts in smoothly. 'This one is very fruity. Very good, signora. Now for you, signor, I have something very special to try.' He leads Todd away to show him a bottle, an expert in defusing difficult situations.

The rest of the tasting passes without incident, and then Antonio asks us to follow Stefania outside to the courtyard for a late lunch. I find Todd at my elbow.

'Hey, I hope you know I was kidding about the black-currant,' he says. 'I didn't mean anything by it.'

'Don't worry, it's fine,' I say, keen to keep the peace.

In the courtyard garden, the table is laid under the shade of a tree, all white linen and polished silver. At each place setting there's a menu written in elegant black calligraphy on thick cream card. There's no sound other than the faint buzzing of bees in the lilac, the chirp of cicadas and the distant hum of farm machinery. Stefania pours water into heavy, rounded tumblers as we take our seats. There are two empty places – there's no sign of Trina or Andrew.

'We seem to be missing two of our party,' Julian says to Stefania, who looks confused. 'Missing?' Julian says, pointing to the empty seats.

'Ah, si. I think . . . toilet?'

We chat for a few minutes about the wines and the upcoming menu, and then Trina joins us.

'Have you seen Andrew?' I ask.

'I was in the loo. I mean – yeah, he's on his phone in the car park,' she says.

'Who's he talking to?'

'I've got no idea,' she says. 'Why would I?'

'Sorry. I hope it's nothing to do with the kids, that's all. Although they're with my parents so I'm sure they would have called me rather than him if there was a problem.'

As Stefania is serving our first course of baked figs stuffed with blue cheese and pine nuts, my phone pings. I look at it under the table. It's a text from Andrew.

Sorry, feeling a bit under the weather. Ordered a local taxi to take me back to the villa. Send my apologies. See you later x

'Everything all right?' Poppy says.

'It's Andrew. He says he's not feeling well and he's getting a taxi home. I'll see if I can find him.'

'Oh darling, he's just in a mood,' Saffie says, waving her fork at me. 'Best to leave him to it.'

Maybe she's right. I return to my figs, which I'm sure are delicious but may as well be stuffed with dust for all the pleasure I get from them. Stefania clears the plates. As we wait for the next course, and Todd launches into another interminable story that not so subtly reminds us about his enormous wealth and status, I stand.

'I'm going to go and check on Andrew.'

Poppy catches my hand as I go. 'Do you want me to come with you?'

'No, it's OK. I'll be back in a sec.'

There's no sign of him inside so I head out to the car park. He's not there either. I try calling him again, but there's no answer. I'm about to cut it off when I hear, very faintly, Andrew's ring tone. He's still here. I take the phone away from my ear and listen intently. It sounds like it's coming from down the driveway, but I can't see him from here. He must be on the road, but he's not answering my call. Why would he wait for the taxi down there? I start to make my way along the drive, but as I do, I hear a car pulling up, the door opening and then slamming shut. A small, battered maroon car drives past the entrance, reverses in and returns the way it came, a puff of dust from the ground the only sign it had ever been there. Andrew has gone.

Chapter 17

Liz

Saturday afternoon, Villa Rosa

'Do you think it was a mistake to do the wine tasting the same day as Todd's birthday dinner?' Saffie says anxiously as we sit on the terrace watching catering staff lugging trays of food from their van into the kitchen. 'I don't know if anyone's going to be up for it.'

'I don't know either. Andrew's still asleep so I'm not sure how he's going to be.'

I went to look for him as soon as we got back. He was asleep on our bed, his breathing slow and rhythmic. I'd put a tentative hand on his arm but he hadn't stirred.

'Mi scusi.' The small, wrinkled woman who was so upset at me loading the dishwasher last night steps out of the house holding an overflowing bin bag. 'It is ... where is ... ?'

'The bins are at the end of the drive,' Saffie says.

The woman gazes at her uncomprehendingly.

'Big bins. Blue. End of drive.' Saffie gestures towards the drive.

The woman shakes her head, baffled.

'Oh, for God's sake,' Saffie huffs.

'I'll do it.' I stand up and smile at the woman, signalling for her to give me the bag.

'Grazie.' She hands it over gratefully and scurries inside.

'They could have done that, Liz. Christ knows we're paying them enough.'

'It's no trouble. I'll take it to the bin and then go and check on Andrew.'

At the end of the drive, I place the bag into the large wheelie bin and stand for a moment, savouring the warm air on my skin and listening to the cicadas. I wish it was me and Andrew here on holiday alone. I imagine he's having a siesta, and later we'd change into our evening clothes and wander down to a beachside restaurant, serving fish grilled over charcoal and cheap wine. We'd reminisce about how we met and the holidays we took before we had the boys, and later we'd stroll back to our room which would have a ceiling fan and a wardrobe with only two hangers instead of air con and gold taps. He would slowly take off my clothes like he used to, unwrapping me like a Christmas present.

I walk up the drive and around the other side of the house to go in through the front door, avoiding the terrace and Saffie. As I'm going up the stairs, I hear footsteps on the landing and almost bump into the young, dark-haired woman who was clearing up the kitchen last night.

'Mi scusi,' she says. 'I was looking in bedrooms for any … cups and plates … for the … ' She mimes washing-up.

'OK.' I'm not sure why she feels the need to tell me. Once again, I feel unnatural in this position as an employer of domestic staff. I don't think it will ever sit easily with me, even on a holiday where someone else is paying.

I walk along the landing and slowly push the door to our room open. The curtains are drawn. Andrew turns onto his back as I do so, his eyes half open.

'How are you feeling?' I lie down next to him, resting my head on my arm.

'Better, thanks. Sorry for running out like that.'

'I was worried about you.'

'I know. I'm sorry.'

'Were you really ill, or was it something else?'

He rolls to face me, our noses inches apart. Stubble is forming on his chin, despite him having shaved this morning.

'A bit of both, to be honest.'

I reach out and stroke his cheek, knowing every con-tour of it before my finger touches his skin. I'd come up prepared to be angry if he wasn't ill, but all I feel is compassion.

'Tell me. I won't be cross.'

'It's Todd, mainly. I know you think I'm predisposed not to like him because of Owen, but I truly believe I wouldn't like him anyway. And now hearing they're engaged, knowing the impact that's going to have on Owen, and if I'm honest on our life too. I don't want to spend any time with him once this weekend is over.'

'I get that, I do. Owen's my friend, too, and it is weird seeing Saffie with someone else. And to be honest, I'm not the biggest fan of Todd either. But Saffie and the others are also our friends – this group is our main social life. If we stop going to things . . . '

'To be honest it's not only Todd. The whole thing has become too claustrophobic recently. I wouldn't mind a break from it. We can spend more time together as a family.'

'I spend loads of time with the boys as it is. I don't want to stop seeing my friends.'

'Fine. I'm not going to stop you going.'

'So . . . what? You're never going to come to any social events again?'

'I don't know, Liz. I haven't got it all worked out. I just know I don't want to spend any more time in that man's company than I have to.'

He gets up to open the curtains and sunlight comes streaming in as he stands with his back to me looking out over the gardens. I try to process what he's told me. Try to imagine what my life will be like, always going to group events on my own, knowing that Andrew is sitting at home stewing. I'll spend every night out with a knot in my stomach, knowing that Andrew will be waiting for me when I get home, sullen and resentful.

There's a knock at the door.

'Yep!' I'm grateful for the interruption.

Poppy's head pokes round the door, pillow marks on her face, her curls flattened on one side.

'Can I come in?'

'Sure.' I shift over to Andrew's side to make room for her on the bed. 'Have you been asleep?'

'Yeah, for a bit. You?'

'No.'

'Are you feeling better, Andrew?' she says, oddly formal. She and Andrew are usually so familiar – she spends more time with him than I do during the week.

'I'm fine,' he says shortly. 'I'm going to have a shower – I'll leave you two to it.'

'Is he really OK?' Poppy asks once he's gone into the bathroom.

'He's not ill. He's pissed off with Todd.'

'He's not the only one.'

'What do you mean?' I look at her sharply.

'Never mind. Tell me about Andrew.'

'I think the engagement thing has forced him to recognise that Todd's here to stay, and Owen's never going to be a member of this group again. He's saying he doesn't want to come to any social things if Saffie and Todd are going to be there.'

'That's ridiculous! That's basically all your social things!'

'I know. I wish we'd never come.'

'So do I,' Poppy says.

'What – you wish we'd never come?'

'No! Me.'

'Why?'

'Oh …' She scrunches up her nose in the way she always used to when she had something unpleasant to tell me when we were at university – she'd blocked the bathroom sink, or needed to borrow money to pay her rent, or had slept with someone unsuitable.

'Sorry, girls.' Andrew darts out of the bathroom in a robe and grabs his towel from the back of a chair where he'd left it earlier. Once he's locked in the bathroom, I turn to Poppy expectantly.

'Doesn't matter,' she says. 'I'm being an ungrateful cow – I mean, look at this place. I think I need a cup of tea – do you want one?'

'Yeah, good idea. I'll come down with you.'

We get up from the bed and leave the room. I try to banish the notion that something bad is going on with Poppy, but it lingers like a bad smell. I hope she'll tell me in her own time.

Chapter 18

Liz

Here we are again, on the terrace. It's like last night, but everything's turned up a notch. There's classical music playing from two massive speakers, giving the impression that there's a string quartet hidden in the undergrowth. Light spills into the garden from real flaming torches set at intervals around the terrace. Waiting staff circulate keeping our glasses topped up with champagne and offering exquisite canapés. Last night, the men were in chino shorts and T-shirts or casual shirts and the women in linen trousers and vest tops or maxi dresses. Tonight, suits and smart shirts are the order of the day for the guys and we're all dressed up to the nines. I'm wearing an absurdly expensive, simple black dress that I bought last week in a panic, worried as ever that everyone would be better dressed than me. It's straining across my chest and upper arms – I needed a bigger size but they didn't have it so I decided to make do. Something's scratching the skin at the back of my neck.

'Can you check if there's a label digging into me?' I lift my hair and offer my neck to Andrew. His fingers are rough between my shoulder blades. A muscle memory flickers through me of all the other times he's run his hands over my body, and I sigh.

'Sorry, I'm just trying to help.' He thinks it was a sigh of frustration.

'No! It's not that, it's . . . ' I can't explain it to him, not out here with everyone else in earshot. I don't want to tell him how his touch has reminded me of what we used to have, what we no longer have now that kids and work and life have exhausted us.

'It's the zip, it's sticking out,' he says, fiddling with it. 'There you go – better?'

'Yes. Thank you.'

'No worries. You look great,' he says, softening.

'Thanks. So do you.' For a minute, the backdrop fades and it's as if we're alone. For a second, the weekend delivers what I'd hoped it would: me and Andrew properly seeing each other, knowing in our bones why we're together. He leans in to kiss me, but at the last moment my eye is caught by a movement behind him in the garden and I draw back, distracted.

'What?' He turns.

'I thought I saw something moving . . . in the bushes at the end of the garden.'

'Probably a cat or something. I've seen loads of feral ones around.'

'No, it was bigger than that. I thought someone was down there.'

'Really?' he says sceptically. 'You can barely see – if it wasn't an animal it was probably a reflection from one of these ludicrous torches.'

'Yes, I suppose so.' I turn my face up for the kiss but the moment has passed.

'Hello, lovebirds!' Julian bowls up in a bold pink-and-purple-striped shirt. He appears to be a few glasses of champagne down already. 'I wish my wife would look at me like that.'

Trina is a few feet along, facing away from us, chatting to Todd. She doesn't look round but I see her shoulders tense before she throws her head back and laughs uproariously.

'I'm sure she does, Julian,' I say. I've always thought of them as being one of the strongest couples I know. Secretly, I ascribe this to not having had children, although I would never say it out loud, this heretical thought that having children is bad for your relationship. Yet so many times, including in my own marriage, I have seen the difference it makes when you go through the unprecedented upheaval of going from being a couple to being co-parents.

'You're sure, are you? What about you, Andrew? What do you think?'

Andrew squirms. Neither of us are used to Julian being

on edge like this. We are accustomed to genial, jolly, out-going Julian. How much has he had to drink?

'I think you should talk to her about this,' I say.

'You're joking, aren't you? It's like blood out of a stone.'

Poppy wanders over. While Trina and I are straight out of the Boden catalogue's evening wear section, Poppy is spectacular in a rose print full-length satin dress that manages to be cool and alternative but also heart-stoppingly sexy. She's left her conker-shiny, pink-streaked curls loose and they tumble magnificently over her bare shoulders. Not for the first time, I wish I had her confidence. Growing up, my mum wasn't particularly interested in clothes and we had little money for such things. Somehow I never developed my own style. If I look passable these days it's because I copy other middle-aged middle-class women, putting together a uniform that enables me to pass as one of them. Poppy, on the other hand, is always extrava-gantly herself.

'Can I borrow Liz a minute?' she says to Andrew and Julian, grabbing my elbow and hustling me away to the rear of the terrace without waiting for an answer. We sit down on the bench.

'What's up?' I say.

A waiter appears as if from nowhere and tops up our glasses.

'Saffie and Todd ... don't you think it's too soon for them to be getting engaged? She hardly knows him.'

'It is pretty quick,' I say. 'But what can we do? If we

say anything she'll get defensive and marry him even quicker – you know what she's like.'

'Maybe it'll run its course before they get to the wedding. Saffie's not divorced yet, is she?'

'No, not yet. It's definitely going to be a while before anything can happen. And if it goes wrong, it goes wrong. We'll be there to pick up the pieces.'

'Yeah, I guess. I just don't know how many more of these things I can get through with him.'

'He's not that bad, is he?' I say curiously. 'He's brash, I know, and Andrew's not a fan, but that's mainly because of Owen.'

'It's just a feeling, I guess.'

'Poppy, is there—'

I'm interrupted by the handsome man who is in charge of tonight's proceedings coming out of the double doors and banging a small bronze gong.

'Signors and signoras, dinner is served.'

Inside, the dining room has been transformed into a fairy tale with candles everywhere and elaborate arrangements of white lilies on every surface. The imaginary string quartet is playing in here, too, although I can't see the speakers. Poppy and I scan the place cards and I note with relief that Andrew and Todd are nowhere near each other. Poppy's face falls when she sees she's been seated next to Todd.

Once we're all in our places, Todd stands up and raises his glass.

'Thank you all for being here on my birthday, it's

fantastic to have you here and to spend time together. I'd especially like to thank my gorgeous fiancée who's done such an amazing job of organising everything. I hope you enjoy the meal – let's have a great evening.'

We all clink glasses, and he sits down. Saffie gives him a grateful kiss. On his other side, Poppy fusses with her serviette.

The bin-bag lady from earlier moves around the table pouring a citrussy white wine that tastes good even to my unsophisticated palate. The young woman I saw upstairs this afternoon serves us a salad composed of delicate green leaves, warm goats' cheese, honey and walnuts. I thank them effusively at every interaction. Wine glasses need refilling with alarming regularity, my own included. I'm thankful I didn't drink too much last night or earlier today.

'When do you two think you'll get married?' Trina asks.

'Obviously I've got to wait for my divorce to come through,' Saffie says.

'*Obviously*,' Kitty says, almost but not quite under her breath. I don't know if Saffie didn't hear or chooses to ignore her.

'And on that note, I'd be grateful if none of you would tell Owen about the engagement – I appreciate he needs to know,' she flicks a worried glance at Andrew, 'but I want to be the one to tell him. I understand it's not going to be easy for him.'

I bet I'm not the only one thinking of the first time Saffie introduced us to Todd in a wine bar in town. Owen

120

had somehow got wind of it and turned up steaming drunk and plonked himself down at our table. *Well, isn't this cosy?* he had said. It was Andrew and I who had persuaded him to leave, taken him off to a pub and listened to him for hours.

'None of this has been *easy* for him,' Andrew says.

'Jesus Christ,' Todd says. 'It's been six months. He needs to man the fuck up.'

Andrew tenses beside me. I put my hand on his leg and press down, a tacit plea to keep the peace. He shakes it off, and I wait for the explosion, but instead he pushes his chair back and leaves the room.

Saffie looks nervously at Todd, who seems faintly amused.

'I know it hasn't been easy for Owen,' she says tightly. 'But there are two sides to every story.'

'Of course there are,' Poppy wades into the fray. 'Relationship breakdowns are never clear cut, no matter how it looks from the outside. I should know, I've been in enough of them. And somehow it's always the woman who comes out as the villain.'

'Come off it,' Julian says. 'Don't make this into a feminist issue. It's purely a matter of who is at fault. The one who's lied and cheated is the one who's in the wrong, and that's all there is to it. If one of your friend's husbands did the dirty on her, you'd all be sitting around slagging him off till the cows came home. It works both ways.'

'Maybe,' says Poppy. 'But don't try and tell me society judges him as harshly as it does a woman who's unfaithful – especially a woman who has children. It's not the ideal way to end a relationship – or start a new one. But we don't live in an ideal world, and nobody knows the circumstances that have led to it.'

'Thanks, Poppy,' Saffie says.

I like to think of myself as a feminist, but I recognise a disagreeable nugget of truth in what Poppy says as far as my own reaction to Saffie's unfaithfulness. Yes, I would have been shocked if Owen had had an affair (although I have a faint memory of Andrew telling me years ago that Owen had cheated on a girlfriend at university) but was it more than that, when I found out Saffie had been having an affair? Did I . . . disapprove?

Andrew reappears as the salad plates are being cleared. We've all done our best to steer the conversation onto less controversial ground, and he takes his place in silence. The waitress serves a large ceramic bowl to each of us, containing a steaming, fragrant tangle of spaghetti studded with prawns, clams, mussels and squid. Bin-bag lady is back round again with a different white wine. I'm not involved in the conversations either side of me, and for a moment it's as though I rise above the table, observing it like an audience member at a play. It sounds ridiculous and melodramatic but something feels very wrong. I push the thought away but it's still there, bubbling away under the surface. Waiting for its time to strike.

Chapter 19

Liz

Saturday night, Villa Rosa

The waitress places a large, square slate in front of me. In the centre sits a wobbling half-sphere of panna cotta, creamy and flecked with vanilla, surrounded by succulent berries and topped with a caramel shard shaped like a lightning bolt. It's almost too beautiful to eat.

Whilst we ate our main course we'd reminisced about pasta bakes and other culinary delights from our student days and the virtually condemned houses we'd lived in. Now we've fallen back on the familiar topics of the middle-aged middle classes – jobs, house prices and schools. Andrew hasn't said much, coiled tightly like a spring beside me. We just need to get through dessert and then he can make his excuses and go to bed. Tomorrow is a free day with no organised plans, and Monday we fly home.

The wine is still flowing. There's red and white on

the table from earlier plus the maître d' is coming round with a dessert wine, sickly sweet and cloying to my palate although Julian is exclaiming over it. He motions for the guy to hand him the bottle, reads the label and gives it back without thanks.

'We had this one after lunch at the vineyard,' he says. 'Delicious. Who remembers it?'

'Not Andrew,' Todd says, falsely jocular. 'He'd beaten a hasty retreat by then.'

'He wasn't feeling well,' I say quickly.

'Right, of course,' Todd says genially. 'How you feeling now, Andrew?'

'Much better, thank you,' he says through gritted teeth.

I reach out for the water jug and hear a rip. I snatch my arm back but it's too late – the sleeve of my dress has finally given into the pressure and a gaping hole has opened in the armpit.

'Oh dear,' Kitty sniggers. 'Maybe you shouldn't have that pudding.'

I shouldn't care what she thinks or says – I don't really – but nonetheless heat spreads from my chest up to my face.

'Kitty!' Todd tries to sound reproving but I detect a hint of laughter behind it.

'It's funny,' Andrew says conversationally to her. 'I'm sure I've seen you somewhere before, but I can't think where.'

She sits back, darkening. 'That's funny, I was going to say the same to you.'

'You should consider that before you're rude to my wife,' he says. 'I'm sure it'll come back to me sooner or later.'

Kitty's body draws in on itself, like a cobra about to strike.

'Andrew, it's fine,' I mutter. What is he talking about?

'No, it's not fine. None of this is fine.' His words are slurring – God, how much has he had to drink?

'Look here, old chap.' Julian is gruff and awkward. 'Why don't you come outside and get some air?'

'No thanks.' He downs the contents of his wine glass and pours himself another.

'I think you've had enough,' Julian says.

'I think that's down to me, *old chap*,' Andrew says. 'And I wouldn't be so worried about me if I were you. I'd take a look a bit closer to home.'

Julian takes the linen napkin from his lap and folds it in half and half again, smoothing it flat.

'Andrew, stop,' Trina says. 'You've had too much to drink.'

I'm mortified, every muscle in my body clenched.

'Go to bed,' Saffie says to him. 'You're embarrassing Liz.'

'Really? That's your angle? Protecting Liz? You should have thought of that before you—'

'That's enough!' Saffie says. 'If you can't be respectful when we've offered you nothing but hospitality—'

'Ah, there it is. You're paying for everything so we have to toe the line. Well, sod that.' Andrew stands

125

up and drains yet another glass of wine. 'I know what type of a man your fiancé really is. I can't stand this any more.'

He strides from the room and we hear the door to the terrace open. Todd, puce with anger, goes after him. I try to breathe deeply. I don't want anyone to see me cry.

'That's my dad,' Kitty says. 'Lord of the fucking manor.'

'He is hosting everyone,' Saffie says defensively. 'You can't expect him to take that sort of rudeness lying down. Sorry, Liz. Are you OK?'

'Not really.'

'Things can't go on like this.'

'What d'you mean?' I sit up straight. I'd been expecting sympathy.

'We're not going to be able to socialise together after this – Todd won't want to.'

'Andrew won't want to either,' I say.

'Quite. So you're going to have to choose. Either you come alone, or you don't come at all.'

The weeks, months, years stretch out ahead of me. Having to tell Andrew where I'm going and coping with his disapproval. Checking my watch throughout the day, or evening, knowing that the longer I'm out the worse mood he'll be in, trying to come up with excuses to get away early without alerting my friends to the reason.

'Why do I have to choose? Why don't you?'

'To be fair, Andrew's the one who's making things difficult,' Trina says.

'I see. So you agree?' I say, a catch in my throat. 'You too, Julian?'

He squirms, unable to meet my eye.

'Poppy?' I say in a small voice.

'You're my best friend,' she says. 'You're never going to lose me.'

That doesn't answer my question. I stand up.

'I'm going to find Andrew.'

As I leave the room, Todd is coming back in. He brushes past me without looking at me.

Andrew is sitting on the terrace with a bottle of whisky and a glass on the table in front of him.

'Andrew, please. Come back inside.' I sit down next to him.

'It's better if I don't,' he says dully.

'What did Todd say?'

'It doesn't matter. I'm sorry.' His anger has dissipated leaving a despairing sadness behind. 'I'm sorry, Liz.' There's a weight to his words. He's not only apologising for the scene tonight. 'I've got a lot going on, things you don't know about.'

'What? Andrew, you're scaring me.'

He holds my face in his hands and rests his forehead against mine. 'There are so many lies.'

'What do you mean, who's lying?'

In his pocket, his phone pings. He ignores it.

'I'm going for a walk,' Andrew says.

'I'll come with you.' I can't bear to go back in there to be confronted with the inevitable questions and sympathy.

'No, don't. I want to be on my own for a while. I'll see you later, OK?' He walks down the steps and across the lawn without looking behind him.

I scurry up the stairs to our bedroom, brush my teeth and climb gratefully between the cool sheets. I am convinced sleep will elude me, but find myself falling towards it after a few minutes. My last thought before I tip into oblivion is of my friends: Trina, Saffie and Poppy. I could probably manage without the group socialising stuff if Andrew sticks to his guns, but I'd never cope without my friends. They're the ones who know me best in the world. The only people I can count on never to hurt me. I'd be lost without them.

Chapter 20

THE SURREY JOURNAL

LOCAL MAN DROWNED IN ITALY

A forty-five-year-old man from Haverbridge who was on holiday in Italy has been declared presumed dead by drowning. He was staying with his wife and a group of friends in a villa on the Amalfi Coast, and was last seen around 10 p.m. on Saturday at the villa.

It's thought that the man, who could not swim and had been drinking, went for a walk on a local beach, a small cove which becomes completely submerged at high tide. It is not believed he was familiar with the tide pattern.

His wife, who had gone to bed before him, awoke in the early hours of the morning and raised the alarm when she realised he hadn't returned.

His body has not been recovered, but local police in Italy say they do not believe there are any suspicious circumstances and there is no reason to suspect foul play.

As well as his wife, he leaves two young children.

PART TWO

After the Funeral

Chapter 21

Liz

Everyone has left. The kitchen is spotless – they all helped clear up before they went. Poppy was the last to go. I hate that even as I watched her sweep crisp crumbs off my kitchen floor and take the bottles out to the recycling bin, I was wondering if I could trust her. She's my best friend – the only one of the women that I brought to our group who wasn't originally Andrew's friend. Surely she wouldn't be able to look me in the eye if she'd been sleeping with my husband? She asked me if I wanted her to stay the night, but I said I'd prefer to be alone. It's not true. When I'm alone it's harder than ever to quiet the questions that won't stop forcing their way in about how well I really knew my husband, and whether one of my friends was sleeping with him. But being alone is preferable to being around her and the others. My parents offered to stay, too, but I couldn't bear their kind, sad faces any longer – their pain at not being able to protect me was more than I could bear.

133

I stumble upstairs to check on the children, suddenly aware of how much I've drunk since we got back from the funeral. They're both fast asleep, exhausted from a day they'll remember for ever. Josh has dragged his mattress into Ethan's room. They haven't voluntarily shared a room for years. In their sleeping faces I see traces of the babies and toddlers they once were. Will I always see those ghosts of their past selves, even when they're adults? I hope I made today OK for them. I wanted it to be as much a celebration of their dad's life as possible, as opposed to a day of mourning. Those who spoke included humorous recollections of Andrew as well as talking about how much they're going to miss him.

As I crouch down at Ethan's side, picking up the teddy bear he pretends he no longer needs and replacing it next to him, my phone beeps. Neither boy stirs. I creep out and sit down heavily on the top stair. The message is from Owen: *Well done for today, it was as perfect as such a day could be. After my mum died it felt like everyone disappeared after the funeral. Just want you to know I won't disappear. Is there anything I can do?*

I've lost count of the number of people who've said something along those lines to me today: *Let me know if there's anything I can do.* I'm not sure any of them actually meant it and even if they did, it's useless to me. There are so many things I need, and conversely nothing anyone can do to help me. What would be more useful is if my friends would offer to do something specific they can be certain I will need help with. However, as

I don't know what that would be, I can't blame them if they don't either. Unlike the others, I know Owen means it. He's probably the only one of my friends who is straightforwardly mourning Andrew. Everyone else's recollection of him is bound up with the tension of the weekend in Italy.

Thanks, I type, then stop. What I really want to do is ask him to come over. I can't stand the silence and the whirl of my own thoughts. I want someone in whose company I can be myself. Normally, the women who were here earlier could have fulfilled that function, but today all I felt was sick suspicion. It's ten-thirty at night, though, is it fair to ask him? I lean against the wall and close my eyes. I must have dropped off for a moment but my phone beeps again and I jerk my head up.

I saw you were typing! Please, if there's anything I can do, don't feel like you can't ask.

Everyone has gone home. Was going to ask you to come over but I just fell asleep sitting on the stairs so I should probably go to bed! I'm aware as I type that it's kind of a passive-aggressive way of asking him to come over whilst seeming as if I'm not, but I'm too tired to care.

I can't sleep. Happy to come over. See you in ten mins.

I start to message saying he doesn't have to, but stop when I realise I want him to. Surely today of all days I can be selfish. Ten minutes later, a car pulls up outside on our otherwise silent street. I'm waiting at the door as he comes up the path. He envelops me in a huge hug. For a second I resist, and then, as if sinking into a warm bath,

135

I let go and for the first time all day the tears come. I hate crying in front of people usually, although that's not the reason I didn't today. If I hadn't found the condom, I would have been inconsolable all day, as I have been since he died, but finding it closed me up like a fan. Owen lets me cry for a minute or so.

'Shall we go inside?' he says eventually. 'Don't want to wake the neighbours with your bawling.'

I give a choking half-laugh, half-sniff and he follows me down the hall to the kitchen.

'Do you want a drink?'

'Nothing alcoholic, thanks. Driving.'

'God, are you OK to drive? Didn't you drink too much earlier?'

'No, I didn't fancy it. Made it feel too much like a party, if you know what I mean? Plus I didn't want to risk causing a scene with Saffie and Todd. For your sake.'

'Thanks, that was kind. Tea, then?'

'Yes, that'd be lovely.'

'Builders' OK?' I hear myself saying, then instantly cringe. It's a habit I've picked up from Saffie, her patronising name for the type of strong brown tea that until I left home I thought was the only kind. It's a term Owen would never use, having come from a similar background, but he simply nods and sits down at the table.

I lean against the countertop as we wait for the kettle to boil in companionable silence. The panic I felt earlier at being left alone begins to subside. I've known Owen as long as I've known Andrew – a few minutes longer, in fact, if I recall correctly. I met them both at Andrew's twenty-first birthday party.

'How are you feeling?' he says – another question I've heard a lot in recent times.

'I don't know.' There's a certain solace in being able to answer truthfully. *As well as can be expected*, I usually say. *Up and down.* 'I know that sounds weird.'

'Not at all. I don't know how I feel either. It's like I've been flung into this whole new world which I didn't know existed, a world that's been here all along, co-existing within the old one. Does that make any sense?'

'Yes! It's like ... the curtain's been lifted, and how I thought the world, life, was ... it's not like that at all. And you realise there are loads of other people out there who know this, who've lost someone close, but they can't tell you about it. You have to find out for yourself.' The kettle clicks off and I pour water onto teabags and sloosh them around with a too-large spoon, the only one that's not in the dishwasher.

'Exactly. I sort of felt like this after Mum died, but it wasn't the same. I don't mean this to sound heartless, because I was devastated, but she was old and she'd been ill for a long time. There wasn't the sense of shock – of the natural order of things being disrupted.'

'Yes. And now I've got to re-evaluate my entire life.' I place the mugs on the table and sit down opposite him. 'I thought it was going to be one thing, but it's going to be ... I don't know. Something else altogether.'

'That must be scary.'

'Yes.' It is, but there's also a part of me, a part I'm trying not to examine too closely, that feels something else at the thought of the blank page that lies ahead of me. Excitement is not the right word, but there's a shockingly cleansing sensation at having the slate wiped clean. The future I thought was mine has been demolished and I need to build a new one in its place. Putting aside the condom I found today, things hadn't been great between Andrew and me. He'd been uptight, stressed, secretive. The antipathy between him and Saffie and Todd was wearing. Over the course of the weekend in Italy I'd begun to feel something close to trapped in our relationship. I can't tell Owen that, though. I can't ever tell anyone, like I can't tell anyone about the condom. A spark of fury blooms within me, fury at Andrew for leaving me with these questions, denying me the ability to grieve.

'Although . . . ' He takes a sip of tea. 'Never mind.'

'What?'

His knuckles are white against the blue spotted china of the mug.

'I was going to say – and please, tell me if I'm out of line – that one day, you might be able to see that as a positive. You can choose what happens next. Yes, your life won't be what you thought it was going to be, but it can still be good.'

I make a futile attempt to stop the tears falling but they escape anyway, rolling down my cheeks, an unstoppable release.

'Oh God, I'm sorry, Liz.' He comes round the table to crouch beside me, putting his arm across my shoulder. 'I shouldn't have said that, it was insensitive.'

'No, it's OK,' I say, my voice muffled. 'I ... I've had that thought myself.' I speak into his shoulder so I don't have to look at him. 'It feels wrong, though, to say it.'

He draws back, forcing me to meet his eye. 'Hey, nothing's wrong. However you feel – that's how you feel, and it's OK. You know how much I loved Andrew, but you don't have to be scared to tell me these things. I want to be here for you. You've always been my friend as much as he was.'

'Thanks.' There's so little space between us that his face is blurry. I don't know if I'm claustrophobic or stifled or ... something else, something I don't want to examine. A droplet hangs from my nose and I give a great sniff.

'I'll get you a tissue.' He stands up quickly, tears off a couple of sheets of kitchen roll, hands them to me and sits down opposite me again.

'Sorry if I spoke out of turn,' he says. 'Forget I said anything.'

'It's OK. I think I just need to take each day as it comes.'

'Yep, you'll probably feel different every day. Remember what I said though – whatever you feel is OK.' He puts down his half-drunk mug of tea. 'I should go, let you get some sleep.'

'Yes, that's probably a good idea.'

The boys will be up early as ever tomorrow – no

chance they'll sleep in because they had a tiring day. The thought makes my heart sink. I'd give anything to spend the day under the covers in bed, only emerging to make tea and toast. Various friends have offered to have the boys overnight to help me out, but they need to be at home with me at the moment. They need to know their sole remaining parent is reliable. So I'll get up tomorrow and paint on a happy face. I'll take on responsibility for everything, from the blocked downstairs toilet to updating my life insurance. I'll cuddle them and make their breakfast and chat to them about whatever they want – whether that's their dad or their latest build in Minecraft. I will be here, like I will always have to be here, because I'm all they've got now.

'How about we get together with the kids soon? I don't want it to be always Saffie who gets to have family time with our friends.'

'Yes, that'd be great. The boys love Milo and Ben. And it'd be good for them to—' My throat catches and I take a shuddery breath. 'Sorry.' Owen waits patiently while I compose myself. 'Now they don't ... you know ... have a dad. It's nice for them to spend time with a male role model.'

'I don't know about being a role model!' he says. 'But seriously, I'd be honoured to be there for them. For Andrew. They're with Saffie this coming weekend, but how about the following one? We could go to the beach if the weather's nice?'

'Great. I'll text nearer the time to arrange it.'

At the door, Owen kisses me lightly on the cheek and gets into his car. I stand in the doorway and watch as his tail-lights recede into the distance. A noise from across the road – a cough? Something breaking underfoot? – rouses me from my reverie. Just in time, I see a figure turn into the alleyway opposite my house and melt into the darkness. I shiver and close the door. Inside, I stand for a moment, my forehead resting against the opaque glass panel, my fingers lightly touching the spot where Owen's lips met my cheek.

Chapter 22

Liz

Since the funeral two days ago, my phone has been beeping constantly with messages checking up on me. It's nice they're thinking of me but every time I hear it, my heart sinks. A few of them say *no need to reply*, which I'm grateful for, but the ones that don't I feel obliged to, and it's exhausting trying to come up with a response for every one.

Poppy has organised for her, Trina and Saffie to come over for lunch today (she's bringing it so I don't have to do anything). My first instinct was to say no, but I can't keep them at arm's length for long without an explanation. I could confront them, either individually or as a group, but I'm not ready to do that. If one of them was sleeping with Andrew, they've been lying to me for as long it's been going on – why would they tell the truth now? No, my best bet is to take a watch-and-wait approach. Nobody knows I found the condom, so they won't be expecting me to be on alert.

I hoover and mop the kitchen floor in preparation for their arrival, but there's no real need – the house is immaculate. I've not stopped cleaning since the funeral. I need to be active all the time, to stop the bad thoughts from creeping in where I imagine Andrew's final moments in the water, choking and gasping until he's unable to fight it any more. He comes to me in my dreams, demanding to know why I'm acting as if he's dead when he's alive and well, accusing me of forgetting him. I see him everywhere – my heart leaps every time I pass a tall, dark-haired man on the street, or a man who walks like him, or carries his bag in the same way.

To keep these thoughts at bay, I choose instead to consider the possibility that one of my oldest, dearest friends has betrayed me in the most horrible way imaginable. In a weird way it's protecting me from facing the knowledge that Andrew has gone. I imagine myself as a detective, searching for clues or signs that will give the culprit away. Once I know who it is, or if I'm able to discover another reason for Andrew having that condom in his pocket, I can stop suspecting everyone and rely on the rest of my friends again. Until then, I'm on my own.

I finish in the kitchen and make a start on the living room, wiping invisible dust particles from every surface. As I run the duster over the windowsill, I'm distracted by a movement from across the street. There's a vaguely familiar young woman standing at the bus stop, wearing a floral maxi dress and denim jacket, dark hair pulled into a messy bun, most of the top half of her face obscured by enormous sunglasses. She's looking down the road as if expecting a bus, but every now and then she glances over at my house.

I wipe the bright yellow duster across the window as if cleaning it, and she immediately rummages in her bag. She gets out her phone and scrolls, but there's a fakeness about the flip and swipe of her thumb – as if it's a performance for my benefit. I hear voices and see Poppy and the others arriving in convoy. I go to the front door to let them in, pausing for a few seconds to check my appearance in the mirror in the hall. I'm ashen and puffy-eyed, but there's nothing I can do about that. By the time I open the front door, the young woman has gone.

'Hi, love,' Poppy says, giving me a fierce hug and continuing on down the hall towards the kitchen.

'Darling.' Saffie sweeps me into a silk-shirted embrace. 'How are you?'

'You know. Up and down.'

'I bet.' Trina kisses me on both cheeks. 'And the boys?'

'They seem OK. They've gone back to school, which I think has helped. Playing a lot of Minecraft, but no change there.'

'What's Minecraft?'

'Oh God, you don't want to know,' Saffie says. 'The joys of having kids these days!'

Trina's mouth tightens. I've always tried to keep the child talk to a minimum around her. It was her choice not to have children, so it's not exactly a sensitive subject for her, but I am very aware how boring it can be

144

for non-parents to sit through endless discussions about weaning, potty training and speech development.

'Let's go through,' I say.

Poppy is unloading Tupperware boxes from her bag onto the kitchen worktop. 'Some of these need to go in the fridge, unless you want to eat straight away?'

'I thought we could have a drink in the garden first. It's such a nice day.'

'I'll put these in the fridge, then.'

I grab a tray of glasses and a bottle of wine, and we troop out onto the patio. My cleaning frenzy hasn't extended to the garden. A couple of the paving stones are cracked and weeds poke through every available gap. The grass is in terrible need of mowing, and I'm no longer sure which are flowers and which weeds in the beds that line the lawn on either side.

'This is nice,' Saffie says.

It's kind of her to say, but I've seen Todd's garden – hers now, I suppose – which has been recently remodelled. Mine is a slum in comparison. We settle around the rickety garden table, which has several slats missing, into mismatched garden chairs, and I pour everyone a glass of wine.

'Cheers,' Trina raises her glass. 'To you, Liz. You're doing amazingly.'

They all drink to me and I lift my glass too in thanks, although I have no idea what 'doing amazingly' means. I don't have any choice, do I? If it was me alone I could fall apart but I've got the boys to think of.

'So, what's going to happen about the company?' Trina asks with her usual directness.

'We don't have to talk about it,' Saffie says hastily. 'If you don't want to, Liz.'

'No, it's OK. Poppy probably knows more about it than me.' I've been putting off thinking about it. It's been on my list since I got the confirmation of the presumption of death, but I know Poppy will have done anything urgent that needs doing.

'I was going to talk to you about it, when you were ready,' she says. 'But I don't think now's the time.'

'Come on, Poppy, we're all friends here. Liz doesn't mind, do you?' Trina says.

'Er . . . no . . .'

'I'll talk to Liz about it properly in private,' says Poppy firmly, 'but basically there's nothing to worry about. Andrew and I had partnership protection insurance, which means that if one of us died . . . I mean, now one of us has . . .' Her voice cracks. 'Sorry, Liz. The policy will pay out to me so that I can buy Andrew's shares from the estate . . . from Liz, I mean.'

'So you'll own the business outright?' Trina says.

'Yes. There are other options, and none of it's straight-forward. I can't run the business alone – I'll have to hire someone, or find another partner. But we'll talk about it another time, OK Liz?'

'Wow, you've sorted all that out very quickly,' says Trina. 'That doesn't sound like you.'

'What's that supposed to mean?' Poppy says, offended.

'Well ... you're usually kind of ... disorganised, aren't you?' Trina says.

'Not at work, no. That's probably why I lose track of things in my personal life. Anyway, I haven't done anything about it yet. Of course I'm going to wait and talk to Liz.'

'I know, I didn't mean it in a bad way,' says Trina. 'I meant you've done well. Could be a second language thing.'

Trina's English was fluent when she came from Sweden to go to university in the UK. She's practically a native speaker now. Even if Poppy had set the wheels in motion for the insurance, I wouldn't mind – it's her livelihood after all. I can't see any reason for me to hang onto the shares. Andrew had a personal life insurance policy, too, so our mortgage will be paid off and there's a lump sum for me.

'How's Scarlet?' I ask Poppy, keen to move the conversation on to something else.

'Much better, thank God,' she says. 'She's really benefitted from the counselling she's been having over the summer. She goes back to uni in a couple of weeks and I'm hopeful she's going to have a happier time this year.'

'You were lucky to get that organised so quickly,' Trina says. 'I thought the waiting lists were months long.'

'I paid for it privately,' Poppy says tightly. 'When it's your child that's hurting, you do whatever it takes.'

'Of course you do, darling,' Saffie says. 'Any mother would do the same.'

'Yes, I know that,' Trina says. 'Just because I don't have children doesn't mean I'm some sort of ... robot, who doesn't understand human relationships.' She laughs to disguise it as a joke, but it's not.

'Shall we get the food, Poppy?' I say.

She jumps up gratefully and we spend a couple of minutes going back and forth to the kitchen, laying out salads, cold meat, cheeses and bread. Over lunch, the conversation meanders along uncontroversial, safe lines and I have a few moments where things feel normal. At times, I almost forget that Andrew is dead and one of my friends was sleeping with him. As Poppy clears our plates and Trina makes a pot of coffee, Saffie leans across the table and takes my hand.

'Darling, I want to say sorry.'

'What for?' My heart skips a beat.

'What happened in Italy. What I said about you having to choose between us and Andrew. It wasn't fair, I shouldn't have made it into an ultimatum. I feel terrible.'

A small voice inside me asks why she was so keen to shut Andrew out of the group. Had she been sleeping with him, but things had gone sour? Was she scared that Todd would find out?

'Todd's so sorry, too, about rubbing Andrew up the wrong way,' she goes on blithely. 'He knows he behaved badly. He's not generally an angry man but he was finding it hard that Andrew was so ... hostile towards him. It's very sweet of you to be so kind about it, but we've been feeling frightful. So I've been thinking, now that the funeral's out of the way, why don't I organise a charity auction for the Landell Trust?'

The Landell Trust is a UK charity that supported me through the logistical nightmare that began the moment Andrew was declared missing, presumed dead, in Italy. They helped me deal with the police, medical and legal services and so much more.

'I don't know, Saffie ... ' Apart from my lurking suspicion that she's doing this to assuage her guilt, it feels uncomfortably like an opportunity for her and Todd to flex their muscles, make themselves look good.

'No, it'll be brilliant. Todd knows everyone, he'll be able to get some amazing lots – things money can't buy. We'll raise a fortune.'

'OK,' I say weakly.

'Fab. Why don't you come over Sunday lunchtime for a barbecue, bring the boys? They can have a swim in the pool and we can thrash out the details.'

'Thanks, they'd love that.' I can't help thinking, with a pang of guilt, how much more tricky accepting her invitation would be if Andrew was still alive.

'Great. No, no coffee for me thanks, Trina, I've got to run.'

I see her to the door. When she's gone, I stand in the hall for a moment, listening to the indistinct chatter from Poppy and Trina in the garden, and it comes to me like a blow to the skull. I know who the young woman was – the one I saw earlier at the bus stop opposite. It was the woman I didn't recognise at Andrew's funeral.

Chapter 23

Liz

A vast, raised deck opens out from the kitchen, partly shaded by a mechanically controlled awning to protect from the sun. On one side, a low coffee table is surrounded by squishy outdoor sofas and armchairs and on the other, a huge wooden table with a parasol and eight chairs commands a view of the garden. Steps lead down to a manicured lawn bordered by tastefully colour-coded flowers and shrubs. The hedges on either side are high. This is not the kind of neighbourhood where people want to chat over the garden fence. At the end of the garden, positioned to catch the maximum possible amount of sunlight, is a solar-heated azure blue swimming pool complete with a wooden chalet-style changing room.

Sunlight sparkles on the pool's surface as my youngest Josh, along with Saffie's sons, Milo and Ben, races down the garden towards it, whooping with excitement. Ethan, who at eleven has a more nuanced understanding of our situation, curls into me on the pale grey sofa. He's sucking his thumb, something he gave up years ago.

'Are you going to go and swim with the others?' Saffie asks him. 'The water's lovely and warm.'

He burrows further into me.

'Go on, darling,' I say. 'You'll enjoy it once you get in.'

He takes his thumb out. 'Do I have to?'

'No, but ... why don't you go down and watch the others and maybe you'll change your mind?'

'OK,' he says in a small voice. He stands, picks up his swimming bag and heads slowly down towards the pool, reluctance personified.

'The poor darling,' says Saffie. 'Josh seems OK, though?'

'Yes, but that worries me too. It's like he's not affected at all – I mean, that's not normal, is it?'

'I think it probably is for a kid his age.' Todd flips a burger on the barbecue, improbably manly in Saffie's Cath Kidston apron over a polo shirt and shorts. 'Kitty was the same when Maddison and I split up, didn't show any emotion. Her therapist said it was pretty standard. At that age, they don't have the emotional intelligence to process what's going on, so they tend to carry on as normal – at least on the surface. She said it's more likely to come out in their behaviour – which it certainly did with Kitty.'

I'm impressed. Before the Italy weekend, I'd thought of Todd as a one-dimensional, handsome, financial rich guy. In Italy, he'd come across as a bully. Either way, I'd rather assumed his emotional intelligence to be fairly low, but I'm reminded now that Saffie and he met at the therapist's office. Perhaps I shouldn't be surprised.

'That's the thing though – his behaviour's been fine too. A little more hyper and manic than usual, but nothing major.'

'You'll just have to keep an eye on it,' Saffie says. 'Have you sorted any therapy for them?'

'Not yet. I have mentioned it to them but they weren't keen, and I don't want to force them.'

'There's no rush. Take your cues from them.'

My gin and tonic, with a slice of pink grapefruit and a bay leaf in a frosted tumbler, is utterly delicious. I feel guilty at the pleasure it gives me. Surely I shouldn't be capable of any positive emotions right now?

'Right, about this auction,' Saffie says, suddenly business-like. 'I don't want you to have to worry about anything – I'll organise the whole thing. I've spoken to the fundraising woman at the Landell Trust and she was delighted, I've found a venue and already got promises for some amazing lots for the auction from Todd's colleagues.'

'Blimey, you don't mess around, do you?' I'm grudgingly impressed, although there's that voice again, asking me if she's doing this because she feels guilty about sleeping with Andrew. I try not to listen to it – I would like to raise money for the Trust. I shouldn't have been so mean-spirited when she first mentioned it.

'No use in waiting. I need something to do when the boys are with Owen.'

'Talking of which,' Todd says, trying to rescue a slice of halloumi that's fallen through the grill, 'has Saffie told you the news?'

'News?'

'About Owen.'

'No. What?' I try to shake off the thought of Owen's face, inches from mine, as we said goodbye. In the cold light of day, I'd realised how ridiculous I was being to consider for a nanosecond that there was anything romantic in my feeling for him. They say that grief is love with nowhere to go, and that's all it is. I'm looking for a place to put my love, and Owen is a safe target because of our long-standing, easy friendship.

'I don't know if it's because of . . . Andrew . . . ' he waves the tongs in my direction, 'but he seems to have turned a corner.'

'How so?' I look from him to Saffie.

'He dropped them off as usual on Thursday morning,' she says. 'Normally he pulls up in the drive, they get out and he leaves. If something happens while they're with him that I need to know about, he texts me. But this time, he got out and came to the door. I was quite worried – I thought something must be wrong with the boys.'

I take a quick peek down the garden. Ethan has changed and is dipping a toe in the pool. Josh splashes water up at him and I wince, anticipating a blow-up requiring my intervention that will send Ethan racing back to my side, but instead he retreats from the edge and sits on a sun lounger, wrapping his towel tightly around him. I sink into the cushions and take a sip of my gin.

'I asked him straight away if something had happened, but he said no, and came out with this speech that he'd patently been preparing. It was all about how it wasn't good for the boys for us to be on bad terms, and how he knew it was his fault and that he was going to try to be civil, and he hoped I would too.'

'What did you say?'

'I was so shocked I couldn't get a word out. To be honest, in the three months since we announced our engagement I've been waiting for him to kick off like he did when we first got together. I managed to say I'd like that, and then he left.'

'Wow. That's great.' I wonder if it's not only Andrew's death that has led Owen to reconsider his behaviour. Is it possible that the anger Andrew harboured towards Saffie and Todd on his behalf had infected Owen, meaning he held onto his own rage and hurt longer than he otherwise would have?

'Let's see,' says Todd. He bends over Saffie to place a dish of burgers on the table, briefly kissing the side of her neck on his way back to the barbecue. She squeezes his thigh. God, these two are sickening. Would Saffie really have slept with Andrew and put all this in jeopardy? 'It's only been three days,' Todd goes on, 'so it's too early to tell if he's going to put his money where his mouth is.'

'I think he will,' says Saffie. 'He was different – like the old Owen, the one I was married to.'

'Hey, I am here, you know.' Todd's tone is determinedly light, but there's a set to his jaw that indicates something else at play.

'Don't be silly, darling, I didn't mean it like that.'

'I mean, the old Owen can't have been that great, can he?' He's still presenting it as if it's a joke, but there's no mistaking the deadly seriousness behind it. 'Or you wouldn't be here, would you, enjoying all this?' He waves the tongs around at the house, the deck, the pool.

'Darling, you know I didn't mean . . .' Saffie's colour is high and she's clenching her glass so tightly I'm afraid it will shatter.

'Jesus, Saff, I'm teasing. Don't get your *knickers in a twist*, as you'd say.'

Saffie's laugh is brittle, and I join in, in an attempt to ease the tension. She asks me to go and get the boys out of the pool for lunch while she heads inside to fetch bread and salads. I follow the path that leads down the garden, through tropical foliage that I'm astonished can be persuaded to grow in this climate. This place is a paradise. I only hope Saffie hasn't had to pay too high a price to live in it.

Chapter 24

Liz

The wind whips across the huge expanse of beach, whirling sand into the air. The sky is a pale, washed-out blue with an occasional strand of candyfloss cloud, the air all salt and seaweed and childhood holidays.

'Once we get this up, we'll be OK,' says Owen, forcing the poles of a striped windbreak into the sand. I take out my picnic rug and it flies up like a banner. Milo, Ben and Josh leap on it, pinning it to the ground, breathless and laughing. Ethan sits in silence, hoodie drawn up tight around his face. I put the heaviest things out of my bag around the edges of the rug, taming it into submission.

'Let's go in the sea!' says Milo. He and his brother and Josh strip down to their swimming trunks. They ignore my futile cries to put their clothes away, and race down towards the shoreline, leaving me gathering up T-shirts and socks and stuffing them into any available receptacle to prevent them from blowing away.

'You not going in, Ethan?' says Owen as he pushes

the last pole into the sand and sinks gratefully down out of the wind.

'Too cold.' He pulls his sleeves down over his fists.

'It'll be lovely once you're in. The temperature's quite warm today, it's the wind makes it feel colder.'

'No thanks.'

'Why not, darling?' I say. 'You love swimming in the sea.'

'I said no.'

'OK,' I shrug. 'Coffee, Owen? I brought a flask. Where did I put it?'

I'm rummaging in one of the many bags when there's a nudge at my elbow. Owen gestures towards Ethan, his knees drawn up to his chest, furiously wiping silent tears from his cheeks.

'Oh sweetheart, what's wrong?' I regret the question as soon as I've asked it. How stupid am I? What could possibly be wrong with an eleven-year-old who's recently lost his dad? An eleven-year-old who's recently lost his dad in a drowning accident. In the sea. What was I thinking, bringing them to the beach?

'Is it . . . do you not want to go in because of . . . because of what happened to Daddy?'

He puts his forehead on his knees and gives an almost imperceptible nod. I think of last weekend at Saffie and Todd's when he wouldn't go in the pool. How could I have been so dense?

A lump forms in my throat. Owen comes over and sits down next to Ethan, looking out to sea.

'Ethan, mate. What happened to your dad was awful. I'm desperately sad about it too. Your dad was one of my best mates. It's natural that you feel sad. That just shows how much you loved him, how much we all loved him. But what happened to him was an accident, and it's really, really rare for something like that to happen. Plus, he was on his own in the water, and the currents where he was were very unpredictable. On this beach, when the tide's out like it is now, the sea is so shallow, it's completely safe. And see, there's a lifeguard there, so in the very unlikely event that anyone did get into trouble in the water, he'd be in there like a shot.'

Ethan contemplates the lifeguard.

'How about I come in with you?' Owen says. 'Just for five minutes if you like. See how you feel, and if you still want to get out, we will.'

'OK. Just for five minutes.'

'You got it.'

They both undress down to their swim shorts. I try to avert my eyes from Owen's broad shoulders and surprisingly hairy chest that tapers to a thin line of hair leading down to the waistband of his shorts.

'Right, let's do this.' He offers Ethan his hand, but he refuses and picks his way slowly down the beach, avoiding the pebbles. Owen heads after him, turning back to give me a thumbs-up. I mouth *thank you*, swallowing down grief. At the water's edge, they stop and I fear Ethan's going to change his mind, but then Owen runs through the breakers and dives in with a great splash. He turns onto his back, feet kicking out of the water, and beckons. After a pause, Ethan does the same, emerging out of the waves screeching in what I think for a moment is terror, but quickly realise is a mixture of delight and the shock of the cold. The others come barrelling over, jumping and splashing, and I relax as Ethan joins in. They're in there for a good twenty minutes, and without making it obvious to the others, Owen doesn't let Ethan out of arm's reach. When they finally scurry back to the windbreak, shivering, sand crusting on their wet skin, I wrap Ethan in a towel and hug him close to me. Owen gives me a broad smile as he helps Milo and Ben change.

'That was good fun, wasn't it, boys? Right, is it time for lunch? The wind's dropped a bit.'

I give Ethan a final cuddle and get the sandwiches out of the cool bag. He joins in with a good-natured squabble about who's having which flavour crisps, and Owen lays out plastic plates and cups. It's so nice being a member of a team again. It's been one of the hardest things of the past few months – being the lone adult in the house, solely responsible for every single thing and person.

After lunch, the boys take spades down to the shoreline to dig an enormous hole. The wind has dropped, and I lie back with my head on a rolled-up towel, luxuriating in the warmth of the September sun on my skin. I can't help questioning whether, if Andrew was sleeping with someone, Owen knew about it. It's unlikely he would have chosen Owen to confide in given how hurt Owen was by Saffie's infidelity, and because Owen and I have always been close, but there's a chance.

'Owen,' I say.

'Mmm?' he replies, on the verge of drifting off to sleep.

'Do you think Andrew was ... different ... before he died? I mean, in the last few months.'

'Different how?' He sounds wary, but not overly defensive.

'I don't know, exactly. Not himself.'

'You'd know better than anyone. You were with him all the time. Although ... '

'What?' I roll onto my side. He's lying on his back, about a metre away.

'Last time I saw him, I did get the sense he wanted to tell me something.'

'Like what?' I try to sound unconcerned. I don't want him to stop because he's afraid of upsetting me.

'I don't know. He didn't actually say as much, it was just a feeling I got. It was when we were talking about the weekend away. He wasn't much looking forward to it – he was very upset about the Saffie-and-Todd thing – very protective of me.' His voice softens. 'And then ... I think there was something else, some other reason he didn't want to go, but he closed down and didn't say any more. I didn't push it – to be honest, I didn't want to give Saffie and Todd any more headspace. They've taken up too much of that over the last nine months.'

I can't be sure, but I don't think he's lying to me. Andrew was his best friend, but he and I go back a long way too. I trust that if there was something to tell, he'd let me know. But what was Andrew keeping from him? I return again and again to that bloody condom. I push the thought away.

'Saffie said you'd had a change of heart when I saw her last weekend. About being more civil for the sake of the boys.'

'Yeah. I thought it was time I stopped being such a dick, basically.'

'Good for you. Although no one could blame you for being upset.'

'I'm grateful to you and Andrew for sticking by me. But the thing is – what's happened has happened. I can't change it now. I can only control how things are going forward, and it's incontrovertibly better for the boys if their parents are on reasonable terms. I just wish it hadn't taken me so long to understand that. It's partly losing Andrew that prompted it. Life's so bloody short. I've wasted too much of it on bitterness and hate.'

'So – this other reason why he didn't want to go – did you get any impression as to what it was about?' I can't let this go without getting everything I can out of him.

'He really didn't say much. Sorry.'

We lapse into silence. Owen's breathing slows into a rhythmic pattern punctuated by the occasional snore. The boys are digging a complicated network of channels in the sand. I try to focus on the crashing of the waves and the wild cries of the seagulls, but it's no good. All I can think about is Andrew, and what he was hiding from me.

Chapter 25

Liz

'Do you want a coffee or anything?' Poppy stands in the doorway to her office readjusting her hair, which is held back with a tortoiseshell clip.

'Yeah, that'd be nice. God, I haven't been here for ages.' I perch on the sofa that just about fits in the tiny reception area of Andrew and Poppy's rented office space in a business park on the outskirts of Haverbridge.

She unclips the canister from the coffee machine, fills it with water and replaces it, then tries to slot a capsule into the little drawer at the front.

'God, sorry, I don't know how to work it. Lola normally does it when we have clients in and I only drink tea.'

'I know,' I say, laughing. 'I'm your best friend, remember? Here, let me do it.'

'Thanks. I need to send a couple of emails and then we can talk.'

She disappears into her office, and I sit down with my coffee, oddly nervous. For one thing, it's strange being in a work situation with Poppy. Although she and Andrew worked together for years, I never got involved. I'm used to Poppy being flaky and disorganised but here she is assured and in control. The other reason I'm nervous is I don't know how Poppy's going to react to what I'm about to suggest. Since the day they all came over for lunch and she told me about the insurance, the cogs in my mind have been turning. I even spoke to Owen about it at the beach last weekend. I need a challenge – something to distract me, to breathe life back into me, to give me a purpose. This could be the perfect thing.

'Right, sorry about that.' Poppy sits down next to me and places the paperwork on the coffee table in front of us. 'I'll take you through this, and then you can let me know if you have any questions, OK?'

'There's something I wanted to run by you first, if that's OK.'

'Oh. OK, sure.'

She takes off her glasses and lays them on top of the papers.

'I've got a proposal for you. You know how bored I've been at work over the last few years, right? And when I worked in events, in those dim and distant days when I actually had a career, I really enjoyed the parts of my job that crossed over into PR. I was thinking that maybe I won't sell the shares, but instead I could keep them and work in the business with you.'

'What?' Poppy looks flabbergasted. 'But ... I don't

mean to be horrible … you don't know anything about PR. It was a long time ago that you worked in events.'

'I know, but I reckon I've got lots of transferable skills. And I can learn on the job! I'm not expecting to come in as a partner – I could take on a lot of the stuff that you do at first – the financial stuff, for example, which I already do at work – which would leave you free to deal with the clients. And we could take on a PR bod part-time at first to help with the clients whilst I'm learning. I don't know how it would pan out in detail but I think we could make it work. What do you say?'

'Gosh, I … er … I'm not sure, Liz. It would need a lot of consideration.'

'Yes, I know, but …' I tail off, crestfallen. I knew she'd have doubts, but I thought she'd be more excited at the prospect of us working together. 'I thought you'd be pleased. It would mean you wouldn't have to shoulder everything alone. And we'd be working together. I thought it might be … fun.'

'We're not twenty-five any more, Liz. It's not like when you worked in London twenty years ago and went to events and had drinks after work every night with your mates from the office. I know everyone thinks I'm this kooky oddball who can't get anything done, but work is different, always has been. This is a small business. It's hard work. Everything depends on our clients getting a good service from us, getting a return on their investment. It's stressful. There's not a lot of fun.' She's like a totally different woman to the one who brought lunch round the other week. I guess this is her work persona.

'Yes, I know,' I say in a small voice. 'But Owen said—'

'Owen? What on earth has he got to do with it?'

'Nothing. I wanted to discuss the idea with him.'

'When? At the funeral?'

'No! Last weekend. I went to the beach with him.'

'What, just you and him?' She looks at me askance.

'No, with the kids. He's keen to make sure they still socialise with the rest of the gang when they're with him, not only when they're with Saffie and Todd.'

'Is he? How does Saffie feel about that?'

'Does it matter? She cheated on him, remember.'

'God, you're starting to sound like Andrew.'

'So what if I am?' Heat rises to my face. 'Andrew was my husband, and Owen was his best friend – and one of my best friends too. Sometimes it feels like he's the only one who cares that Andrew's dead.'

'Oh God, I'm sorry, love.' Suddenly my friend is back, the woman I love. 'He's not the only one who cares. I miss him terribly. And not because of the business. I miss him as a friend, and I can't begin to imagine what you're going through. I'm just not sure that now is a good time to be making any big decisions, like leaving your job and starting a new career.'

'It's the ideal time. It's a terrible cliché, but it's true: life is short. I don't want to waste any more of it filling in spreadsheets and waiting for three o'clock to roll round so I can leave to pick up the kids.'

'But there are loads of spreadsheets here. Especially if you take over some of my responsibilities.'

'Yes, but it'd be different. I'd be more invested. I'd care more.'

'I get that, but . . . I'll need to think about it.'

'Owen said—'

'Jesus, Liz. Why are you so hung up on what Owen thinks? You know what he's put Saffie through.'

'What about what she put him through? Anyway, that's all different now. Owen's realised he needs to have a better relationship with Saffie for the sake of the kids. And before you say anything, that came from her, not Owen – she told me herself. Things are a lot better.'

'Liz, love, I can't believe I'm asking you this right now, but there's nothing . . . going on . . . between you and Owen, is there?'

'No! God, no. Of course not.' My face is on fire, but hopefully she'll think it's from anger.

'Good. I mean, I suppose he's attractive if you like that type of thing, but you're incredibly vulnerable at the moment. Plus, you need your friends.'

'You're right, I do. Owen is one of my friends.'

'I know, but I mean Saffie, and the rest of us. It would be so complicated, and I wouldn't want to see you taken advantage of.'

'I'm not going to be. There's nothing going on. Can we go back to the business, please? I really would like to give it a go.'

'Well . . . ' She takes a tissue from a box on the coffee

166

table and rubs at an imaginary smudge on the lens of her glasses. 'I don't mean to sound ... whatever ... but it's not up to you.'

'What do you mean?'

'We had it written into the partnership agreement when we set up the business that the surviving partner would have the right to buy out the one who had passed away. You can't legally hold on to your shares if I want to buy them.' Work-Poppy has returned in full force.

'I see. Presumably you could choose not to buy my shares?'

'Yes.'

'But you don't want to?'

'Liz, you've rather sprung this on me. I need time to think about it.'

'Fine.' I gather up my jacket and bag and head for the door without another word. Poppy doesn't try and stop me.

I manage to wait until I get into the car before I let the tears fall.

Chapter 26

Liz

As I get ready to go out for drinks with the girls, arranged by Saffie, I can't shake the sensation of being watched. I haven't seen the young woman from the funeral again, and I'm beginning to think it wasn't her after all. There have been several times when I could have sworn I'd seen Andrew, so I know I can't rely on myself at the moment. Grief does strange things to you. But still, several times I've had a prickling sensation on the back of my neck and spun round. There's never anybody there. The evening sun slants through my bedroom window as I sit in front of the mirror making a futile attempt to disguise the bags under my eyes. When I've done the best I can, I walk over to the window. There's nobody around but I draw the curtains.

'Do you have to go out?' Ethan sidles into the room and flops down on my bed.

I screw the lid onto my concealer and lie down beside him, guilt invading me.

'Do you not want me to?'

He doesn't reply but nestles into me, thumb firmly in his mouth.

'I don't have to go, no.'

'But you want to.'

'Yes.' I think of all the advice I've read. *You must be honest with your children*, all the books say. *Don't hide your sadness from them, or they'll think it's not OK for them to be sad.* 'I'm sad about Daddy like you are. Spending time with my friends helps me feel better.' This is sort of true, although all my interactions with them are tinged with suspicion.

'Owen's coming to babysit,' I add.

He pulls away from me and removes his thumb.

'Will he play Minecraft with us?'

'We can ask.'

'OK, then.'

The doorbell rings and I go downstairs to open it. Owen fills the doorway. With the evening sun behind him his face is in darkness for a second. He steps forward to hug me.

'Hi,' I say into his shoulder. 'Thanks again for doing this. Are you sure it's OK?'

'Of course.' He steps back. 'I'm so glad you finally took me up on the offer. I'm delighted to have something useful and concrete I can help you with.'

'Help yourself to whatever you want,' I say as we go through to the kitchen. Josh comes thumping down the stairs and into the room.

'Owen! Ethan says you're going to play Minecraft with us!'

'I hope that's OK,' I say. 'He was a bit funny about me going out.'

'I warn you, I'm terrible at it,' he says to Josh ruefully.

'Come on!' Josh tugs at his sleeve.

'OK, show me the way,' he says, and then turns back to me. 'Have a good night, Liz. Stay as long as you like.'

Before I leave, I poke my head into the living room where Ethan and Josh are rolling with laughter at Owen's attempts at the game. The boys wave casually in my direction and I experience a fierce burst of gratitude to Owen.

I decide to walk into town and get a cab home so I can have a couple of drinks. As I clip my way down our leafy street, I hear footsteps behind me. I force myself not to turn around, telling myself there's nothing sinister about it. It's no more than an innocent person walking behind me at seven in the evening. It's not even dark. Nevertheless, I double check I've got my phone. The footsteps speed up. I unlock my phone and go to Owen's number, my thumb hovering over the ring icon, feeling faintly ridiculous. I'm minutes from home. A hand grabs my elbow and my phone slips onto the pavement with a clatter.

'Sorry, Liz, did I make you jump?'

It's my neighbour, Sophie, head to toe in pink lycra, out for her evening run.

'Not to worry. I'm just a bit antsy.'

She pivots to pained sympathy. 'Yes. How *are* you?'

'I'm good. I'd better get on, I'm late. You carry on with your run.'

'OK. Let's get together soon, yeah?'

I agree, knowing that'll be the last I see of her until the next time we accidentally bump into each other and discuss plans for a get-together that will never happen. When she's jogged off, I make myself take a few deep breaths. I need to pull myself together or I won't get through this evening.

By the time I get to Saffie's wine bar of choice, which is expensive enough to ensure that the clientele is as middle-aged as we are, I've recovered my composure. Saffie and Trina are waiting for me, a bottle of champagne in an ice bucket beside them, three glasses on the table. I would have preferred something else.

'Is it just the three of us?' I say.

'Yes,' Saffie says. 'Poppy couldn't make it – something came up at the last minute.'

Either Poppy lied to her, or Saffie's lying to me now, but I don't call it out. Clearly Poppy doesn't want to see me after our last encounter. I put the hurt that causes me aside. I can't dwell on it. Trina and Saffie get their *how are yous* out of the way over the first drink, which I fend off with a mix of *up and downs* and *not too bads*, and then Saffie moves on to bitching about Kitty.

'She's been worse than ever recently – even more so than when we announced our engagement. She never seems to be at work during the day – keeps turning up at the house on some pretext or other, moping about with a face like a wet weekend – and then swans off to work in the evening doing God knows what.'

'She works in events, doesn't she?' Trina says. 'So it would be a lot of evening work?'

'I've never quite been able to get to grips with what she does, to be honest. Whatever it is, she has a lot of free time in the day to hang around trying to make me feel uncomfortable in my own home.'

'Give her time,' Trina says. 'She'll have to come to terms with it sooner or later. How are the boys doing, Liz?'

'Not bad. Josh seems normal. Ethan's been very quiet.'

'Who's with them tonight?' Saffie asks.

'Owen.' I watch her face, knowing she'll be at best surprised.

'Really?' She's shocked, although she has no reason to be. Owen was Andrew's best friend, and she's always known that both Andrew and I have seen him regularly since the split. Plus, I haven't noticed her offering to babysit my children. 'That's kind of him,' she says grudgingly.

'Yes, it is.' I must have sounded more pointed than I meant to, as she leans across and presses my hand.

'Sorry, darling, I didn't mean to sound disapproving. Sometimes I forget that the rest of you still have a relationship with him now that I don't. But of course you do – especially you, with Andrew and Owen being so close. I mean, you've known him as long as you knew Andrew.'

'Longer, a tiny bit,' I say. 'I met him earlier the same

evening I met Andrew – it was Andrew's twenty-first, in that funny house in Exeter where one of the bedrooms had a shower cubicle in it – do you remember?'

'Oh God, yes. That was Owen's room, I think, although that was before we got together, thank goodness, so I never had to shower in it,' Saffie says, laughing.

'No, it was Andrew's room!' says Trina. 'I was still going out with him when they first lived in that house. I used to make him leave the room while I was showering. It was so weird. Obviously, this was well before you met him,' she says hastily to me.

'I know,' I say. 'You and Julian got together the same night Andrew and I met.'

'Did it ever bother you,' Saffie asks, 'that Andrew was still friends with Trina? Not now, I mean, it's ancient history, but back then, when you guys first got together?'

'No!' says Trina. 'I mean … sorry, Liz … didn't mean to butt in, but Andrew and I had split up a month before, which I know doesn't sound very long, but it's a lifetime when you're twenty-one, isn't it? You didn't mind, did you?'

'No,' I say. 'Not really.' It's not true. It bothered me hugely at first, especially as for the first couple of months of our relationship we were long-distance and Trina was very much a part of his everyday life, although she was with Julian. It got better when she went travelling. Before I found the condom I would have said all this to them, but now I can't bear the thought that one of them could have lied to me then and is lying to me still. What if

Trina has always held a candle for Andrew? Worse, what if he held a candle for her? I need to keep my cards close to my chest.

'What about Julian?' Saffie asks Trina.

'I think he found it hard at first, to be honest,' Trina says. 'He's . . .' she pauses as if choosing her words carefully, 'not without jealousy.'

'I would have struggled,' Saffie says. 'Todd definitely would. He hates it if he senses I'm even attracted to anyone else. I told him about this one time when I'd come onto someone who turned me down, and he didn't like that at all.'

'Hang on, when was that?' Trina says.

'It was . . . before I met Todd . . .' she says vaguely. 'I know it sounds bad, but I was unhappy with Owen well before Todd and I got together. Nothing happened anyway. It was a silly, drunken moment that came to nothing. That's the point – Todd was jealous even at the thought of me liking another man, even though he didn't know who it was, and it was before we met.'

'Really? Oh gosh, Julian's not that bad, although he can be surprisingly Neanderthal when he wants to be.' She gives a shaky laugh.

'I think it's kind of hot,' Saffie says with a smug smile. 'I love how much Todd wants me all to himself.'

'It sounds kind of controlling to me,' I say. 'Does he talk to you about women he fancies?'

'Yes, but only in fun,' she says. 'He wouldn't do anything about it.'

'So it's fun for him to tell you about women he likes, but you're not allowed to mention a passing fancy for a bloke off the telly?' Trina says.

'For God's sake, you're reading too much into this! Let's change the subject. How are things with you and Julian? You guys seemed a little spiky with each other in Italy.'

'We're fine,' Trina says in a stilted tone, her eyes straying anxiously my way.

'Don't worry about me,' I say. 'You don't have to censor yourselves or wrap me in cotton wool – that's the last thing I need. What I need is for things to be normal, for my friends to be able to moan about their husbands around me.'

'No honestly, it's not that,' she says. 'There's nothing to tell.'

'What were you and Andrew talking about on the terrace in Italy, the night of Todd's birthday dinner?' Saffie says, determined to keep the conversational heat off her and Todd. 'You were having a right old deep and meaningful. I thought maybe it was about Julian?'

'I've no idea,' Trina says. 'It was months ago. I'm surprised you noticed what with lavishing all your attention on your *fiancé*.'

'Shut up,' Saffie says laughing, and as quickly as it appeared, the ill feeling dissipates. The three of us dissolve into giggles until I find my laughter turning to weeping, unexpectedly struck by the realisation that hits me like a wave out of nowhere that I'm never going to see Andrew again.

'Oh, darling.' Saffie tops up my glass with champagne. 'Here, drink up.'

'That'll make me cry even more,' I say, scrabbling in my bag for a tissue.

'That's OK – it's good,' Trina says. 'We've been worried about you – you've been coping so well – too well. You don't have to soldier on pretending everything's OK.'

'Let it out – I've got all night. The longer the better. Todd won't be home till late and Kitty's not working tonight so she's probably hanging around at ours waiting to make my life hell.'

I find a clean, if dusty, serviette from a sandwich shop in the depths of my bag and blow. As my nose clears, so does my head, and a new and hideous suspicion entwines its tentacles around my heart. What if the reason Kitty's been so awful since Italy isn't Saffie and Todd's engagement? What if Andrew wasn't sleeping with one of my best friends? What if he was sleeping with Kitty?

Chapter 27

Liz

Owen gets two tall glasses down from the cupboard and mixes us both a gin and tonic. I shouldn't really have it – I had too much to drink in the wine bar – but as the gin glugs in over the ice and the tonic fizzes and spits, I allow myself a moment of pleasure at having something done for me. Not only that, but done by someone who knows where the glasses are because he's been here so many times before, and who understands why I pretend to like wine when I don't.

We clink glasses across the kitchen table. Everything is blissfully quiet. The only time I can let my mask drop at home is when the boys are asleep, and I'm so exhausted I'm often asleep then too.

'Did they go to bed OK?'

'Good as gold. If a touch later than you'd ideally like, I suspect.'

'Bedtimes have gone out the window, to be honest. Pretty much as soon as they're in bed, so am I.'

'I know you must be fed up with this question, but how are you doing?'

I am, but I don't mind it so much from him.

'Most of the time, I'm OK. I have to be, for the boys.' I feel sick at the thought of what it would be like for them if I wasn't OK. If I couldn't get out of bed, wasn't cooking for them or keeping up with the washing or making them brush their teeth or all the other millions of tasks I've continued to do with a smile on my face. 'But then I get moments where it hits me like a wave, like I've been knocked off my feet. Last night I was sitting on the sofa watching TV and I looked over to where he normally sits . . . sat, I mean . . . and I couldn't believe he was gone. How can he have been here, and now he's not? Like, I know this sounds stupid, but where is he?'

'I know exactly what you mean. I had it with Mum, and I've had it with Andrew too. I'll get caught up in something and for a short while I almost forget, and then it hits me, and it's like it's happened again, you've lost them all over again.'

'Yes!' I lean forward. 'And it's unbelievable that it can have happened. I have to say it out loud, even if I'm alone. *He's dead. He's actually dead.*'

'Yep, I get it. I think that's normal. You know, something else that's normal is having mixed feelings about someone after they've died. You don't have to only remember the positives. It's OK to acknowledge all the parts of them.'

I try to remain composed, but it's such a relief to hear those words, to have permission to feel the way I do about Andrew since I found the condom, that I can't stop the tears falling.

'God, sorry, Liz, I didn't mean to upset you.'

'You haven't. It's . . . ' Being with Owen is so easy, and drink has weakened my resolve to keep quiet. 'On the morning of the funeral, I found something in his bag, the one he took to Italy.'

'What?' He leans forward across the table, full of concern.

'A condom.'

He draws back as if I've hit him.

'Presumably you and he didn't use them.'

'No, not for years.'

'Are you sure it was his?'

'No, how can I be? But why else would it be there? It was a new bag, he'd never used it before. The condom was in the pocket of the shorts he was wearing during the day.'

'So if he *had* taken condoms to Italy . . . ' he says slowly.

'Yep. He was sleeping with someone who was there.'

'God.' He takes a long pull on his drink.

'Why aren't you saying, *of course he wasn't, Andrew wasn't like that, he wouldn't lie to you?*' I say, tears threatening again.

'Well . . . there are always secrets, aren't there? Nobody ever knows every single thing about another person, even those closest to them.'

He runs his fingernail along a groove in the table, dislodging dust and grit.

'Owen – what is it? Do you know something about this? Was Andrew having an affair?'

'Oh Liz, no, nothing like that. I'd be truly shocked if he was sleeping with one of your friends.'

'But there is something, isn't there? Tell me, please.'

He sighs.

'It doesn't feel like the right time, but ... OK. There was one time at university, about a month after he met you, that Trina stayed over at mine and Andrew's house. With Andrew, I mean. I don't think they knew I was there – Andrew never found out that I knew.'

'What?' Suddenly, there's not enough air in the room.

'I'm really sorry, Liz.'

'Are you sure they ... ?'

'Yes. I ... I heard them. My room was next to Andrew's.'

'And you're sure this was after he and I got together?' A wave of anger rolls through me. Fractured memories of the party where we met flash through my brain. Chatting to Owen in the kitchen and then Andrew coming over, the birthday boy, so handsome and self-assured; talking to him for hours with the sensation of a key slotting into a lock. Of coming home.

'Yes. I know it was because she got together with Julian at Andrew's twenty-first party, the same night you met Andrew, and she was definitely going out with Julian when I heard her with Andrew. Julian was away for the night.'

'He doesn't know?'

'Not as far as I know. I suppose Trina might have told him, but I doubt it.'

'Was it just that one time?'

'I never saw or heard them together again. Maybe I shouldn't have said anything.'

'But . . . how did it happen?'

Andrew always told me he fell in love with me that very first night. We hadn't seen each other again for a month or so after because I was still living in Manchester and he was in Exeter and we were all embroiled in our final university exams, but we'd spoken on the phone almost every night.

'I don't know. Like I said, he never told me about it and I never asked. I'm sorry, Liz.' I don't know if he's sorry he never told me before, or sorry he's told me now, but either way, I don't blame Owen. Andrew was his best friend and he barely knew me then. I blame Andrew – and I blame Trina who was going out with Julian.

'My God, Owen. Did I know him at all?'

'Don't think like that. It doesn't make your whole relationship a lie.'

'Doesn't it?'

There's been a part of me all along that thought there must be an innocent explanation for the condom, because deep in my core I trusted Andrew and I trusted my friends. What Owen's told me has shown me that I couldn't have been more wrong. Trina has been lying to me for years. Who's to say she's not lying to me now?

181

Chapter 28

Liz

I ring the doorbell with some trepidation. Poppy and I haven't spoken since that day in her office.

'Hi.' She opens the door wearing an ancient striped apron stained with the debris from a thousand meals. The wooden spoon in her hand drips a vibrant tomato sauce onto the scuffed wooden floorboards. 'Come in.'

I follow her down the hall to the galley kitchen at the back of the house. She closes the door between the kitchen and the hall behind us. Steam rises from a bubbling pot of water on one of the gas rings and the sauce simmers on another.

'It's boiling in here, shall I open the back door?'

'It's stuck,' she says. 'I need to get someone to come and sort it. Open the window.'

I force the rusty key into the lock and prise open the top window. Even by Poppy's standards the house is in a state of some disrepair.

I hand her the bottle of wine I've brought. I would

have said I'm entirely myself with Poppy, but I still make the adjustments I make for everyone, to make sure I don't reveal myself as being not quite one of us.

'Here, sit down.' She swipes up a pile of paperwork from the tiny table to make room for me. 'Who's got the boys?'

'Owen's babysitting.'

'That's kind of him.' She remains neutral, not betraying any of the opinions she voiced last time about me and Owen. She pours me a glass of wine and takes a big gulp of her own as she stirs the pot with overdone vigour.

'How's everything?' she asks.

'OK.' Unbidden, my imagination conjures up a vision of a young Trina and Andrew locked in a passionate embrace in Andrew's student room in that house in Exeter. I had so many happy times there, but I'll never be able to think of it again without pain. I want more than anything to confide in Poppy, but everything is different between us since I found that condom. If you'd asked me before that day if I thought she'd ever betray me I would have said no way on earth, but I'm not sure of anything any more.

'We missed you the other night,' I venture.

'Sorry about that – I was snowed under with work. How's Saffie? Planning her big day?'

'Yeah, although her divorce still isn't finalised. Why are you so anti her and Todd?' I ask.

'I still think it's too soon. What's the rush?'

'Or you could ask why wait?' I say, playing devil's advocate. 'Life is short, as I know.'

Her shoulders drop. 'Sorry, I didn't mean to be unsympathetic to your situation.'

'It's fine, you weren't.'

As she's draining the pasta, there's a ring at the doorbell.

'Shall I get it?'

'No, leave it,' she says.

'It's no trouble, it might be a parcel and it's annoying to miss them.'

'No, leave it,' she says sharply. I look at her in surprise.

'Sorry,' she says. 'There's loads of people selling at the door round here at the moment. It'll be one of them. Best to ignore.'

The caller gives three sharp raps on the door. Poppy places the pan softly back on the hob, as if to minimise the noise.

'Is everything OK?' I say.

'Yes, of course. How's Owen? I feel bad that I haven't seen much of him.'

Like the others in the group, Poppy has barely kept in touch with Owen since Saffie left him. You think when you're married that your friends like the two of you equally, but there's no hiding the stark reality of the situation when you split up. People choose their sides, and everyone chose Saffie's, apart from Andrew and I who were stuck uncomfortably in the middle.

'He's good. I told you he's making more of an effort to be civil with Saffie?'

'Yeah, that's great.' She puts two bowls of pasta on the table and sits down opposite me. 'Do you see a fair bit of him?'

'Quite a bit. He's been brilliant with babysitting,' I say.

We shovel forkfuls of pasta into our mouths in silence. It's hard to swallow. I can't bear that there's this space between us when there never has been before. This thing with the business is making it worse, and realistically I'm not in the right frame of mind to launch into a new job. I can't contemplate going back to my old one at the moment, although my compassionate leave won't last for ever.

'Listen, Poppy,' I say without giving myself much chance to think about it, 'if you'd rather I sold you my shares, that's what we'll do. I don't want to fall out with you about it.'

'Are you sure?' Her eyes glisten. 'I wanted to talk to you about it again but I didn't want it to come between us.'

'I don't want that either. If you say it's not the right thing for the business, I trust you.'

'Thank you. Thanks for understanding. I've got the paperwork here, if you want to check it over later?'

'Sure. How's Scarlet getting on back at uni?'

'So much better. She's moved in with a girl from her course and they're getting on really well. I can't tell you how relieved I am.'

When we've finished our pasta, she pours us both more wine and goes upstairs to get the papers. While she's gone, her phone – which she's left on the table – pings with a message and I look across to see who it's from. My heart leaps. It's from Todd. Why is he messaging Poppy? When she comes down, she sits opposite me, looks at her phone and puts it aside without reading the message. I could ask her – if everything was normal, I would. But nothing is normal and it feels like it never will be again, and so I say nothing.

'There's loads of facts and figures here, but these are the important ones.' She turns the paper round so I can see it. 'That's what the business is currently valued at,' she points to a figure at the bottom of one column, 'Andrew and I were fifty-fifty, so that ...' she points to another figure at the bottom of the next column, 'is how much it will cost me to buy you out. As I said, we had partnership protection insurance, which will just about cover it.'

'Oh. Right.' I wasn't expecting any particular figure, but I had thought it would be higher than that.

'Is that ... are you OK?' Poppy says anxiously.

'It is what it is, I guess, and I'm OK for money. Andrew had life insurance. I suppose I thought, I don't know ... that it might be more than that.'

'Do you remember a few years ago we invested in that new IT system?'

'Vaguely.'

'That was a fairly large expense as you can see here,' she points to an entry on the spreadsheet, 'and we'd agreed – Andrew and I – to depreciate it over the last three years, which reduced the share value for that period. So that could be why it's a bit lower than you thought.'

'Like I said, I'm not really sure what I was expecting. It's fine. You need to crack on with things. I'll sign everything now.'

'Are you sure? You don't want to let your accountant have a look at it?'

'I don't have an accountant – part-time admin assistants don't need them! It's OK, I trust you.'

I sign the papers where she indicates, and she puts them away and pours more wine. We spend the rest of the evening chatting about our kids, old times and the Landell Trust charity auction next Saturday that Saffie's organised. I try to avoid any discussion of Trina, not wanting to give away that there's something wrong. Poppy doesn't mention or check her phone. I try to store Todd's message and what it means away with all the other troubling questions in my mind, but I can't ignore it. Poppy is lying to me about whatever's going on between her and Todd. If she can lie to me about that, what else is she capable of?

Chapter 29

Liz

Todd's rich friends surround our table on all sides, dressed up to the nines, guzzling champagne and braying with laughter. I barely notice them because all my attention is focused on Andrew. He's standing there at the back of the room, leaning against the wall, smiling at me as I stare at him open-mouthed, delight and anger and disbelief fighting for supremacy inside me. He starts walking towards me and I stand up from the table as if in a trance. I can feel Poppy and Trina looking at me curiously, wondering what I'm doing. My heart is racing. Andrew smiles and waves, but he's not looking at me, he's heading for another table, bending to kiss a red-haired woman.

Oh, God. It's not Andrew. I sink back down, pressing my hands to my eyes. Of course it's not Andrew, just as that dark-haired man on the street the other day wasn't him, or the broad-shouldered dad at the school gate waiting for his children. When will it stop, this seeing him wherever I go?

None of this feels right. I'm at a round, white-linen-clad table with our group of friends (and Kitty). All the talk on the tables around us is of school fees, house prices, the trials of finding a decent cleaner or nanny. I'd be considered middle class these days (although I've never had a cleaner or a nanny, and the boys go to a state school) but I'll never be part of this world. I'll always be separate. Other. Less.

I'm the guest of honour, apparently. I'll be forever grateful to the Landell Trust, and to Saffie for raising funds for them, but an auction catering to the whims of the rich doesn't feel like the way to do it. I know it shouldn't matter. The charity needs money to help people who find themselves in the situation I did, and it shouldn't make any difference how they get it, but it makes me feel sick. I've been blocking out those terrible days in Italy because it's the only way I'm able to get on with my life, but now the memories crash over me in wave after nauseating wave. I force down a mouthful of champagne, the bubbles pricking my tongue and throat, the taste sharp like vinegar.

I'm grateful that Saffie bought a table for us, so I don't have to spend the night talking to Todd's hedge fund pals and Saffie's prep-school mum friends. I know we need them here because they've got cash to spend, but they don't have any connection to me, to Andrew, to what happened. They're here for a fun night out, a chance to boast about the deal they've cut this week, to show off their latest designer dress or facial peel. An opportunity

189

to feel good about themselves and impress their friends by forking out for a whole table.

The lots consist of 'things money can't buy'. Saffie and Todd have tapped up everyone they know to tap up everyone *they* know, and have come up with a host of incredible lots: private helicopter rides, tours of football stadiums including meet and greets with premiership players, catered boxes at Lords and Ascot and Wimbledon, VIP backstage passes for gigs and music festivals, a cooking class in your home with a Michelin star chef. The list goes on.

Poppy looks tired and isn't saying much. There's been little to no interaction between her and Todd, and I still have no idea why he texted her the other night. I suppose it could have been to do with the business. Saffie told me the other night that he'd been asking her what was going on with it. When she told him Poppy and I had come to an agreement, he said I should let him know if he could help in any way, which was kind of him.

Trina and Julian are chatting away gaily, but it's all on the surface – underneath they seem as brittle and disconnected from each other as they were in Italy. I try to keep any thoughts of what Owen told me about her and Andrew at bay – tonight is about Andrew, and raising money for the charity that helped me so much – but I can't. Every time I look at Trina, unwanted images of the two of them together fill my mind. It's like being transported back to when Andrew and I first met and I didn't like the fact that he was still close to her, his recent ex-girlfriend. If I'd found out then that he'd cheated on me with her, I doubt our relationship would have continued. My life would have been totally different.

Next to Trina is Kitty, insanely sexy but sullen as a teenager in a black silk fishtail dress, drinking fast and only speaking when spoken to. When she gave me a perfunctory air kiss on arrival, I was almost asphyxiated by her perfume, a grown-up, musky scent that evokes cocktails and cigarette smoke and smudged make-up.

'Are you OK?' Poppy says quietly, under another of Todd's anecdotes about the items his brilliant rich friends have donated to the auction, and what he's planning to bid on.

'Yes, not bad.'

'Is this all a bit weird?' She gestures around the candlelit room.

'Yeah, a bit.' My panic subsides at being able to admit it.

'Think about the money, what they'll be able to do with it.'

'I know, you're right. Thanks.'

The waiters come round and clear the main-course plates. The auction will start as we eat our dark chocolate mousse. Saffie wanted to give the punters a chance to get well oiled before the bidding begins. Anita Standlish, a local minor TV celeb, is acting as the auctioneer, and she gets a huge cheer from the crowd as she comes on stage.

'Good evening, everyone, and welcome to this auction in aid of the Landell Trust. We've got tons of amazing lots coming up, so don't go anywhere! Before we get going, I'd like to invite the woman who's made all this possible to come up and say a few words – please give a big hand for Saffie Kesterton!'

An even bigger cheer goes up as Saffie, elegant in a floor-length, high-necked midnight-blue dress that highlights her gym-taut body and probably cost as much as my car, threads her way through the tables and up on stage. She did ask me to say a few words, but I said no, unable to countenance the thought of standing up in front of all these rich people, feeling them pitying me, observing me like a curiosity, an animal in a zoo. Watching with prurient interest to see if I would break down and cry. Analysing my dress and shoes and vowel sounds to work out whether I was one of them.

'Thanks so much for coming, everyone. As Anita said, we've got lots of fabulous experiences up for auction tonight and competition's going to be stiff, so I hope you're feeling generous.'

'Something's feeling stiff!' brays a florid man from a table at the front who has already abandoned his bow tie and loosened his collar. There are whoops from the other men at his table.

'Jeremy!' the blonde woman beside him remonstrates, smiling indulgently as much as she can with her suspiciously smooth skin. Opposite me, Todd sits still as a statue although I sense a change in the set of his jaw. On stage, Anita Standlish grimaces, sensing trouble.

'All right, gentlemen, settle down,' Saffie says as if speaking to Milo and Ben. 'Let me be serious for a moment. A few months ago, I went on holiday to Italy with a group of dear friends to celebrate my fiancé's birthday. Tragically, while we out there, one of those friends, Andrew Morgan, got caught out by the tide and drowned.' A hush falls over the crowd. Jeremy's smooth-faced companion has him in a vice-like grip, willing him to read the room and keep quiet. 'Andrew's wife Liz was overwhelmed by both an emotional rollercoaster and a logistical nightmare. Even with friends like us to help her, the red tape was confusing and endless. I contacted the Landell Trust, and I don't know how we would have managed if it wasn't for their support. Tonight is about ensuring that everyone who finds themselves in this terrible situation has access to that help. And make no mistake, it could happen to anyone.'

They have their serious faces on, but I know no one here thinks this will ever happen to them. They're under the impression that their wealth and privilege protect them from it, as from so much else.

'So please, don't hold back – I don't think you'll be able to when you hear the details of what we've got on offer tonight. With no further ado, I'll hand you over to Anita to get on with the business of the evening, and urge you to have your chequebooks at the ready!'

There's a buzz of excitement, Andrew and his fate instantly forgotten as the guests leaf excitedly through their catalogues. Anita announces the first lot, a VIP driving experience at Silverstone, donated by one of Todd's friends who is on the board.

An hour and a half and many thousands of pounds later, we're down to the final lot, a week at a luxury resort in Kenya with a personal guided safari. The bidding goes higher and higher, bidders reluctantly dropping out until it's only Todd and Jeremy, the red-faced man on the front table, left in the running. Jeremy takes longer each time before inclining his head to indicate he's willing to add yet another hundred pounds to the mounting tally. By contrast, Todd has agreed to each increment almost before Anita has offered it. Saffie leans over worriedly at one point and whispers in his ear, but he dismisses her, unwilling to remove his laser-beam concentration from the stage for a second. Eventually Jeremy admits defeat and flings his napkin to the floor, beaten. Todd smirks as he goes up to sign the agreement, his satisfaction undeniable.

'Is Todd particularly into safaris, Saffie?' Trina asks.

'God, no,' she says. 'I doubt we'll go, he's so busy at work. It's about winning. That was the final lot, the ultimate prize.'

'He's paid all that for a holiday you might not even go on?' says Poppy, knocking back a glass of champagne. 'So that what? Todd can feel like a big man?' She's enunciating her words with exaggerated care.

'Does it matter?' Saffie says coldly. 'It's about the money, for the Landell Trust. To help people like Liz. And he'll give the holiday to someone else if we can't use it.'

'That's big of him.'

'Yes, it is, actually,' she says.

'What's big of who?' Todd reappears, sliding an expensive-looking pen into the breast pocket of his tux.

'Never mind,' Saffie says tightly. 'All done?'

'Yep.' He slides into his seat with a self-satisfied smile. 'Well bid, sir.'

Oh Lord, it's Jeremy, the other bidder. Over at his table, his companion is watching as anxiously as her face will allow. He staggers and holds on to the back of Todd's chair to steady himself.

'Evening, all.' He waves a hand around the table at the rest of us, stopping short in surprise when he gets to Kitty.

'Aha, good evening to you!' he leers.

Kitty looks horrified. Todd straightens his back, ready to tell this revolting lech twice his daughter's age where to go, when Jeremy continues.

'Fancy seeing you again. Who are you ... *accompanying* tonight?'

Kitty's horror turns to panic.

'I don't know what you mean,' she says but she's clearly rattled.

'Don't worry, we've met before – I'm a friend of Simon Carlton. You've ... escorted him to several events.'

'This is my daughter, Kitty,' Todd says through gritted teeth.

'Oho! I see! In that case, I assume you know what she does for a living, old chap. She's the crème de la crème – the very highest of the high-class escorts, aren't you, dear?'

'That's enough!' Todd looks like he's going to explode.

Kitty is close to tears, too upset for any denial she could put forward to be worth anything.

'Oh dear, old chap,' Jeremy looks like he's won the lottery. 'It seems I've been the bearer of bad news. Congrats on the auction.' He stumbles away towards the bar, leaving a shocked silence in his wake.

'Kitty, can we have a word in private?' Todd is stretched and taut, like an elastic band pulled to its limits.

She pushes back her chair and stands, then catches sight of Saffie, who can't hide her shocked fascination.

'I bet you're loving this, aren't you?' she says.

'Kitty! In private!' Todd barks.

'Why bother?' she says coldly. 'They all know now. But do they know whose fault it is? You're the one who insisted I make my own way in life, who refused to help me when you could easily have done so. If this is the way I choose to make money, it's none of your concern. Or that of your gold-digging little fiancée.'

Saffie looks like someone's thrown a bucket of cold water over her.

'That's not fair,' I say. For all Saffie's faults, I don't believe she's with him for his money, and it's a bit rich coming from Kitty. Todd was well within his rights to encourage her to make her own way in life. 'There are millions of young women your age living hand to mouth in crappy bedsits, scraping the money together for a trip to the discount supermarket, who would kill for the advantages you've been given. Yet still it's not enough for you.'

'Seriously?' She turns on me, radiating a fierce energy. 'You're going to have a go at me, Liz?'

'Don't you dare speak to my friends like that.' Saffie's expression turns sour.

'I'll speak to them however I want.' She turns back to me. 'I wouldn't look so smug if I were you.'

'Stop this.' Poppy is determined, protective. 'Remember why we're here.'

'What are you talking about?' I say to Kitty, bewildered.

'Your husband, Andrew? The one we're all here for? I recognised him straight away, the first night in Italy. If I hadn't seen it all before, I would have been surprised to learn he was a family man. Think you knew him, do you? Well, guess who hired me as an escort one month before our little trip to Italy? That's right. Your devoted husband.'

She sweeps out of the room in a blaze of perfume, champagne and fury, leaving the rest of us in stunned silence.

Chapter 30

Liz

We sit amidst the debris of the meal, the tablecloth stained with wine and scattered with crumbs. I am motionless, trying to get to grips with Kitty's revelation about Andrew. Could she be lying? Why, though?

'If she thinks she's getting another penny out of me, she can think again,' Todd says.

Saffie is holding one of his hands in both of hers and she squeezes it.

'Let's not talk about it now, darling,' she says. 'We've had such a good night. Why don't we go home? The auction's over.'

'What the fuck is wrong with her?' Todd says, as if she hasn't spoken. 'I can't believe she would lower herself to that kind of work. It's disgusting.'

'Is it really?' says Poppy with a hint of danger.

'Poppy, this isn't the time for one of your speeches about sex work and feminism,' Trina says. 'I think we'll make a move too. Julian?' They start gathering up their things but Poppy speaks again.

'No, it's not about that, Trina. Todd knows what I'm talking about.'

'Poppy, you're drunk,' Saffie says. 'Todd, let's go.'

'No, let's have it, Poppy,' Todd says, not taking his eyes off her. 'Spit it out.'

'OK, I will. When we were in Italy,' she says to the table at large, 'I confided in Todd that I was having some ... financial difficulties, which I've now managed to sort out, thankfully. I thought he might be able to offer advice.'

'And what was the nature of these financial difficulties, Poppy?' Todd says faux-pleasantly.

'That's not important,' she says steadily. 'What's important was what you offered me as a way out.'

Todd's face is like thunder. Saffie, Trina, Julian and I are transfixed, unable to move, speak or intervene in whatever it is that's unfolding in front of us.

'You can't have forgotten, Todd? You said you'd pay off everything I owed if I would do you one little favour. All I'd have to do was fuck you.'

We all flinch. Saffie looks like she's been punched in the stomach, all the air taken out of her.

'Seriously? That's where you're going with this?' Todd looks around the table. 'You do all know she's a total fantasist, right?'

'Why the hell would I make this up? Saffie, I swear it's true. Liz, I came to your room in Italy to talk to you

199

about it but I lost my nerve. I was going to go through with it – I even had a condom in my pocket ready. He wanted to do it there in the villa, right under every-body's noses – that's the kind of man we're dealing with here.'

'Did you . . . did you drop the condom? Did you lose it? The day you came to our room to talk to me?'

'Yes,' she says, confused. 'I did, actually, but the point is, you have to believe me.'

Oh my God. Despite the drama that surges around me, I am giddy, as if an enormous weight has been lifted from my shoulders. The condom didn't belong to Andrew. He must have picked it up and put it in his pocket and forgotten about it. He wasn't having an affair. In Poppy's eyes I see reflected all twenty-seven years of our friendship, everything we've been through together. She's not lying.

'I believe you,' I say quietly. 'It's OK, I believe you.'

'Thank you,' she says. 'That's all that matters.'

'Why's that, Poppy?' Todd's question slithers over to us like a snake. 'Is that because Liz is your absolute best friend?'

'I'm leaving now,' she says, standing. 'Will you come with me, Liz?'

I pick up my clutch bag and go to push my chair back but Todd has other ideas.

'Don't go yet, Poppy,' he says in the same dangerous tone. 'Let me tell Liz the precise nature of your financial difficulties.'

'It doesn't matter,' I say, repulsed. I can't believe Saffie is planning to marry this man. He's vile.

'How about this? Poppy was stealing from the company she co-owned with your husband, Liz.'

'What?' I say. Beside me, Poppy freezes.

'Yep,' he says, satisfied he's finally got my attention. 'She'd got behind on her mortgage payments, got herself in all kinds of trouble – debt collectors beating down her door.' I think of that night at Poppy's where she wouldn't let me answer the door. Was that what was going on? 'So she helped herself from the company bank account – just a little, just to tide her over. She was going to pay it back, weren't you, Poppy?'

Poppy's gripping the back of her chair tightly, her knuckles bone-white, as if to stop herself from falling.

'But she found she couldn't, so she took a little more and a little more again. That's where she was when she came to me, in Italy. We discussed various options for her – none of them what she's now suggesting, incidentally. But I did tell her a story that takes on a whole new significance when you look at what's happened since.'

'Todd, what are you talking about?' Saffie says, bewildered.

'When Poppy asked my advice in Italy, we got into a more general conversation about small business and finances. One of the things I told her was about a friend of mine whose business partner died. They had insurance against something like that happening that meant he was able to buy his late business partner's shares from his wife. But when the time came to buy her out, he fudged the figures to show that the business was worth much less than it really was. Ring any bells, Poppy?'

A chasm opens in the heart of me as I think of the figure at the bottom of that spreadsheet indicating the value of the business that was lower than I had expected. I feel sick.

'Of course that was before Andrew was so tragically taken from us.' His words drip with poison. 'I never dreamed that this would happen – and even if I'd known I never would have suspected that Poppy would do that to her best friend. But when Saffie told me what you and Poppy had agreed, Liz, I had to wonder. I suspect if you examine those figures more closely, you'll find that Poppy has grossly undervalued the business, effectively defrauding you of what you're owed. Some friend, huh?'

I can't bear to look at her. I hear her give a stifled sob. She pushes the chair away from her with such force it topples over, and runs from the room.

Todd stands up, grimly satisfied. 'Saffie, we're leaving.'

'I . . . don't know.' Saffie is white-faced.

'You don't believe what that dumbass friend of yours said, do you?' Todd snarls. I've seen him be unpleasant before, but never anything like this. It's as if finding out about Kitty's escort job has made him determined to burn everyone else's world to the ground. 'Because if you do, we're done. Now, are you coming?' He holds out his hand to her. The rest of us hold our breath.

She picks up her bag, stands and puts her hand in his.

Todd surveys the table triumphantly, but Saffie doesn't take her eyes from the floor.

'Good night,' he says, and leads Saffie from the room like a child. Neither of them looks back.

Trina picks up Poppy's chair, sits down next to me and puts her arm around me.

'I know this is horrible, but try not to listen to Todd,' she says. 'Hear Poppy's side of the story before you jump to any conclusions. Todd's vicious, I wouldn't trust a word he says. And if Poppy did do this, she must have been absolutely at the end of her tether.'

Rage pulses through me. I would never have done this to Poppy, no matter how desperate I was.

'Don't try to defend her,' I say coldly, ducking out of her embrace. 'Or are you trying to make yourself feel better about you lying to me as well?'

'What do you mean?' She eyeballs me warily.

'Owen told me you slept with Andrew after he and I got together.' She inhales sharply. 'Did you know about this, Julian?' He sits very still, utterly impassive, as if he's wearing a mask of his own face. 'Owen told me everything, Trina.'

'How did he . . . ' she whispers.

'He heard you. He lived there, for Christ's sake,' I say. 'The fact is you've been lying to me for years – and to Julian, by the looks of it. I know it was a long time ago, but don't think for a second that means it doesn't hurt.'

We stare at each other across this chasm of lies. I've never had a falling-out with my friends like this before – it's so alien it could be a dream, but I know it's not. Into the silence, my phone rings. It's a withheld number, but I answer in case there's a problem with the boys who are being babysat by my neighbour's teenage daughter.

'Signora Morgan?' It's a woman with a soft Italian accent that stirs up painful memories of the days following Andrew's disappearance.

'Yes.'

'This is Elisabetta Stella.' She was the officer in charge of keeping me up to date with the police investigation while we were in Italy, their version of a family liaison officer. 'I'm sorry to call so late, but I wanted to let you know as soon as possible.'

'Yes?' There's a catch in my throat. The others around the table grow still as they sense that something serious is happening.

'We have found your husband's body. It was washed up on the shore down the coast from the beach at Villa Rosa.'

'Oh my God.'

I knew there was no way Andrew was alive, but I hadn't realised until now, when that shred of hope has been taken away, that on some level I've been hoping it was all a terrible mistake and Andrew was going to come walking back through the door. That's why I've been seeing his face in every dark-haired man I pass on the street, hearing his voice everywhere I go. In some ways that's what's been keeping me going, and now I'm toppling like a jenga tower that's had a fundamental piece removed.

'I'm afraid there is something else I need to talk to you about. I have bad news,' Elisabetta says. Bad news? How much worse can it get? 'Do you have someone with you, or someone you can call to come to you? A friend or relative?'

Trina is wiping away tears while Julian sits impassively, not touching or looking at her. I thought they were two of my best friends but I have no idea any more.

'Yes,' I say to Elisabetta. 'What is it?'

'There has been a post-mortem on Andrew's body. He didn't die by drowning. The post-mortem found that he was killed by a blow to the head. He was already dead when he entered the water.'

'What? I don't understand.' I grip the phone so hard it feels as if it might crumble in my hand. My vision wavers.

'Signora Morgan, I am afraid we are now treating this as a possible murder investigation.'

PART THREE

Andrew

Chapter 31

Andrew

The first time Andrew saw Liz, she was talking to Owen – laughing, head thrown back, shoulders open. It was Andrew's twenty-first birthday party. Later, he would look back on it as the last birthday when he had a party like this, in a boys' house shared with Owen and Julian. The bath crammed with ice and cans of beer. Couples snogging on the stairs. A girl puking in the bathroom, a queue of people with their legs crossed shouting at her to hurry up. A beautiful stranger laughing in the kitchen.

After this his birthdays would, like his life, become more sedate. More grown-up. Quiet drinks. Dinner parties. Romantic meals out with Liz. But on this particular night, he stumbled into the kitchen, beer and wine mingling ominously inside him, an argument he'd just had with an extremely drunk Trina still echoing through him. It had been a month since they'd split up and he'd thought she was over it. She'd seemed fine all the times he'd seen her – he'd been congratulating himself on how adult and civilised the break-up had been. It could have been difficult as they shared the same friendship group and neither of them wanted to lose that, but he thought they'd managed to pull off the feat of remaining friends with no hard feelings on either side.

He couldn't have been more wrong. She'd arrived at the party early and hit the vodka hard, radiating a glittery, sharp-cornered but contained anger. It had subsequently descended into vengeful fury culminating in her dragging him into his bedroom to give him chapter and verse on everything he'd done wrong during their year-long relationship, and over the last month since they split up. He'd tried to remain calm, not wanting to hurt her more than he already had. After fifteen minutes of her ranting and him saying very little, he'd had to make his escape before he said something he'd regret. He made an excuse about needing the loo and left her crying on the bed with no intention of returning.

The kitchen was thronged with people, the air hazy with cigarette smoke. Whatever Owen was saying to Liz was making her laugh like a drain and it called out to Andrew over the hum of conversation. When he found the source, he was instantly drawn to this five-foot-two bundle of sparky energy, all thick, wavy dirty-blonde hair and an extraordinary thousand-watt smile. He was gripped by a wave of stomach-clenching jealousy of Owen. He wanted to be the one who could make this girl throw her head back like that. He made his way over to them, avoiding Saffie's efforts to waylay him and attempting to shake off the heaviness of the conversation with Trina.

'All right, mate? Want a beer?' Owen opened the fridge next him and passed one over without waiting for Andrew to answer.

'Cheers. Yeah, not bad.'

'What's up?' Owen knew him too well for him to be able to pretend.

'Nothing. Not much. Trina.'

'Ah. Crazy ex-girlfriend,' he explained to the blonde girl.

'Oh dear,' she said. 'I did hear someone arguing up there when I went to the loo but I didn't know it was you. What's up?'

'Long story.' Andrew cracked open the can and took a long drink.

'I'm always suspicious of blokes who say their ex-girlfriends are crazy,' she said. 'They've usually treated the girl like crap, and either she's being perfectly reasonable under the circumstances and they're trying to excuse their own behaviour, or the girl is acting a bit crazy, but only because the bloke's been such a dick to her.'

'I didn't say she was crazy,' Andrew said anxiously. 'That was Owen. It's ... complicated.'

'It always is. I'm Liz, by the way.'

'Andrew.'

'Aha, so you're the birthday boy! Sorry for having a go at you today of all days.'

'You're forgiven. Anyway, I wouldn't call that having a go.'

'True. I'll come back tomorrow and have a proper go at you.'

A silly smile spread helplessly across his features.

'You're welcome any time.'

'Did you guys meet on your course?' she asked.

'No, we go way back,' Andrew said. 'We were at school together.'

'Where did you go to school?'

'Winchester.'

'Oh right, which school? My cousin lives there, she's at … Henry Something School?'

'No,' Andrew said, apologetically. 'We were at Winchester. Winchester College.'

'Ohhh.' It was more of an exhale than a word. 'You're posh boys.' She was teasing but at the same time Andrew sensed a withdrawal.

'Correction – *he's* a posh boy,' Owen said.

Here we go, Andrew thought. Comrade Owen waving his red flag.

'I was on a full scholarship. As you can imagine, I felt right at home – not.'

'Was it all skiing holidays and horse riding, dahhling?' She put on an exaggerated cut-glass accent.

'You bet it was,' Owen said.

Andrew was fed up with this 'man of the people' schtick Owen launched into whenever he got a sniff of a council-house upbringing. It smacked of inverse snobbery.

'The first time Andrew mentioned his nanny to me I thought he meant his grandma, but no, he was talking about the woman who was paid to bring him up. What did Mummy do again, come into the nursery and kiss you goodnight?'

He was exaggerating grossly, based on a moment of weakness where Andrew confessed that when he was little he'd seen more of his nanny than his mother, and used to sometimes wish she was his mother instead.

'I had a nanny before I went to boarding school because my mum was running her own company,' Andrew said coldly. 'Not because we were super posh. Someone had to look after me. She's actually a great role model for working mums.' God, he sounded middle-aged. Owen and Liz fell about laughing.

'Working-class women work too, you know,' Owen said. 'But they can't afford one-to-one childcare, so they have to scrabble around and ask relatives and friends for favours, or take their kids to work with them.'

'Right,' Liz agreed. 'My mum worked as a cleaner when I was little, she used to take me with her.'

'Me too!' Owen exclaimed. 'I liked helping her, so she used to give me little jobs, dusting and stuff.'

'That's so cute!' Liz cooed.

'There was a good mix at Winchester,' Andrew said, although when he saw the sceptical looks on their faces, he realised he'd made a mistake.

'A mix, really?' said Owen. 'I remember the deathly silence that fell when I said I'd never been abroad. It wasn't even that they took the piss. They simply couldn't comprehend that someone would never have been to another country.'

'I still haven't been to another country!' said Liz cheerfully. Andrew tried not to look appalled.

'Cheers to that!' Owen raised his beer glass towards her.

Andrew was assailed by the fear that Owen was going to be the one to find out all about this girl, to know her. He would be the one to ask why one of her front teeth was slightly wonky, and whether that little indentation above her right eye was a childhood scar.

'Are you at uni here?' It was a feeble question but he needed to claw his way back into the conversation somehow.

'No, Manchester. I'm down visiting a friend.'

'Kara – from my course,' Owen said.

'Oh yeah.' A tall, buck-toothed girl in clumpy boots. 'So do you finish this summer too?'

'Yeah. Bit scary really.'

'Will you stay in Manchester?'

'No, I'm hoping to move down to London if I can find a job.'

'Me too!' said Andrew, deeply grateful to the capital city and all its delights that had drawn this girl to move there. 'What kind of job are you looking for?'

'Something in events. I like planning things from start to finish, and having a defined end point where all your hard work comes together. I'd find that really satisfying.'

'That's the key, isn't it?' Andrew said. 'Finding that

satisfaction in an ordinary job. I feel the same about PR – I've got an internship at TDW starting in September. Sure, it's not one of those dream jobs – footballer or West End star – but who actually gets to do those? The thing is to find the joy in what you do, celebrate the small wins.'

'Life is what happens when you're making other plans, as John Lennon said.' There was an edge of sarcasm to Owen's voice, but Andrew chose to take him literally.

'Exactly. This is life . . . this, right here, now.' He waved an arm around the smoky kitchen, aware as he did so that he was drunker than he'd thought. 'What could be better? We're young, we're clever, we've got great friends . . . ' He gestured at Owen. 'I know it's a cliché but we've got our whole lives ahead of us. This is it! Don't miss it!'

'Very inspiring,' Owen said drily. 'Liz can book you as a motivational speaker at her first event.'

He'd blown it. He mentally admitted defeat and looked down at his beer can, twisting the ring pull until it bit into his finger, sure Liz would be laughing at him along with Owen. But when he looked up, her blue-grey eyes were sympathetic. She understood the point he was trying to make, and didn't think him as ridiculous as Owen clearly had.

Gradually, and without Andrew or Liz really noticing, Owen and everyone else at the party melted away. It was one of those magical nights where everything faded into the background, as if they were the only two people in the room. Occasionally, someone would join them for a while, but it wouldn't take them long to recognise the chemistry in the atmosphere, the spark that zinged between the two of them, and the third party would gracefully retire as soon as was decent. Owen drifted back every now and then but couldn't penetrate the force field created by the growing interest Andrew and Liz had in each other. Andrew had the sensation of falling into something he'd never want to get out of.

After an hour or so he reluctantly dragged himself from Liz to use the loo. The downstairs one was occupied so he headed up the stairs which were in near-darkness and partially blocked by a frantically snogging couple. He tried to squeeze past without disturbing them but accidentally kneed the girl in the back. They broke apart for a second and he saw that the girl was Trina, dark smudges of mascara beneath her eyes from where she'd been crying a couple of hours before.

'Sorry, mate,' said the guy.

'Jesus!' The word slipped out in shock before Andrew could stop himself. The man kissing Trina so passionately was Andrew and Owen's other housemate, Julian.

'Calm down, Andrew,' Trina slurred. 'I can do what I like.'

'I know you can. Sorry.'

Andrew stumbled past and up the stairs into the safety of the bathroom. He stared at himself in the mirror, his dark hair rumpled. It had only been surprise that had made him react like that – he couldn't care less who Trina kissed. As she rightly said it was none of his concern and anyway Andrew's mind was full of Liz – the curve of her nose, the way she spoke not just with her hands but her whole body, her dirty laugh. If anything, he was oddly protective of Julian, who hadn't had much luck with girls over the three years they'd been at university together. He couldn't see things lasting between him and Trina – it had all the hallmarks of a classic rebound relationship with someone who was known, safe, unlikely to hurt her. Andrew's fear was that Trina had gone for Julian because it was a way to stay close to him, and that was a situation that was bound to end badly for all parties.

By the time Andrew came down, Trina and Julian had disappeared and Saffie was slumped in their place on the stairs, her black dress rucked up above her knees, make-up smudged. He was dying to rejoin Liz in the kitchen but Saffie looked in a bad way. He plumped himself down next to her.

'Are you OK, Saff?'

'Andrewwww!' She laid her head on his shoulder. 'Hellooooo, baby!'

God she was hammered.

'Do you want me to call you a taxi?'

'No, I'm fine! I don't want to go home yet! Gonna have another drink!'

'I'm not sure that's a good idea, but OK.' He went to stand up but she pulled him down again.

'Don't go! Stay here with me.' She nestled into him in what he thought was meant to be an alluring fashion. He used to have a secret suspicion that Saffie fancied him, but it was hard to tell with her as she flirted with everyone.

As nothing had ever come of it he'd assumed it was just her way. Not that he was interested. Saffie was gorgeous but not his type – too needy and high-maintenance.

'Leave it out, Saff.' He tried to disentangle himself but she clung on like a limpet, her dress slipping further up her thighs and threatening to expose her underwear. He reached to pull it down but she took it as an invitation and before he knew it her lips were on his, her tongue slipping into his mouth. He pushed her away with such force that she cannoned into the bannisters behind her.

'Ow! For God's sake!' She put her hand to the back of her head.

'Sorry, Saff, but I'm not ... interested in you in that way.'

She seemed more angry than hurt. He supposed she wasn't used to being turned down, looking the way she did.

'I mean ... I don't want to ruin our friendship,' he amended, hoping that would make rejection more palatable for her.

'Right.' The knock to her head had sobered her up. She clambered to her feet, yanking her dress down, and made her way unsteadily up the stairs. Andrew almost ran towards the kitchen, to see Liz where he had left her, thankfully alone. A few hours later she was in his bed, and by the morning, he was in love.

Chapter 32
Andrew

In the month since they'd met at Andrew's birthday party, he and Liz had fallen into the habit of nightly phone calls. If either of them was going out, they'd do it early, around six. If they were both in, one of them would call the other around eight and they'd stay on the call until one or both of them needed to go to sleep, or one of their housemates forced them to terminate the call because they needed to use the phone. Tonight was an early one.

'So whose birthday is it?' Andrew asked.

'My friend Steve. It's his twenty-first.'

'I don't think you've mentioned him before.' He tried to sound casual but his stomach lurched in panic. He forced himself not to bombard her with questions about how long she'd known Steve and what he looked like and whether he had a girlfriend. He'd never experienced this before. When he and Trina were going out he'd never felt a moment's jealousy, but then he'd never felt for her a tenth of what he did for Liz.

'He's on my course. The party's at his girl-friend's house.'

Andrew offered up a prayer of thanks. Steve had a girlfriend.

'We might go on to a club later.'

In his mind's eye he saw Liz downing shots and shim-mying onto the dance floor, some guy sliding up and holding her close. She'd dance with him (Andrew hadn't seen her dance yet) and they'd sit on high stools at the bar and the guy would fascinate her and make her laugh and open her eyes to Andrew's many shortcomings. He forced the images away.

'How are you getting on with your job applica-tions?' he said.

'Yeah, not bad.' She sounded hesitant, but it wasn't always easy to tell over the phone.

'Yeah? Have you got any interviews?'

'I have got one. It's a company that does big corpor-ate events. The job's menial – filing and photocopying mostly – but it'd be a great foot in the door.'

'That's brilliant! Where's the office?'

'That's the thing. It's not in London.'

'Oh right. Where is it?'

She didn't speak for a few seconds and Andrew thought they'd been cut off.

'Liz?'

'I'm still here. It's in Edinburgh.'

It was his turn to be silenced.

'Andrew?'

'Yeah, sorry, I'm ... Edinburgh? Are you ... are you going to go to the interview?'

'It's a really cool company, they do amazing events. It's not an easy industry to get into.'

'So you are going.'

'Don't be like that. This is my career we're talking about. It's important to me.'

'I know. Sorry.' He tried to push down the panic that rose in him like vomit. 'I'm supportive of that, I really am. But my internship at TDW begins in a couple of months in London. I can't turn that down.'

'I wouldn't expect you to.'

'But what about us?' Andrew was aware he sounded like a plaintive child whose toy had been taken away but he couldn't help it. 'We've been making all these plans for when we're both in London. Didn't that mean anything to you?'

'Of course it did. I really like you, Andrew, but I don't want to throw away an opportunity like this. We could do long-distance?'

'That never works,' he said firmly. 'How many people do you know who arrived at university still going out with their school boyfriend or girlfriend who'd ditched them by Christmas?'

'That's different – university's like going into a whole new world.'

'That's what this would be like, though! You'd be meeting all these new people, having all these experiences ... it would never work.'

'What's the solution, then?' There was a touch of annoyance there, and fear surged in him again.

'There must be loads of cool companies in London you could work for.'

'This might be the only interview I get. It's really competitive – especially in London because that's where everyone wants to work.'

'But Liz, I love you.' The words came flying out before he'd had a chance to consider whether it was a good idea.

'What?' She sounded flabbergasted. It wasn't the ideal answer.

'I love you. I'm in love with you.' Maybe if he kept saying it, she'd say the right thing back.

'Andrew, this is ... a lot to ... we've only known each other a month. We haven't seen each other since the night we met.'

'That's circumstance, though. You live in Manchester, and we've had our exams. If you lived round the corner we would have spent every minute of the past month together. And we speak every day. Don't you feel there's something good between us?'

'You know I do. I really like you. But I need to be sensible, protect myself. What if I turn down this interview and then you dump me?'

'Are you not listening to me? I would never do that. I never will do that.'

She sighed and he heard voices in the background, a man calling for her.

'My friends are here. I've got to go. I'll talk to you tomorrow.'

'No, Liz, wait. Please.'

'I've got to go,' she repeated. ''Bye.'

Andrew sat in the hall, the dial tone buzzing at him for a minute or two, then went to the kitchen and made himself a drink which was more vodka than tonic. After three of them, the world finally began to soften around the edges the way he'd hoped it would. When the doorbell rang, he had to put his hands either side of him on the walls as he staggered down the hallway.

'Are you OK?' Trina was dressed in a yellow embroidered cotton sundress, her skin golden. With the evening sun behind her, it looked like she had a halo.

'Fine!' He waved airily and grabbed onto the door jamb. 'Come in!'

He led her down the hall into the kitchen.

'Sit down! Drink?'

'OK. Thanks. Where's Julian?'

'He's at his parents', isn't he? Is he meant to be here?'

'Yeah, he's coming back today. He said to come over at half-seven.'

'I'm sure he'll be here soon. Have a drink with me.'

Andrew sat at the kitchen table and splashed vodka into his glass and another and topped them both up with a dash of tonic. Trina sat down opposite him and picked up her drink. An hour later there was still no sign of Julian and she was nearly as drunk as Andrew.

'How are things with Liz?' she asked.

'OK. We had a bit of a row tonight on the phone. Well, not a row, as such. I don't know. I'm not sure how that's going to pan out, to be honest.'

Even in his drunken, befuddled state he knew he shouldn't be discussing his new relationship – if it was a relationship after tonight – with his most recent ex.

'How's it going with Julian?' Changing the subject felt like the best policy. 'You seem to be getting on well.' Trina and Julian's relationship, which had run on apace since Andrew's birthday party, hadn't been mentioned between them before.

'It's good.'

'You don't sound convinced. You can talk to me.'

Andrew felt very mature – how grown-up he was to be discussing his ex's new relationship with her.

'Julian's lovely – well, you know he is, he's one of your best mates.'

'He's a diamond. He's the absolute best. I love him.'

He banged his glass down on the table with too much force and liquid slopped out.

'Yes.'

'But?' Andrew leaned forward, brow furrowed.

She sighed.

'He's almost too nice. So sweet, so kind, so . . . safe.'

'Those are good things, aren't they?'

'Ye-es. It's just there's not much . . . passion.' Her cheeks flushed. 'We haven't . . . you know . . . '

'You haven't slept together?'

'No. I don't know if he thinks he's being respectful by not pushing me but ... it's not like I'm a virgin.'

'You certainly aren't,' Andrew said, unable to keep the suggestion from his voice. Her face got even redder. Was she remembering the things they'd done together in the dark, as he was? He held her gaze a moment too long – and then the phone rang. Andrew stumbled to get it. It was Julian. They spoke for a couple of minutes and Andrew came back to the kitchen. It was too much trouble to walk around to the other side of the table, so he sank into the chair next to Trina.

'He's not going to be back tonight. Trains are all messed up. He's going to stay at his parents overnight and leave in the morning.'

'Oh.'

She shifted on her chair. Her dress got snagged on a splinter of wood on the seat and it rose up, exposing a couple of inches of smooth, tanned thigh. Andrew resisted the urge to reach out a finger and stroke it. Liz. He was in love with Liz.

'Where's Owen?' she said, her voice cracking in a way he'd always found very sexy.

'Out. Won't be back till late.'

'Oh,' she said again.

The heat between them was unmistakeable. Andrew forced himself to concentrate on Liz but all he could think of was her horror when he'd said he loved her. She blatantly didn't feel the same. What was the bloody point? It was then that Trina put her hand on his leg.

At five in the morning, Andrew awoke with a pounding headache to the sight of Trina wriggling into the yellow sundress in the grey morning half-light.

'Where are you going?' he muttered, his tongue like sandpaper.

'Home. I know Julian won't be home for hours but I don't want Owen to see me and tell him.'

'Did Owen come back last night?' Great chunks of the evening were missing from his brain. He remembered kissing Trina in the kitchen with a white-hot passion he had never experienced when they were going out. They must have decided to move into the bedroom but he couldn't recall much of what happened in there. He knew they'd had sex but wasn't convinced he'd acquitted himself all that well. Hopefully she couldn't recall it any better than he could.

'I heard him come in after we … when you were asleep,' she said. 'You won't tell him, will you?'

'No, of course not.'

'Can you do my zip up?'

She lowered herself onto the bed and he sat up. As he ran the zipper up from the small of her back to between her sharp shoulder blades, he had a flashback to doing the opposite last night and a wave of guilt engulfed him.

'Thanks.'

She turned to Andrew, a wisp of her ash-blonde hair falling across her face. Automatically, he reached up to push it back and she put her hands either side of his neck and kissed him on the lips. He recoiled and she jumped up from the bed.

'Sorry, Trina. Look, last night was a mistake. I mean, not a mistake,' he added hurriedly when he saw her expression, 'but I shouldn't have done it. Me and Liz had a row and like I said, I'm not sure what's happening between us, but I ... I really like her. I want to work things out with her.'

'Right.' She hunted around for her bag. 'I was going to say the same, about me and Julian.'

'But I thought you said last night ... ' he trailed off. If she wanted to frame this around her great relationship with Julian, let her. It would get him off the hook. 'God, I can't remember. We were both pretty drunk, weren't we?'

'Yes, exactly. Let's forget it ever happened.' She found her bag slung over the back of the battered armchair by the window and checked its contents. 'I'll see you around.'

'OK. 'Bye.'

As soon as she'd gone, Andrew fell back into a sheet-tangled, dream-ridden half-sleep. When he woke again, he scrubbed himself under the pitiful trickle that passed for a shower – a shower that for some reason the landlord had decided to install in his bedroom. He changed the bedsheets and cleaned his room from top to bottom as if to expunge the night's activities. At six o'clock as he anxiously awaited Liz's usual phone call, there was a knock at the door. The sun was higher in the sky than it had been when Trina arrived yesterday and at first he was dazzled and couldn't make out who it was, but as she stepped towards him and into his arms, he was astonished to find it was Liz. He pulled her close to him and inhaled the scent of her hair, tears springing to his eyes.

'What are you doing here?'

'I realised how stupid I'd been,' she said. She was crying too. 'I remembered what you said the first time we met, about finding the joy in the everyday, ordinary things. You bring me joy. You are my joy. I'm not going to the interview. I love you too.'

Chapter 33

Andrew

Until today, one month since his night with Trina, Andrew had been doing a good job of locking it away to the extent where he could almost pretend that it had never happened. But as he stared at the white plastic stick in his hand, the colour leaching from his face, he knew the period of denial was well and truly over.

Trina sat opposite him at the other end of his bed, twisting the strap of her bag around her finger until the end bulged like a blister.

'That second line's quite faint, Treen. Are you sure?'

'Positive.'

An appropriate word in the circumstances.

'That line,' she released her finger and pointed to the first little window, 'means the test is working properly. Any line in the other window means I'm ...' She swallowed, and he could tell the word was foreign on her tongue when applied to herself. 'Pregnant.'

'Right,' Andrew said, rigid. 'OK. And are you sure it's . . . I mean, I'm sorry to ask but . . . is it definitely mine?'

'Yes,' she said coldly. 'I told you Julian and I hadn't slept together.'

'And you still haven't?'

'Not that it's any of your business but no. It's yours, Andrew.'

'It must be very early? I mean, it was only a month ago that we . . . '

'It was four weeks.'

'OK, good.' Too late, Andrew hoped she hadn't clocked his obvious relief. A vain hope.

'I see you want me to get rid of it, then.' She snatched the stick from him with a shaking hand and shoved it into the depths of her bag.

'I didn't say that.'

'You didn't have to. I can see how pleased you are that it's early enough for you not to have to feel like it's a real baby. I can have it sucked out of me and you'll never have to tell your girlfriend about it. Lucky old you.'

'I'm not *pleased* about anything, Trina.'

'I hope you're not blaming me? Do you think I wanted this?' She stood up and ducked through the strap of her bag, looping it across her. 'It's all right for you, you're not the one who'll have to go through pregnancy and labour. You're not the one who'll have to look after it. You're not the one who has to tell your boyfriend you slept with someone else before you'd even slept with him.'

Andrew would have to tell Liz, though. He imagined

230

it for a second – how he would have to sit her down and how she would gradually morph from worry to rage. It would be the end of their relationship. She would never forgive him.

'You're jumping ahead. Calm down a minute and let's think.'

'How can I calm down? That's the situation. Either I get rid of it . . . ' her mouth twisted in an attempt to suppress a sob, 'kill it, like you want, or I have it and ruin my life. Those are my two choices. That's it. There's no other way, no compromise.'

'I didn't say that's what I wanted. I . . . ' Andrew groped for the right words, reaching for phrases he'd heard in television dramas. 'I'll support you whatever you want to do.'

She sank down on the bed, nearer him this time.

'Really?'

'Yes.' He reached out to her, relieved that he had said the right thing, and she didn't pull away. 'We'll figure this out together. You don't have to do this alone.'

Perhaps Liz would understand,. They had been on a sort of break when it had happened, after all. Maybe, somehow, it would be OK.

Two weeks later, Andrew found himself sitting on his bed once again, but this time the object he held, twisting it over and over, his fingers rough against the pillow-soft cotton, was a tiny white hat.

He had bought it in a kind of fugue state, drawn into the shop almost against his will, and now he couldn't put it down, engulfed in a complex range of emotions.

A primal instinct kicked in at the thought of holding his own child in his arms. Images came to him: a chubby little girl with blonde pigtails flinging herself into his embrace; a serious, dark-eyed boy in cricket whites listening attentively as Andrew showed him how to bat; a teenager struggling with friendships, grateful for Andrew's wise and considered advice. Liz would forgive him and the baby would bring out the maternal side of her. She would treat the baby as her own when it was with Andrew.

However, his brain insisted on offering alternative scenarios: pacing the floor night after night holding a screaming baby; turning down the low-paid internship that he hoped would lead to a dream career in favour of a better paid but boring job, in order to afford nappies and nursery fees; a lifetime tied to Trina, whether he liked it or not. Liz storming out the moment he told her, never to reappear.

He thought of Trina last week when she told him she was going to keep the baby. He had said all the right things, and at the time he had meant them. He had vowed to support her, and he intended to keep that vow. But every time he'd spoken to Liz on the phone since, he couldn't make the words spill from his throat where they were held so tightly, because he knew once they were out, even if Liz was able to forgive him, nothing would ever be the same.

He was roused from his reverie by the sound of the doorbell. Owen greeted someone at the door, but they were speaking too quietly for Andrew to make out who it was. He heard footsteps coming up the stairs and the door of his room was pushed slowly open. Trina, looking washed-out and strained, stood uncertainly in the doorway.

'Hey! Are you OK?'

She eyed him warily.

'Come in.' For reasons he didn't fully understand, he slipped the little white hat under his pillow as he made a show of smoothing the bedcovers so she could sit down. She perched gingerly on the far end of the bed, as if poised for flight.

'Trina, are you OK?' he repeated.

'Sort of.' She looked out of the window, down at her hands, at the floor. Anywhere but at him.

'What's the matter?'

She shook her head, but still said nothing.

'You're scaring me!' Andrew's heart was thudding in his chest. 'What is it? Is it ... the baby? Is everything OK?'

'There isn't going to be a baby.' Her face crumpled.

'Oh no.' He shifted up the bed towards her and laid a hand on her arm, but she recoiled, shaking it off.

'Don't pretend you're not happy about it.'

'I ...' He thought of the pigtailed girl, the cricketing boy. The little white hat. The words stuck in his throat. He swallowed. 'What happened? When did you start bleeding?'

'Bleeding?' She looked him full in the face for the first time. 'I didn't have a miscarriage. I did what you wanted me to. I got rid of it.'

They sat, eyes locked, in a cold silence, Andrew's mind racing. The truth was that if the choice had been his alone, then yes, he would have wanted her to have an abortion. They were too young, too ill-suited; both in relationships with other people.

'I . . . I never asked you to do that.' It was important to say it into the silence, even if she refused to hear it. He needed to say it for himself, to check that it was true.

'You didn't have to. Can you look me in the eye and tell me you wanted this baby?'

'Not wanted, exactly, but . . . '

'I know, I know. You would have "supported me no matter what".' She made cruel speech marks with her fingers. 'But that's not enough. I wanted you to want it, really want it. With me.'

It was his turn to say nothing. He couldn't lie to her about this.

'That's what I thought,' she said, standing. 'That's what I fucking thought.'

She didn't wait for him to respond, slamming the door behind her. Andrew waited until he saw her turning the corner into the next street before he retrieved the hat from under his pillow. He could hear Owen watching the football on TV in the lounge as he crept into the kitchen and tore a bin bag from the roll in the drawer. He stuffed the hat inside and rolled the rest of the bag around it several times. He poked his head into the lounge.

'I'm popping to the shop, mate – do you want anything?'

'No, I'm all right. Has Trina gone?'

'Yes, she ... couldn't stay.' He had to force the words out.

'Everything OK, mate?' Owen dragged his attention from the football.

Andrew hesitated. He could confide in Owen. He wouldn't judge. 'Yeah, not bad.' Or would he? 'Back in a mo.'

As Andrew left the house, he stopped by the wheelie bin. He half lifted out a bin bag that had ripped and was disgorging its contents – torn teabags, empty ready-meal cartons with a thin sprinkling of mould, used dental floss – and stuffed the bag containing the white hat under it, deep, deep down where no one would ever find it.

Chapter 34

Andrew

'Hello, darling.' Saffie opened the door, a vision in a pineapple-print silk jumpsuit. She kissed Andrew on the cheek, landing nearer to his mouth than he was expecting.

'I feel underdressed now,' he said as he followed her down the hall. He'd been working from home and hadn't changed out of his jeans and check flannel shirt.

'Nonsense, darling, you look lovely. Drink?'

'Yes, please. Where's Owen?'

'Still at work, I'm afraid, but hopefully he won't be long.'

'I thought the civil service was meant to be a doss. Don't they have an early finish on Fridays?'

'Ha! You'd think so, wouldn't you, especially on the crappy wage they pay him, but no. Some kind of fisheries crisis, although what on earth that could be I have no idea.'

'And the boys?'

236

'In bed, thank God. Both knackered after the school week. They push them frightfully hard at Westwell.'

It sounded like a complaint, but Andrew knew her better than that. It was a subtle reminder that her and Owen's boys were at a prestigious private prep school while Andrew and Liz's kids were slumming it in the state sector.

'Champagne?' She'd popped the cork before he had a chance to answer. 'Well, it's Prosecco actually – story of my bloody life.'

'What are we celebrating?'

'I can't think of a single thing, sweetheart – can you?'

'This sounds bad, but I've got the weekend to myself. Is that worth celebrating?'

Liz had taken the boys to her mum and dad's for the weekend, so he had two blissful days stretching ahead of him with lie-ins and no ferrying the boys to swimming and football and birthday parties. He'd stayed at home to catch up on various bits of DIY, but even that would be a luxury without anyone getting in the way or enquiring after his progress.

'You bet it is!' Saffie clinked her glass to his. 'I will definitely drink to that. God, I'd kill for a weekend alone.'

'Couldn't Owen take the boys to his dad's one weekend?'

'He's got this tiresome thing about us spending the weekends together *as a family*. It's different for him, he doesn't see much of them all week so he wants to spend time with them. Quite frankly, I've had my fill of them by Friday night.'

Looking forward happily to his uninterrupted lie-in in the morning, Andrew sat down on a high stool at the breakfast bar next to Saffie. His Prosecco went down like water and they were into their second bottle by the time Saffie's phone rang. It was Owen.

'Oh, right,' she said flatly after he'd spoken for thirty seconds or so. After a few *mm-hmm*s she hung up.

'He's not going to be home for another couple of hours.'

'What's up?'

'God knows. Something to do with briefing the minister about fish and Spain . . . or was it France? I don't know. Let's have another drink.'

'I don't have to stay for dinner, if you've got stuff to do, or . . . ' It was funny, he'd known Saffie since he was eighteen years old but Andrew couldn't remember the last time they'd spent an evening together, just the two of them. When they were younger they socialised in big mixed groups, and since they'd been married and had kids they got together as couples or families. He had an unbidden flashback to the night of his twenty-first birthday party when a drunken Saffie had tried to kiss him.

'Don't be ridiculous, darling, I'm not going to eat that boeuf bourguignon on my own.'

'OK, thanks. I'll stay.' She was right, he was being ridiculous. That party was a million years ago. Saffie was married to his best friend. 'Boeuf bourguignon – that must have taken you ages.' The only thing he could recall Saffie cooking in their university days was jacket potato with cheese and beans.

'It would have done if I'd made it myself. I got it from that fancy ready meals place in town – don't tell Owen. I've buried the packaging in the recycling.' She raised her glass conspiratorially.

'Not a word. But why – he wouldn't care if you hadn't made it yourself, would he?'

'It's not that, it's the money.'

'Oh.'

'Yes, we can't all be brilliant and entrepreneurial like you, sadly.'

'Running your own business isn't all it's cracked up to be.' Andrew downed his Prosecco, thinking of the two clients whose contracts were up for renewal and who hadn't returned his calls this week. Saffie refilled his glass without asking.

'Come off it, you're raking it in, aren't you?'

'Not really. And it's bloody hard work. There are days I'd kill for a job I could leave behind me at the end of the working day.'

'But Owen doesn't have that – he's always stressed, always checking his email, yet he's working for a pittance.'

Andrew thought Owen was on a fairly decent salary – and one which would go a lot further if Saffie hadn't insisted on educating the boys privately – but he didn't want to pursue it with her.

'Then he has the cheek to have a go at me about my Instagram stuff! It may not be bringing in much revenue yet, but it's a start and who knows what could happen if it takes off? Some people make a fortune from it.'

'True.'

'I just wish Owen had a bit more get up and go, like you. He'd never in a million years start his own business.'

'He is fairly risk averse. Always has been. But that's not necessarily a bad thing.'

'Isn't it? God, sometimes I miss the ...' she waves her half-full glass around the kitchen, drains it in one and pours herself another, 'the *excitement*, the possibilities. Don't tell Owen, but there's a guy I keep bumping into after my therapy session. He's frightfully attractive. American. His name's Todd.'

'Ah, Saffie, don't tell me this. Owen's my best mate.'

'No, no, I wouldn't ever do anything. That's not what I'm saying.' She leaned forward and pressed his arm for emphasis. 'It's ... seeing a gorgeous man like that reminds me I'm not totally dead inside. I've still got a life to live.'

'With Owen,' Andrew said doggedly.

'Yes, yes, of course.' She released his arm from her grip.

'You wouldn't want to get involved with someone who's in therapy anyway.'

'Oh darling, everyone's in therapy. Including me. Todd's only there because his lawyers said he had to. His ex-girlfriend made a ridiculous, made-up claim about him being controlling and violent, and they said it would look better for him if he went to therapy.'

'You've actually spoken to this guy?'

'Just in passing. You're barking up the wrong tree if you think I'm considering an affair – I'm just trying to explain to you how I feel.'

'I should go.' Andrew got down off the bar stool, stumbling as he did so. 'This is going to my head – I didn't have any lunch today.'

'Me neither – I'm doing this fasting diet where you can only eat during a set eight hours of the day and then nothing for the rest of the time. So I've been saving myself for supper. Don't go – we'll eat in a minute.'

'You don't need to go on a diet.' Andrew had said it automatically, trained by years of experience that this was the best thing to say when a woman told you they were on a diet, but Saffie simpered.

'Oh darling, that's very sweet of you to say.'

'You always look great.' He felt he'd better follow his auto-compliment up with something, and it was true. Saffie was an extremely attractive woman, if a little polished for his taste.

'I wish you'd tell Owen that,' she said, shaking her hair out.

'He knows, Saff.'

'He's got a funny way of showing it. He hasn't come near me in months.'

'Right. I see.' Andrew sat back down and took a large swallow of his drink to cover his unease at his best friend's wife discussing him in this fashion.

'I've been trying to get him to come to counselling with me, but he won't. So I'm going on my own. Maybe I'll jump on Todd in the waiting room after therapy after all.'

'Saffie!'

'Sorry,' Saffie said, not sounding sorry at all. 'Does that make you uncomfortable?'

'No, not at all,' Andrew lied. Saffie suddenly seemed very close although he hadn't noticed her moving towards him.

'It's just that I feel so trapped.' She didn't take her eyes off him.

'What do you mean?' Andrew traced his finger through the condensation on his champagne flute.

'In this life. Marriage, kids, housework. Do you ever wonder if this is it? No more fun. No more excitement. Remember when we were at uni, we thought we were going to go out into the world and do great things? And now what have we got to look forward to? Standing on the side of a sodding kids' rugby pitch or putting together Ikea furniture? Don't you ever want more?'

'I know what you mean,' he said, trying to be supportive, but he didn't, not really. All he'd ever wanted was to come home every night to Liz and his children from a job he enjoyed.

'I thought so,' Saffie said and leaned forward to kiss him.

'Jesus, Saffie!' Andrew jumped up and his bar stool clattered to the ground. 'What the hell are you doing?'

'I thought you were . . . we were . . . '

'You're married to my best friend! I'm married!'

He righted the stool and moved away from her towards the door.

'I'd better go.'

'Don't tell anyone.' Saffie crossed the floor towards him, reaching out for him. He flinched and stepped further away. 'Please, don't tell Owen or Liz. I'm drunk and maudlin and things aren't great with Owen. I've been thinking a lot about when we were younger and how everything was so much easier then and . . . I got carried away. Call it a moment of madness. OK? Please?'

'Fine,' he said, although he would have agreed to almost anything for the sake of getting the hell out of there as quickly as possible. 'We'll put it down to too much Prosecco. But Saff, don't give up on Owen. Give him a chance.'

'What if he's the one who's given up on me?' she mumbled through the beginnings of tears. 'I don't know if he ever loved me in the first place. I always felt like second best.'

'Don't be silly, he's crazy about you. Look, Saff, I've got to go.'

Not wanting to prolong the agony by waiting with Saffie for a taxi to arrive, he walked the half-hour home in the freezing cold, weighing up his options. By the time he let himself into his blissfully warm house he'd decided to honour Saffie's wishes and not mention anything to Liz or Owen. It wasn't likely to happen again after the reaction she'd got from him, and telling them would throw a grenade into the friendship group causing damage it would be impossible to recover from.

Chapter 35

Andrew

ONE MONTH BEFORE VILLA ROSA

Andrew was putting on his coat ready to go to a meeting he hadn't told Poppy about – one he'd explicitly told her he wasn't going to take – when he heard a noise from her office. He poked his head round the door.

'I thought you'd gone home ages ago!'

'Just catching up on a few things.' Her hair, secured in a knot with a pencil, was unwashed and there were dark circles under her eyes.

'You look knackered, why don't you leave it? Finish whatever you're doing in the morning. Actually, can we go over a few things tomorrow with the accounts, if you've got time?'

'Tomorrow's really busy. I've got the GreenEc meeting to prepare for, and some other bits and bobs. Can we do it another time?'

'Sure, there's no rush.'

Guiltily, Andrew thought it was good if Poppy was absorbed in the GreenEc stuff as it would give her less time to question what he was doing. In the five years since they'd set up the business, he'd never kept a secret like this from her. They didn't live in each other's pockets – they'd always divided the work according to their strengths, which was what had made them a successful team. They each had their own clients whose accounts they worked on. In addition to that, Poppy did the company accounts and managed the financial and HR side of things, whereas Andrew was responsible for business development and bringing new clients on board. They kept each other updated as far as was practical, but an essential element of the relationship was trust. The company was never going to make them a fortune but they were each able to draw a decent salary. In the early years there had even been the occasional bonus, but those had been in short supply recently.

The original USP of the company was that they would deliver PR campaigns for brands with sustainability at their core, but attracting new business was becoming ever more challenging, and Andrew had been forced to put out feelers in other industries. When a friend from an old job had told him that financial services company DOSH were looking for a new PR company, Andrew had mentioned it to Poppy. She had flown off the handle at the mere idea of it. It was the first time they had ever had a blazing row since they'd started the agency.

In the end, Andrew had said he wouldn't pursue it,

but he had been lying. His first responsibility would always be to ensure that the company was profitable. Without profit – and that meant attracting new business – there would be no company. If Poppy couldn't get on board with that – well, he didn't know what would happen. He couldn't easily fire her – they were equal partners in the company. They'd set up procedures and processes when they started out, but in a company this size there was no HR manager, and he had no idea how he'd go about it. In his lower moments, although he'd never say as much to Liz, he'd wished she would mess up big time, making it easier for him to remove her from the agency. But that was unlikely to happen. Poppy was whiter than white.

When he and Liz got together, Andrew had been delighted to discover that Poppy, Liz's best friend, was in PR like him. It made the prospect of meeting her so much less daunting, knowing they would have this big thing in common that they'd both enjoy talking about.

'She loved you!' Liz had said, on the tube journey home after his first time meeting her, shortly after they'd all moved to London. 'I mean, I knew she would, but . . . she really loved you! She told me when you went to the toilet.'

'And she wasn't just saying that to make you happy?'

'No, she's not like that. She'd tell me the truth.'

Andrew had been so relieved, had known Poppy was the important one, the one he had to impress, even more than Liz's parents. In fact, he suspected that Liz had been more worried about her parents embarrassing her in front of Andrew, rather than the other way round. No matter how many times he reassured her that he couldn't care less if their house was tiny and they didn't have real coffee, he knew how anxious she had been the first time she took him home to meet them. He'd got angry with her at one point, accusing her of thinking him a snob who would look down on her parents for not being from the middle-class world that he himself inhabited. Couldn't she tell he wasn't like that? Out of all the privileged boys at his private school, he had gravitated towards Owen, the scholarship boy from a council estate. A snob was the last thing he was.

As he left the office, dodging a question from Poppy about whether he was going straight home, he checked his messages. There was one from Don, the Head of Public Relations from DOSH who he was on his way to meet in London.

I've arranged some company to make the evening more pleasant. See you soon. Andrew tapped out a quickly reply: *No worries, happy to meet any of your colleagues.*

He shoved his phone into his pocket and hurried to the train station. An hour and a half later, he scanned the wine bar where they'd agreed to meet. Andrew had initially suggested a daytime meeting at their offices, but Don had said he'd prefer something casual and low-key so they could get to know each other and get a better idea of how they would work together. Andrew was in no position to argue. He needed the business badly. He knew deep down that Poppy was right, that DOSH was unethical and went against everything they stood for as a business. But Don had said they were keen to clean up their image and become more socially conscious. Even though Andrew knew it would mainly be a matter of appearing to be more ethical while continuing the same shady practices, it was enough for him. Quite frankly, beggars couldn't be choosers.

At first, Andrew couldn't see Don, despite having studied his profile picture on LinkedIn to make sure he'd recognise him. Andrew's mistake was that he was scanning the bar for a lone man or, given Don's earlier message, a man with a couple of colleagues dressed in business attire. What he wasn't looking for was the man waving him over imperiously, a man in an expensive suit, shirt unbuttoned at the top and tie loosened raffishly, flanked by a pair of extremely glamorous women young enough to be his daughters.

'Andrew! Come and sit down.'

Andrew leaned forward and shook Don's proffered hand, lowering himself gingerly onto the white leather circular sofa. Don poured him a glass of champagne from the bottle in the ice bucket next to him and passed it to the dark-haired young woman on his left.

'Give this to Andrew, darling,' he said. She brought it over and sat down beside him. She was wearing a burgundy dress cut so low at the back you could almost see her bottom. Her sweet, musky perfume was overpowering.

'This is Kitty,' Don said. 'And this,' indicating the immaculate blonde on his right, wearing a figure-hugging, emerald-green silk dress, 'is Chantale. I thought it might be nice for us to have some company tonight.'

'Right.' Andrew felt like he'd walked onto the set of a seventies TV show, or possibly a soft-porn film. People didn't do things like this in real life, did they? Hire escorts, if that's what these women were?

'So Don,' Andrew said, trying to ignore the fact that Kitty was as close as she could be without actually touching him, 'why don't you tell me more about what you're looking for in a PR agency?'

'We can talk about that later,' Don said, reclining, his arm outstretched along the back of the sofa. Chantale slid closer to him and his hand snaked down around her waist. 'We're here to enjoy ourselves. Tell you what,' he said with a mischievous twinkle, 'anyone fancy a snort of the old Colombian marching powder?'

Jesus Christ. Andrew shifted away from Kitty. 'Not for me, thanks.'

'Ooh, yes please,' said Chantale.

'Kits?' Don said.

'No thanks,' she drawled. 'Not my scene.'

'Come on then, Chantale. Back in a minute, you two. Be good!'

Once they were out of sight, Andrew moved ostentatiously out of Kitty's range.

'You don't seem altogether comfortable with this situation,' she said. Now Don had gone, she'd dropped the

Bond girl act and was more like someone who could have been one of his friends' daughters.

'You could say that. I was expecting a business meeting, not . . . all this.'

'It's what he does,' she said. 'He's hired me for this type of thing before. It's a test, to see if you can be "one of the boys". He basically only hires men who are as much of a dick as he is. God knows what happens if a woman applies for a job.'

'So he's a regular . . . client for you, is he?'

'Yeah – well, for the agency. I don't think he particularly cares which girl he gets. We're all the same to him.'

'God, this is horrible.' Andrew's skin was crawling. He'd never wanted more to be safe at home with Liz eating a lasagne and arguing about whose turn it was to put the bins out.

'What else could I do that would make as much money for a night's work?' she said defensively.

'Sorry, I didn't mean . . . I meant him, not you.'

'Yeah, he's a creep but he tips well.'

'You don't have to . . . do . . . other things, do you?'

'Are you interested?' Kitty observed him slyly from under her lashes.

'God, no! I'm married.'

'So are a lot of my clients.' She looked him steadily in the eye, the invitation to take things further abundantly clear. Andrew thought about what it would be like to accept that invitation. How it would feel to touch this beautiful young woman's body, to experience the thrill of being with someone new after all these years with his wife. There might be things she would do, or let him do, that he'd always been curious about. No one would ever have to know.

'I can see you're thinking about it,' she said softly. 'I'd be happy to do anything you want.'

'You two seem to be getting on like a house on fire.' Don tumbled into his seat, wrestling a giggly Chantale down onto his lap. He rubbed his nose and gave a sniff. 'Let's get some more champagne!'

It was the prompt Andrew needed. He wasn't a Don, and what's more he couldn't go into business with one. He had an overwhelming longing to get into a shower that was as hot as he could stand it and slough off this experience like dead skin.

'I'm sorry, Don, I've got to go. Not feeling well.'

'Sorry to hear that,' said Don coldly. 'Are you sure?'

'Absolutely,' Andrew said. 'It was nice to meet you, Kitty. Good luck.'

He didn't wait to hear any more. As he hurried away from the bar as fast as his legs would carry him, Andrew thought about what he would say to Liz. She'd known he was going to meet with DOSH tonight so he couldn't altogether lie, but it was so grubby and disgusting he didn't want to tell her about it. She didn't need to know about Kitty and Chantale and she definitely must never know about that moment – seconds, really – where he had considered taking Kitty up on her offer. He'd burned his bridges with DOSH by leaving like that, and he would never see Kitty again. He would keep quiet, tell Liz it hadn't worked out with DOSH for some other reason. There was no way she would ever find out about this sordid episode.

Chapter 36
Andrew

Andrew stood alone sipping a whisky, warmth spreading down from his throat into his stomach. He hoped it would calm the jittery feeling the conversation at dinner had left in its wake. Would he ever be able to sit and be civil with Todd and Saffie, after what they'd done to his best friend? It would help if Todd showed any remorse or understanding of how it was for Andrew, but he seemed instead to be deliberately goading Andrew, pushing different buttons to see which one would make him explode. He had an overwhelming longing to be in bed with Liz, wrapped around her warm, soft body, but she was laughing happily with Trina and Poppy on the bench at the rear of the terrace. He didn't want to take her away from her friends.

'Can I have a quick word, Andrew?' One side of Saffie's face was cast into shadow by the lights in the flower bed, giving her a ghoulish air.

'OK.'

He took a sip of his drink in readiness for what he assumed would be either an apology for Todd's boorish behaviour at dinner or an appeal for Andrew to be civil with him.

'You didn't reply to my text the other day,' she said quietly.

'Oh. That.'

'Yes. That. Look, I'm sure you wouldn't tell anyone, but I need to be certain. What I did ... I didn't mean it, I never would have gone through with it ... '

Andrew had done his best to forget that evening, and had been largely successful. He'd always been good at compartmentalising, expunging the memory of that one night he spent with Trina after he and Liz had got together until it was like something that had never happened at all. He'd put Saffie's clumsy pass at him into a mental box containing things that should never have happened. He found if you never spoke of the things in this category, it wasn't long before they could be re-categorised as things that never did happen.

'I need to know you're not going to mention it to Todd,' Saffie continued. 'I know he's been needling you tonight, and I'm sorry about that. He might appear to be full of confidence but he's very aware that he's the interloper in this group. He feels under pressure and it's coming out in the wrong way.'

Andrew doubted Todd felt anything of the sort and was simply an arsehole, but he didn't need to share this with Saffie.

'Of course I'm not going to tell Todd. That's entirely up to you.'

'Oh, thank God.'

'Jesus, Saff, would it really matter that much, though?'

'I know it sounds a bit ... controlling, but he's genuinely not. I just think it would be too much for him, knowing what had happened, and having to be around you, and ...'

As Andrew thought. He was a complete arsehole.

'Like I said, it's none of my business. But to be honest, I have thought about telling Liz.'

'No!' Panic flared. 'Why now? It was what? Eight months ago? Can't we forget it ever happened?'

'I don't like having secrets from Liz,' Andrew said. 'It doesn't sit well with me.' Things had been off between him and Liz recently, although he wouldn't confide in Saffie about that. It wasn't the only secret he was keeping from Liz, but the idea of unburdening himself at least of this had been more and more appealing of late.

'Please, please, no. What if she tells the others and it gets back to Todd?'

'So you don't care if she's upset with you? You're only bothered about Todd finding out? What is wrong with you, Saffie? Todd isn't hurting you, is he?'

'No! God, no! Why on earth would you say that?'

'What you told me that night. About Todd.'

'What about him?' Saffie said, puzzled.

'You said he was at therapy because an ex had accused him of being violent towards her. I know you said he denied it, that she was making it up, but . . . I have wondered. He seems pretty volatile.'

'I don't remember telling you that.' Saffie looked terrified.

'We were both pretty drunk.'

'Don't tell him you know. Please, Andrew.' She clamped her hand around his arm, biting into his flesh.

'I wasn't planning to, but . . . why not?'

'He doesn't like anyone to know. Even though obviously he didn't do it, he knows people will say there's no smoke without fire. He'll kill me if he knows I told you.'

'*Kill* you?'

'It's a figure of speech.' She let go of him. 'I mean he'll be angry.'

'Fine. If he stays off my case, I'll stay off his.'

'Are you OK, Saffie?' Trina had wandered over, leaving Liz and Poppy on the bench.

'Yes.' Saffie collected herself. 'I think I'll go and see the girls.'

Andrew watched as she went and sat down next to Liz.

'Is she OK?' Trina asked.

'She's fine,' he said dismissively.

'Andrew, I need to talk to you about something.'

'Oh God, what now?' He'd been half joking, but then he saw the tremble in her hand as she brought her glass to her lips and downed the contents in one go.

'Trina, what is it?'

'I've been putting it off and putting it off.' She tripped over her words. 'But I can't, I can't any more.'

'You've had a lot to drink. We all have. Why don't we talk about this tomorrow?' Andrew thought longingly again of his bed and Liz.

'No, I need to tell you now or else I never will, and then *she* will and it'll be even worse.'

'Trina, you're not making any sense. Who will tell me? Tell me what?'

'Remember that night,' she said quietly, 'when we ... you know ... after I got together with Julian and you met Liz.'

'Yes.' He looked over at Liz, laughing with Poppy, the light catching her face in such a way that she looked not a day older than when he first knew her. 'But it was a million years ago. Another lifetime. Why are you bringing it up now?'

'And you remember what happened afterwards ... that I was ... I got ... '

'Yes, of course.'

If he allowed himself, which he seldom did, he could call it to mind as if it was yesterday – particularly Trina's insistence that he had bulldozed her into having an abortion. Afterwards he had tried to cling on to what he was sure to be true – that he had offered to support her whatever her decision, and that he had meant it. But the knowledge became malleable as the years went on, bent out of shape by her insistence that day that it had been what he wanted, that she had done it to appease him.

'OK, I'm just going to say it. I didn't have an abortion.'

'So ... you weren't pregnant?'

257

'No, I was pregnant.'

Andrew gazed at her in silent incomprehension.

She looked back, pleading, although what she wanted from him he had no idea.

'You . . . had the baby?'

'Yes.' Tears spill from her eyes. 'I made the appointment, I went to the clinic. But I couldn't go through with it. I sat there alone in the waiting room – and I absolutely 100 per cent believe in a woman's right to choose – but there, in that moment, I couldn't do it. I walked around for hours, turning everything over and over. I knew I couldn't look after a baby – I was a baby myself. And I felt so ashamed that I'd been so stupid as to get pregnant – and I knew I'd have to tell Julian it wasn't his, because we hadn't slept together by then. It was all such a mess. So instead of staying and dealing with it and making an adult decision, I told you I'd gone through with the abortion and I ran away.'

'That's when you went travelling?'

'Yeah, although I wasn't gone for as long as everyone thought I was. I travelled around Europe for a couple of months, then I came back and found this horrible bedsit in the arse end of South London and I basically sat and waited to have the baby. My mum and dad had given me this money to travel the world and I spent most of it on rent and pot noodles.'

'But . . . the baby?' Andrew asked. He had never forgotten the little white hat. His mother-in-law had given Ethan one very similar when he was born, and every time he put it on his soft little head he had thought of that other hat, that other baby, the one that never was. But now Trina was telling him that it had been.

'I knew I couldn't keep it. I was too young, and I hadn't told anyone I was pregnant, not even my parents – especially not my parents. My dad would have done his nut.'

Andrew remembered meeting her parents at their graduation in Exeter. Her father was taciturn, not showing any outward sign of pride or love, her mother equally quiet, deferring to him at every turn.

'So ... what? It was adopted?'

'Yes. Andrew, I'm so sorry.' She was almost whispering although everybody else was involved in their own conversations. 'I should have told you but I didn't and the longer it went on, the harder it became to tell you.'

'Why are you telling me now? Here? For God's sake, Trina.' He'd tried not to be angry because the whole thing was just too sad, but he couldn't help his frustration spilling out.

'Because she's found me.'

'She?' Despite the absolute chaos that he knew this story would create in his life, his heart lifted. 'The baby was a girl?'

'Yes. Her name is Olivia. I got a letter from the adoption agency a few months ago saying she wanted to get in touch with me and stupidly I said yes.'

'Why stupidly?' Olivia, he thought. A round, smooth name. Olivia.

'Because I don't want Julian to find out that you and

I slept together when I was with him! And she wants to meet me, and to meet you, and once he knows the dates and how old she is, it won't take him long to work it out.'

'She wants to meet me?'

'Yes, and she's said if I don't tell you about her, she'll get in touch herself. But I am begging you, please don't meet her, don't see her. Don't tell Liz about her because if you do, I'll never be able to keep it from Julian and he'll never forgive me.'

'Surely he will? He's a good bloke.' Would Liz forgive him the same crime? He could hardly bear to think about that.

'You don't know him like I do. He's so straight, so black and white. Not only have I been lying to him for twenty-four years, I cheated on him when we'd just begun. And you cheated on Liz. Please, Andrew.'

'I need time to think about this. We can't talk about it now. Not with everyone around. But Trina, if I do choose to meet her, you can't stop me.'

Andrew slipped through the French doors into the house without telling Liz, or anyone, that he was going to bed. As soon as he was alone, unaccustomed tears welled in his eyes. He had a daughter. He hugged the fact to him. Whatever happened next, he couldn't wish that it wasn't true.

Standing in the shadows on the terrace, Julian, who had heard every word of the conversation between Andrew and Trina, stared out into the darkness.

PART FOUR

The Truth

Chapter 37

Liz

When the worst of the sobbing has subsided, I lift my face from Owen's now-damp blue chambray shirt.

'Sorry,' I say for the millionth time.

'Stop saying that,' he says, gently smoothing back a strand of hair that has stuck to my wet cheek. 'You've been through so much already, and now this. It'd be weird if you weren't upset. You're doing amazingly under the circumstances.'

The house is strangely quiet without the boys shouting at the PlayStation. I played the widow card and asked my neighbour Sophie to have them for an hour or so. I said I had errands to run, and she didn't question what they were on a Sunday afternoon. In truth, I needed some time alone to try and come to terms with the enormity of last night's drama at the charity auction. I haven't yet told the boys what the police told me about Andrew. I can't begin to imagine how I'll do that, or how they'll react, but I can't hide it from them for ever.

'I still can't believe Andrew might have been killed deliberately.' I can't bring myself to say *murdered*. It's such a violent, horrible word.

'But they can't be certain, right?' Owen asks.

'No, that's the thing. All they know is he died from a blow to the head and that he was already dead when he entered the water.'

'So he could have fallen and hit his head, and then the tide came in?'

'Yes. Which surely is the most likely explanation?' I say, pleadingly.

'Absolutely,' he says confidently. 'The most likely by far.'

'But when they called this morning, it didn't seem like that's what they thought. The questions they were asking . . . and they said they'll be working with the UK police. They're sending officers to interview all of us – everyone who was there that weekend.'

'They can't think . . . '

'That it was one of us?' The words stick in my throat. 'I know. It's unbelievable, ludicrous.'

'He was drunk, in unfamiliar surroundings. The most likely scenario – the *only* likely scenario – is that he fell and hit his head, passed out and got washed out by the tide. He wouldn't have known a thing about it.'

'What if that isn't what happened?' I say, although I can hardly bear to contemplate it.

'Then it was a passer-by, some random unstable person.'

'You don't know what it was like there – there weren't

any passers-by. We were miles from anywhere. The only way down to the cove was from the grounds of the house.'

'Are you seriously saying the police believe Andrew was killed by . . . someone that was there that weekend?'

'They must do.' Tears roll down my cheeks again. 'But how can that be right? I know there's been stuff going on, but this . . . I can't believe it.'

I hadn't planned on calling Owen, but once the boys had gone to Sophie's I found I couldn't bear to be alone. He was the one person I could countenance spending time with.

'What do you mean when you say there's been stuff going on?' Owen says, passing me another tissue.

'To be honest, it doesn't seem so important now but the phone call from the police wasn't the only thing that happened last night. There were a few . . . revelations.'

'Such as?'

'This bloke came over to our table and recognised Todd's daughter, Kitty. Apparently, she's some kind of high-class escort.'

'No! I bet Todd didn't take too kindly to that.' I can't blame Owen for enjoying that, given Todd basically stole his wife, but I need to tell him the rest.

'No he didn't, he went mad, but the worst thing was . . .' Oh, God. I'm breaking down again. I didn't think it was possible to cry this much. I blow my nose and try to compose myself. 'Kitty said that Andrew was one of her clients.'

'What? That doesn't sound like Andrew's thing at all.'

265

'I don't think she was lying – why would she? She said she recognised him straight away in Italy.'

'I swear he never mentioned anything like that to me.'

'He wouldn't, would he? He would have known you'd disapprove.'

'Well, yes . . . I would have disapproved,' Owen admits. 'Could it have been a work thing? What did Poppy say?'

'I didn't have a chance to ask her, but she would never have been on board with him doing something like that even if it was beneficial to the business – although . . .' The words dissolve on my tongue like sugar paper. How can I hope to know what Poppy would think or do about anything, knowing what she's done to me?

'What?' says Owen.

'When it came out about Kitty, Todd blew up and said it was disgusting that she did that type of work, and then Poppy said . . . honestly, Owen, I'm still trying to get my head around this . . . She said that she'd been having financial problems and that he'd offered to give her the money she needed if she slept with him.'

'Jesus Christ. I can't believe Saffie left me for that piece of shit. She didn't do it, surely?'

'No, and he denied it. But then he turned it around on her and said that she'd been stealing money from the agency, and that since Andrew died she's done something – fudged the figures somehow to make it seem like the business was worth less than it is, so it wouldn't cost her as much to buy me out. And I think . . . I think it might be true.'

'Poppy wouldn't do that to you, would she?'

'I don't know any more. I wouldn't have believed Trina would have slept with Andrew when he and I were together, but she did.'

'That's a bit different. It was so long ago.'

'It still hurts.'

'I know,' he says. 'Sorry. I didn't mean to imply otherwise.'

'I'm afraid that came out too – I told Trina you'd told me about it. She was trying to defend Poppy and I lost it.'

'What happened in the end? Did you resolve anything?'

'No. That's when I got the phone call from the Italian police and everything else went out of the window.'

'Have you spoken to any of the others since last night?'

'No. I can't face them. I can't face any of it. I want to stick my head in the sand and ignore it, or go back in time to before we went to Italy.'

'It's such a lot to cope with. I wish I could help.'

'You being here is a help.' I realise as I say it how true that is. Being able to talk to someone who knows the players in this twisted story but isn't involved in the events themselves is the one thing saving my sanity. 'I should go and pick up the boys. I told Sophie I wouldn't be long.'

'Do you want me to stay?'

I'm sorely tempted to ask him to dinner. It would be so nice to cook for someone who wouldn't turn their nose up and demand chicken nuggets, to have someone to share a bottle of wine with, to lay four places around the table instead of the three that kick me sharply in the guts every single time. But I need to get used to it. I need to become accustomed to being the only adult, to being the one responsible for every single thing that has to be done as well as for the happiness of two lost, grieving children.

'No, I'd better spend some time with the boys. But thank you.'

I follow him down the hall. At the front door, we hug. It's so good to feel strong arms around me, to be physically close to someone I didn't give birth to and who wants nothing from me. He's the first to let go so I follow suit. He's just being a good friend, helping his best friend's widow in her hour of need. There's nothing more to it – and even if there was it would be inappropriate and extremely inadvisable.

When he's gone, I don't go and collect the boys straight away. Instead, I sit at the kitchen table running through the people who were at the villa that weekend, trying to imagine one of them killing Andrew. Saffie. Todd. Trina. Julian. Poppy. Kitty. I cannot believe that one of them would have been so angry with him that they would have wanted to hurt him, let alone kill him. It must have been an accident.

Nevertheless, as I grab my keys and walk round to Sophie's to get the boys, I can't stop their names running through my consciousness like a mantra: Saffie, Todd, Trina, Julian, Poppy, Kitty. They've all lied to me about something. Who's to say there aren't yet more lies to be uncovered?

Chapter 38

Liz

'Can you tell me in your own words what happened that evening? Take me through the events as you remember them.'

DS Bowyer adjusts his tie very slightly, so that it's perfectly symmetrical between the lapels of his suit and lying flat against his crisp pale blue shirt. His colleague, DC Randall, watches me impassively through her dark-rimmed glasses, hands folded neatly in her lap. They both turned down the offer of tea or coffee. Randall explained when they arrived that that she'll be our family liaison officer, and offered support in talking to the boys about what's happened. I said I'd prefer to do it myself, but I have no idea how I'm going to explain the truth about how their daddy died.

'We had drinks on the terrace at seven p.m., then dinner was served around eight p.m. There were eight of us on the trip, as you know.' My voice quavers on the last word and I swallow the excess saliva that has gathered in my mouth.

'Can you tell me how you and your husband knew the other guests?'

'My husband was at university with Saffie, Trina and Julian. Poppy is my oldest friend, also from university but a different one. Todd is Saffie's new partner and Kitty is his daughter.'

'And the weekend was to celebrate Todd Blake's fiftieth birthday, is that right?'

'Yes. Todd and Saffie arranged the whole thing.'

'And paid for it?'

'Yes. Todd's pretty wealthy. He does something in finance – hedge funds, I think, whatever they are.' I give a nervous laugh. Neither Bowyer nor Randall reacts.

'And I believe there were staff present in the villa?' Bowyer says.

'Yes. There were a couple of women who'd been around all weekend cleaning and waitressing, and then on the Saturday night there were caterers and waiting staff. Saffie would have the details.'

'Yes, our Italian colleagues are following up on that. DC Randall and I will be leading enquiries in the UK.'

'Right, right. So we all sat down for dinner at eight.'

'How did your husband seem? Was he his usual self?'

I don't know how to answer that.

'I wouldn't say so.'

'How so?' He leans forward. Randall clears her throat. The air in the room seems to thicken.

'He hadn't been feeling well earlier in the day. We went to a vineyard for lunch and he left early.'

270

'What was wrong with him?' DC Randall asks.

'He felt under the weather. But also . . . there had been a bit of tension between Andrew and Todd.'

'What was the source of that tension?'

'This wouldn't be anything to do with . . . ' I look helplessly from one to the other. 'It wasn't anything serious.'

'That's OK,' Bowyer says. 'We're just trying to get a picture of the weekend at the moment.'

'Saffie used to be married to my husband's best friend, Owen Kesterton. They broke up nine or ten months ago and Saffie . . . she left Owen for Todd. Andrew was protective of Owen. He wasn't too keen on Todd. Todd can be . . . spiky.'

'Spiky?' Randall asks.

'Tactless. He rubs people up the wrong way.'

'Was there an argument?'

'No, not really. Just some . . . jibing, I suppose you'd call it.'

'OK,' Bowyer says. 'And you said your husband wasn't his usual self at dinner?'

'He was quiet. Not enjoying himself. I think he was hoping to keep his head down and wait until it was time to go . . . home.' I stumble on the last word. Andrew had always loved our home and seen it as a place of refuge from the outside world. Now he'll never be in it again, never know the pleasure of stepping through the front door and letting the cares of the day roll off him. I'm not sure I will either – it will never be the same to me, without him.

'Around ten p.m., he said he'd had enough, and that he was going for a walk to get some fresh air. I went to bed not long after that and fell asleep. I woke around five the next morning and he wasn't there. I looked downstairs to see if he'd come back and fallen asleep on a sofa or something, but there was no sign of him. I didn't know what to do, so I waited until the others woke up. We looked all over the grounds for him, and on the . . . on the beach. Eventually we called the police.'

'I understand that after extensive searches, your husband was declared presumed drowned, with no suspicious circumstances?'

'Yes. He was drunk, he couldn't swim very well. The sea came right into the cove at high tide. I thought he must have fallen asleep on the beach, or tripped and fallen . . . that's possible, isn't it?'

'Yes,' Randall says. 'That's a possibility. The forensic evidence tells us only that your husband was dead when he entered the water. He died from a head injury, not by drowning.'

I wince. Every time I hear it, it's like the first time, like being plunged anew into freezing water.

'Mrs Morgan,' DS Bowyer says. 'As my colleague says, it's certainly possible that your husband's death was an accident, but we want to make absolutely sure. Is there any reason that you can think of that anyone present at the Villa Rosa, guest or staff, would have wanted to harm or kill your husband?'

I am at a loss as to how to answer that. My instinctive

reaction is to say no, of course not. These are our friends. But they've all been lying to me. Who's to say they're not lying about this? Poppy had been stealing from the company she owned with Andrew, a fact she wouldn't have been able to keep from him for ever. Andrew was a major stumbling block in Todd being welcomed into Saffie's friendship group, which was a huge problem for both Todd and Saffie. If Kitty is to be believed, Andrew had procured her services as an escort, so knew what she really did for a living, a fact she was desperate to hide from her father. Trina and Andrew slept together when they were both in relationships with, respectively, Julian and me – a fact I can't be certain Julian hadn't found out. But if I say any of this, am I implicating innocent people? Surely none of these are a motive for murder. I sit up a little straighter.

'None that I can think of,' I say.

Chapter 39

Liz

In Saffie and Todd's kitchen, it's as if nothing has changed. *A kitchen supper* was how she described this evening, a term I've become familiar with over my years faking it in this rarefied middle-class world. To me, growing up, supper was a glass of milk and a couple of digestive biscuits – chocolate ones if you were lucky – eaten before bed in your PJs. In Saffie's vocabulary it's a meal which may have taken you all day to prepare, even though by the time the guests arrive the work is over and you're just giving it the occasional stir. It's allocated seats and wine that matches the food. As a concession to informality there may be a shop-bought pudding but it'll be from M&S or, at a push, Waitrose.

The room is bathed in a subtle golden glow from a lighting system controlled by phone. A casserole bubbles on the stove, emitting a mouth-watering, meaty, herb-laden scent. Red wine has been poured into a crystal decanter and set on the table to breathe, even though it's only the two of us tonight. I'd made sure before I accepted her invitation that Todd wasn't going to be here, although I'm not clear how things are between the two of them.

'Who's with the boys tonight?' Saffie asks. I've been here fifteen minutes and so far neither of us have mentioned the bomb that's recently gone off in our lives. We both know it's coming – even Saffie can't gloss over something so major – but for now we're sticking to the niceties.

'Owen,' I say.

'Owen?' Sauce from the wooden spoon in her hand drips unheeded onto the marble worktop.

'Yes,' I say defiantly. Why shouldn't he help me out? 'He's been brilliant since I got back from Italy.'

'I didn't realise you were seeing so much of him.'

'Of course I am. He was Andrew's best friend. He's one of my best friends. He's devastated about what's happened.'

'Right, right. I suppose he has always been very fond of you.'

I blush, shame flooding me at the memory of Owen's arms around me at the door, the way I had breathed him in, how I hadn't wanted to let go.

'Have you spoken to Poppy or Trina since the auction?' she asks with her back to me, stirring the casserole. Here we go. I knew we couldn't ignore it for ever.

'No. They've both been calling and texting but I haven't answered. You?'

'Poppy's keeping a very low profile. I'm not surprised she won't see me after telling such a damaging lie about Todd.'

'You believe him, then?'

'Do you think I would stay with him if I thought there was any chance that he'd done what she claims?'

'Well, no, but . . .'

'You don't believe her, do you? After what she's done to you? She was trying to get in there first and divert the attention onto him before Todd had a chance to tell you what she'd done.'

Scenes from the night of the auction flash through my mind – Todd's vitriol, Poppy's bloodless face. I want to believe her regardless of what she's done to me.

'I mean, Poppy's not the most reliable, is she?' Saffie says, warming to her theme. 'I know she's your best friend, but she's always been frightfully scatty. It's exactly the sort of thing she would make up to get herself out of a jam.'

'She's not the most organised, no, but I still don't think she'd make something like that up.'

'So you think Todd did it?' She wipes her hands on her apron. 'Because if you do, I don't know how you and I can remain friends.'

'No!' My stomach churns. I can't lose Saffie too. 'I don't know what I'm saying. Can we . . . not talk about it? Not tonight, anyway?'

'Fine, but you need to know that I believe Todd. Todd and I are going to be together and everyone will have to come to terms with that.'

Is there anything that would persuade her that Todd is

not the man she thinks he is? Or is she so blinkered that she'll never see it? Is it love that stops her from seeing it, or an insane desire not to lose face by admitting that she made a mistake in leaving Owen for Todd?

'As for Trina,' she goes on as she warms a couple of plates in the microwave, 'I have spoken to her, and darling, I do think you should forgive her.'

'Really?' I drain the last of my G&T. I'm not sure why Saffie feels it's up to her to decide who I should and shouldn't believe, or forgive.

'Yes,' she says decisively. 'It's ancient history, you and Andrew had only recently got together, it was a drunken one-off by the sounds of it. Is that worth losing a friendship over?'

Put like that, perhaps not, but it's more than that. For a start, Andrew had told me he was falling in love with me by then, but also it led to a lifetime of lies from both him and Trina.

'I'll think about it,' I say but I'm just trying to get her off my back. Her relentless need to control the narrative is claustrophobic. It was the same in Italy – that's why she was happy to organise and pay for everything, it meant she could have it all her way.

'Have you spoken to the police?' she says.

'Yes, they came to see me this week.'

'Listen, darling, you didn't tell them that Todd and Andrew had argued, did you?'

'I said there was some tension between them, yes. You can't expect me to lie to the police, Saffie.'

'No, I don't expect that. Did they tell you . . . anything about Todd?'

'Like what?'

'You're going to find out sooner or later because the police will want to ask you about it – but you have to understand that it's firmly in the past.'

'OK.'

'You know I met Todd at my therapist's office?'

'Yes.'

'The truth is he was there for anger management therapy. He didn't need it – his lawyers had advised him to do it.'

'His lawyers?'

'Yes, the woman he was seeing before me was a nut-case – she took him to court, accused him of trying to control her, said he'd been violent towards her. It's totally ridiculous.'

After witnessing Todd's outburst at the charity auction, it doesn't seem ridiculous or even unlikely to me.

'His lawyers had the feeling the courts would come down on her side – what with all this Me Too nonsense – so they advised him to plead guilty, but to show that he was remorseful and taking it seriously, they suggested going to therapy.'

'"Me Too nonsense"? You think believing women who've been assaulted is nonsense?'

'Oh, you know what I mean, darling. So is that all you said? There was a bit of tension between Andrew and Todd?'

'Basically, yes.' She's deluded. What would Todd have to do for the scales to fall from her eyes? 'Saffie . . . you're not . . . frightened of Todd, are you?'

'Don't be so silly! I just don't want the police to get the wrong idea and think Todd had anything seriously against Andrew. Obviously, I told them he was with me all night, which he was. The only people who were on their own were Poppy and Kitty.'

'Were you awake the whole night watching him?'

'No, but I'd know if he'd gone out for long. You know what a light sleeper I am. He did get up to go downstairs for a drink around midnight. In fact . . . I wasn't going to say anything, but seeing as we're throwing accusations around, when he was on his way back, he saw Poppy coming in from the terrace. She said she couldn't sleep and had gone out to get some air, but . . . '

'You can't seriously think Poppy killed Andrew,' I say. I am so, so angry with Poppy but I cannot, will not believe that of her.

'You wouldn't have believed she'd steal from you, would you?' Saffie says. 'If she knew Andrew was about to find out she'd taken that money from the business, who knows what she might have done to keep it a secret? And then there's Kitty – she was terrified Andrew was going to tell Todd her dirty little secret. She knows which side her bread is buttered, that one. Although there's less butter on it now,' she says with satisfaction.

'What d'you mean?'

'I didn't know this before, but Todd had set up this

trust fund for Kitty, which she was meant to come into when she turned twenty-five, next year.'

'Meant to?'

'Yes – he's not going to give it to her now, is he? Not now he knows the truth. So if anyone would have bene-fitted from Andrew being out of the way, it's Kitty, what with him – sorry, darling, but it's true – knowing what she'd been up to.'

'For God's sake, Saffie.' I can't bear this speculation, as if Andrew's death is a puzzle to be solved.

'Sorry, darling,' she says unrepentantly. 'But I don't see why Todd has to be enemy number one when there are others who had more to lose.'

A wave of sheer panic washes over me. None of us have got any way of knowing who killed Andrew, if anyone did. I can't believe the change that has been wrought on my life since the night of the auction. Things were bad enough before, but now I'm infected with a sick suspi-cion that bleeds into all my relationships. I don't know if we'll ever find out what happened to Andrew, but what I do know with a dull certainty is that my life as I knew it is over.

Chapter 40

Liz

'Auntie Poppy's here!'

Josh launches himself off the sofa from where he's spied her through the sitting-room window and races to the front door. Ethan stays curled deep in the sofa, staring at the TV screen, although he must have watched this Harry Potter film a dozen times. He's been so quiet since I broke the news to them about the circumstances of Andrew's death. I thought about keeping it from them until they're older, but they've already got access to the Internet via their iPads, and even though I have parental controls in place and monitor what they watch, I couldn't be sure they wouldn't find out. I've spent time with them doing things they like, conscious that whilst my preoccupation with unravelling the events leading to Andrew's death may have served as a distraction from my grief, it has also kept me from properly engaging with them. They need me now more than they ever have.

'Hello, love.' The familiar sound of Poppy's voice runs me through like a sword. 'How are you?'

'We're watching Harry Potter!'

'Brilliant. Where's Mummy?'

'I'm here.'

I step out into the hallway, unsmiling.

'Come and watch!' Josh runs back into the sitting room.

'Can we talk?' She looks tired, her hair lank.

'You haven't left me much choice, turning up when the boys are here.'

'I'm sorry, but you wouldn't answer my calls.'

I check behind me. Ethan is giving every impression of being engrossed in the film but I'm pretty sure he's listening to every word we say.

'Come through to the kitchen. Boys, I'm going to talk to Poppy for a minute in the kitchen. Don't pause it, I'll be back soon.'

'How are they?' she says once I've closed the door behind us and we're seated opposite each other at the kitchen table.

'I don't know,' I say tightly through unshed tears. 'They won't talk about it. Ethan's shut down. Josh has gone the other way, totally manic.'

'He always gets like that when he's stressed, though, doesn't he?'

Now Andrew's gone, she's the only other person who knows Josh well enough to know that. I screw my face up tight. I will not cry, not after what she's done to me.

'Oh, Liz.' She reaches out towards me but I snatch my hand away.

'Don't! Don't touch me.'

'Sorry. Liz, I know I don't deserve it but will you give me a chance to explain?'

'If you must.' There's nothing she can say that will make this better.

'I only ever meant to borrow from the company.' The words tumble out in a rush as if they know they haven't got long. 'The money was just sitting there in the company account and it wasn't going to be needed. Since I re-mortgaged the house I've barely got enough each month for the bills, and then the boiler went and my car failed its MOT and there was the Italy trip, and I'd maxed out all my credit cards and they wouldn't let me have another one. It was getting really serious, they were threatening me with debt collectors. I was in a frightful panic – you know what I'm like, Liz, I've always been hopeless with money.'

'You can't use that as an excuse. There must have been another solution.'

'There wasn't. I was absolutely desperate. I meant to pay it back, truly I did, but there was always something else, and the minimum payments on my credit cards were taking a huge chunk of my salary every month, and I got myself into a terrible mess. I know it sounds weird but it was like someone else was doing it and I was watching.'

'Why didn't you talk to Andrew? He might have let you borrow some money.'

'Partly because I was ashamed,' she says. 'I know what you all think of me: hopeless, chaotic Poppy – can't keep a man, can't manage her finances. The only thing I've ever been good at is my job. Plus, Andrew and I had argued about the agency. We badly needed new clients and he wanted to diversify away from our core business – the ethically sound stuff – but I refused to countenance it. I was scared that he was looking for an excuse to get rid of me. If he'd found out about the money, he'd have had me out on my ear in a heartbeat. I had Scarlet weeping down the phone every night, talking about leaving uni and coming home – I was petrified I was going to lose the house and she wouldn't have a home to come back to.'

'Was Andrew on the verge of finding out what you'd done?' My throat is tight.

'I wouldn't have been able to hide it for ever.'

'It worked out well for you, then, what happened in Italy?' My words are knives and they wound her as I meant them to.

'No, Liz! God, no. I would never have wanted or chosen that. You have to believe me.'

'Why should I? You've lied to me over and over, and what destroys me is how easy you found it. And you not only continued to lie, you tried to defraud me of what was rightfully mine. I don't know you at all, Poppy. I have no idea what you're capable of.'

'Will you let me explain about the agency? I'll tell you exactly what I did – everything. No more secrets.'

'You can tell me whatever you like but it won't make any difference.'

'When Andrew died, I checked the partnership protection insurance. Basically, we hadn't updated it for years, not since we set the business up. It wasn't going to be enough for me to buy you out at what the business was really worth. But I knew that if you kept your shares, I was going to have to admit to you that I'd been taking money out of the business. It was a sort of madness. I'd got so used to hiding it, I couldn't see a way out. I was getting letters and calls from the debt collectors every day, they were turning up at my house.'

Tears are streaming from her eyes. It's all I can do not to reach out to her, as I normally would without thinking if she was this upset about something. I put my hands together on my lap.

'So I lied to you. Todd was right. I did get the idea from him. I told you Andrew and I had agreed to depreciate the cost of the IT system over three years, but it was actually fifteen years. The business was worth much more than I told you it was, but if I'd given you the real figure, I couldn't have bought you out. I can't excuse it, there is no excuse. All I can do for you now is tell you the truth and beg you to forgive me.'

'How can I forgive you when I still don't know if you're telling the truth? How can I ever believe a word you say again? No one can verify where you were on the Saturday night. Saffie says Todd saw you coming in from

285

the terrace in the middle of the night. Did you follow Andrew to the beach?'

'No!' She pales. 'Please, Liz—'

'Mummy, you're missing the best bit!' Josh comes charging into the kitchen but stops short when he sees that both Poppy and I are crying.

'What's the matter?'

I grab him and bury my face in his soft hair.

'We're all right, my love, just feeling sad about Daddy. Like we talked about.'

He wriggles out of my embrace.

'Come and watch the film. And you, Auntie Poppy.'

'I will. Poppy's got to go, haven't you?'

'Right. Yes.' She wipes her eyes. 'I'll see you soon, Josh.'

'OK, hurry up and go, then,' he says, hustling her towards the front door. Normally I'd tell him off for being rude, but I can't bring myself to care. We say a forced, formal goodbye under Josh's impatient eye and Poppy closes the front door softly behind her.

Josh ushers me into the sitting room and onto the sofa. I sit down next to Ethan, and Josh flings himself down on my other side, nestling close. I try to put my arm around Ethan but he shakes it off, glued to the TV, his body unyielding.

Chapter 41

Liz

The boys have gone off to school and I'm steeling myself to make a start on sorting out Andrew's stuff when the doorbell rings. I know from the Facebook forums I've been haunting that the widowed have very different timetables for this – some still have their partner's dressing gown hanging on the door five years after they died, others can't bear to see a single reminder of their loved one and have cleared everything within the first week.

I'm half expecting to see Owen's outline through the frosted-glass panels – he said he'd pop over for a coffee today although I wasn't expecting him until later. However, as I walk down the hall, I can see it's someone slighter – almost certainly a woman. I open the door to reveal Trina. She's gaunt and angular – she must have lost half a stone in the week since I've seen her – and her eyes are puffy.

'Please don't close the door,' she says, before I have a chance to speak.

'I wasn't going to. Come in.'

She follows me down the hall to the kitchen, and we sit opposite each other at the table.

'Sorry to barge in like this, but you wouldn't answer my calls and I need to talk to you. Firstly, I want to say how sorry I am. I never wanted you to know about me and Andrew – not to save my own skin, but to avoid hurting you. It was so long ago and it meant so little, even at the time. Andrew thought you were going to break up with him – you'd been offered a job in Scotland, I think it was. We got drunk and reminisced about when we were together. It was a stupid mistake, and he regretted it massively the next day. As did I.'

'Was that when it was?' I remember that phone call like it was yesterday – especially Andrew's distress when I told him about the job interview in Edinburgh. It was the first time he told me he loved me, and although I was shocked he'd said it so early, there was something in me that knew it was right. I knew we had something special, something extraordinary. We'd spoken on the phone every day for a month, and there was nothing we hadn't talked about – big or small. I'd shared things with him that I'd never told anyone, but we were also able to make a conversation out of absolutely anything. One night we'd spent ten enjoyable minutes talking about coats. After the phone call where I told him about Edinburgh, I'd gone to a party but hadn't been able to relax, my mind full of him. By the end of the night, I'd decided I wasn't going to the interview.

'Yes,' Trina says. 'He really thought you were going to leave him. Can you forgive me?'

She looks exhausted, anxious and hopeful all at the same time. We've been through so much together, and I need my friends more than I ever have. It was one night. Andrew and I had been together such a short time.

'I think so. I want to.' It's the best I can do.

'Oh thank God. Thank you. There's something else I need to tell you – to talk to you about. I don't know what to do.' Her face contorts with the effort of not crying.

'What is it?'

'That night – the night Andrew and I slept together – I got pregnant.'

I try to speak but the air has been sucked out of me.

'Yes.' She pre-empts the question I'm trying to ask. 'It was definitely Andrew's. Julian and I hadn't slept together. To be honest, I wasn't sure it was going to last with him, so I'd been putting him off.'

'Did Andrew know, back then?'

'Yes. He tried to be supportive but I knew he didn't really want me to have it. He knew that would spell the end for your relationship, and that was the last thing he wanted. So I told him I'd had an abortion.'

'You told him?' I manage to draw enough air into my lungs to get the words out. 'What do you mean, you told him? You didn't have an abortion?'

She shakes her head, her face twisting.

'You had the baby?'

'Yes.' It's more of a sob than a word. She scrabbles in her

289

bag for a tissue and blows her nose. 'I was going to have an abortion, but when it came to it I couldn't go through with it. I went travelling around Europe for a couple of months, then I came back and rented a bedsit by myself and waited to have the baby. I couldn't keep it – I was too young and my parents would have disowned me. And by then I'd realised that I wanted to be with Julian – we'd kept in touch by email all the time I was away. The bedsit was above an Internet café – I'd go down there and make up stories about what I'd been doing in various glamorous locations around the world, while staring at the kebab shop opposite. I couldn't tell him the truth – he would have known the baby wasn't his, and he's so black and white with these things, I knew he wouldn't forgive me.'

'So . . . what happened to the baby?'

'She was adopted.'

'She?' Andrew has a daughter. A twenty-four-year-old daughter. Images flash before me: the young woman crying at the funeral and waiting outside my house the following week, trying to pluck up the courage to ring the doorbell. That must have been her.

'Yes. Olivia. She got in touch with me a few months before Italy, wanted to get to know me. And Andrew.'

'Did you tell him?'

'No, I tried to put her off. I didn't want to see her. I couldn't allow her into my life. I was so terrified of Julian finding out. But she was threatening to find Andrew herself. I needed to ask him not to respond, to let it lie. I didn't mean to tell him, but I got so drunk that first night in Italy that it all came spilling out. I begged him not to reply if she contacted him, but he said it wasn't up to me. It was the wrong time, I shouldn't have done it then.'

I remember seeing the two of them talking on the terrace and then Andrew went up to bed. His eyes had been red when I came up to the room – he'd blamed an allergic reaction to the flowers.

'So how did Julian react after the auction night, when he found out about the night you spent with Andrew?'

'That's the thing – he barely reacted at all. The minute I saw his face when you blurted it out, I could tell he already knew. But straight away you got the phone call from the police, so we didn't talk about it. When we got home that night, it all came out. He overheard me and Andrew talking on the Friday night at the villa. He's known about the whole thing – me and Andrew sleeping together, the baby, everything – for three months and never said anything.'

'Why not?'

'I don't know ... that's what frightens me.'

'Frightens you?'

She twists her hands together as if trying to wash off something unpleasant.

'I'm scared about what he might have done,' she says in a low voice, looking down at the table.

'What do you mean? Done what?'

'I didn't tell you at the time, because ... it didn't seem important. But now, with the police saying it possibly wasn't an accident ...'

'Trina, what is it?'

'On the Saturday night at the villa, after Andrew stormed out and you went after him, we all went to bed. No one had the heart for a party. Julian said he'd had too much to drink and he was going for a walk to clear his head. I thought he meant a quick walk around the garden, but when he wasn't back after half an hour, I went to look for him. I thought he must have fallen asleep on the terrace or something. He wasn't there, but I saw Andrew walking down the lawn towards the steps to the cove. I thought I'd try and talk to him about . . . our daughter, ask him again not to respond if she tried to get in touch. I followed him down the garden, but when he got to the top of the steps to the cove, I saw someone coming from the other direction, as if from the driveway. It was Julian. He must have come out of the house the other way, from the front, and round via the drive.'

'Are you sure it was Julian? It must have been very dark.'

'It was, but I could see the fluorescent yellow stripes on the arm of his jacket. It's a ridiculous one he wears out running, but he hadn't thought he'd need a jumper or anything – it was the only warm thing he had with him. They spoke for a minute and then headed down the steps to the beach. I decided to leave them to it and went back to bed.'

'What time did he get back to your room?' I ask, my heart fluttering in my throat.

'I don't know. I fell asleep. He returned at some point because when I woke in the morning, he was there.'

'Did you ask him about it?'

'Not straight away, but yes, when we realised Andrew was missing. He said he hadn't seen him, that he'd just walked down the lane towards the village and then come back and come straight to bed. I let it go – at the time I was so worried about him finding out about me and Andrew, and until the auction night, it hadn't occurred to me that Andrew's death was anything other than an accident.'

'And you didn't know that Julian knew about you and Andrew sleeping together – that he had a reason to be angry with Andrew,' I say slowly.

'Exactly.' Her periwinkle-blue eyes are larger than ever.

'Have you asked him about it?'

'No. He's . . . ' She swallows tears. 'When we got home from the auction, after he told me he knew everything, he packed up his stuff and left. He was so angry that it had come out in front of everyone that I'd cheated on him. He's been staying at his brother's ever since.'

'Have you told the police?'

'No! I don't want them to think . . . if he didn't . . . '

'Didn't what, Trina?' I'm aware how cold I sound. 'Kill my husband?'

'He can't have done,' she says, but she doesn't sound convinced.

'If you don't tell them, I will. Trina, we can't keep this from them.'

'No, I know. You're right.' She locks her fingers together, nails bitten down to the quick. 'I'll call them.'

When she's gone, promising to call the police when she gets home, I sit at the table thinking about how Andrew must have felt when he found out he had a grown-up daughter. Worried about telling me, given that it meant confessing that he'd cheated on me, but he must also have been happy and excited about meeting her. A weight of sadness settles on my chest at the thought of everything he's missed out on. He'll never meet Olivia now, and he'll never get to see our children as adults or know the joy of grandparenthood.

I allow it to sit with me for a moment, and then shake it off. I've only got a few hours until the boys will be home from school, demanding snacks and attention, and I need to be ready for them. The curious thing that I have come to understand since being widowed is the extent to which life has to, and does, go on, no matter what unimaginable pain and tragedy befalls you – especially if you have children. You lose the love of your life, violently and unexpectedly, but meals still have to be cooked, clothes washed and conversations engaged in.

The task I assigned myself today, to be completed by the time Owen drops in for coffee, was to clear Andrew's bedside drawers, and that's what I'm going to do. I set aside my sadness. It will have to wait.

Chapter 42

Liz

I kneel on the floor next to what I'll always think of as Andrew's side of the bed. The top drawer contains the detritus I expected: chargers for devices he no longer owned, a dog-eared pack of playing cards, reading glasses, paracetamol, his father's watch, long stopped. I throw everything into a bin bag, not stopping to look too closely or call up the memories associated with the items. Then I pick the watch out, rubbing dust from the face. He'd obviously kept it for sentimental reasons. I could get it fixed and give it to one of the boys when they're older. I rescue the paracetamol, too, and transfer them to my bedside drawer.

The second drawer contains an expensive camera he bought a few years ago in a short-lived fit of enthusiasm for photography. It came with a battery charger and I dig into the bin bag and fish that out too. I'm not getting very far. There are five or six old phones and his iPad, current but rarely used. It's completely dead. I take it down to the kitchen and plug it into my charger on the kitchen table. It begins to charge but it's so flat it won't switch on yet, so I go back upstairs and turn my attention to the bottom drawer. I open a lined notebook and flip through the pages. It's humdrum stuff – to-do lists, calculations, holiday packing reminders – but the sight of his handwriting – slanted, spiky, heartrendingly familiar – is like a knife to my heart. I close the book and put it back in the drawer. I can't bear to throw his handwriting away. I bury my face in my hands. This is wrong. What was I thinking? I shouldn't be throwing anything away. It's too soon, too sad. I scoop out what's left in the bin bag, put it all back in the top drawer and go down to the kitchen.

As I fill the kettle, the iPad beeps and springs into life. The lock screen is a photo of the four of us on holiday in Cornwall a few years ago. We asked a passer-by to take it. We're bunched up together, Andrew's arms around all of us, a fresh sea breeze blowing pink into our cheeks and whipping my hair around my face. We look happy, like we belong together. I want to gather up those little boys in the photo and protect them from what's coming. The loss of their blind faith in the world as a good place where bad things don't happen has been the hardest thing to bear. I unlock the screen easily. Andrew used the same super-secret code for everything – 1234. I feel guilty, as if someone's going to come and find me snooping, but there is no one coming. I can do what I like. I don't think Andrew had used this for a long time anyway.

I open his email account. There are loads of unread

296

emails but they're all marketing spam. When I get down to the read emails, there's nothing of any interest either. It's mostly confirmations and receipts from online shopping or more marketing stuff. Nobody uses email for personal communication any more, not now we're all surgically attached to our phones. It's all texts and WhatsApp, for the middle-aged, at any rate. I tap off it.

My eyes flicker over the home screen. None of the apps are unexpected – music, YouTube, Safari, the odd game. Then the messaging symbol catches my eye. Seven unread messages. Of course. This being an Apple device, it'll be connected to his account. Even though he hasn't used it for ages all the messages will be up to date. His phone is lost to the raging ocean, but on here I'll be able to see who he was messaging before he died. My head swims. Time slows down. I can feel the chip in the wooden floor from where Ethan once dropped a cast-iron saucepan, rough beneath my bare feet. The iPad is clumsy and too large in my hands. A mother and her chattering child pass on the street outside. The child's voice is insistent and questioning, the mother's patient, hiding her frustration. I tap on the message icon.

I scan them swiftly, trying to take it all in at once. The top two messages are marketing, one from a local pizza place with a weekend offer, the other from Andrew's mobile service provider. The next message thread is from me. I know what the texts say without checking: *Where are you? Please call me. I'm sorry. Come back and we can sort this out.* All the texts underneath mine have been read. I skim down: Andrew's mum, Poppy, Owen, Trina, Julian, Saffie.

I click on Saffie's first, curious as to what she and Andrew had been texting about. The date is a couple of days before we left for Italy.

Thanks for keeping quiet to Owen. I need to ask you again, though. Please don't tell Todd. I know it happened before I met him, but he'd be so angry if he knew I'd tried to kiss you. At you too. I know it sounds messed up, but it's not – that's just who he is. You won't say anything, will you?

I read it again, unable to comprehend. Saffie tried to kiss Andrew? When? The next message down, dating from almost a year ago, answers that question.

Andrew: *I won't say anything but don't try something like that again. I love Liz and I would never cheat on her. You're married to my best friend.*

The relief is a physical sensation, a loosening. I scroll down again, to see what he was responding to.

Saffie: *Please forget tonight ever happened. Don't tell Owen. I was just drunk and lonely. I'm so embarrassed.*

I scroll further. The messages below are chatty, arranging for Andrew to come over for dinner with her and Owen one weekend when I was away with the kids. Jesus Christ. Finding out that Trina slept with Andrew once, over twenty years ago, when things between him and I were uncertain, was one thing. But if I'm reading this right – and as much as I wish there was, there's no other way to read it – Saffie tried to get it on with my husband less than a year ago, when she was still with Owen.

Saffie's always been outwardly selfish, but I thought it was all part of her act, her schtick. *Darling, you've got to look out for yourself,* she'd say. *You can be sure as hell no one else is going to.* I thought that underneath it all, she was fiercely loyal to her friends. How stupid can you be?

I replace the iPad on the kitchen table. Maybe I shouldn't read any more of Andrew's private messages. It's like those listeners who never hear any good of themselves – nothing beneficial ever comes of snooping. But if I hadn't, I wouldn't have seen Saffie's true colours, and surely it's better that I know the truth. I pick it up again.

Feeling disloyal to both Andrew and Owen, I click on the chat thread between them. I have to reread the top message several times before I fully appreciate its significance, but when I do I have to force myself to take a breath. The messages are between Owen and Andrew on the Saturday Andrew disappeared. The day he died. That's who Andrew was texting on the way to the wine tasting. When Andrew stormed out of the lunch, he must have called Owen to ask him to pick him up, because the next text is from him to Owen explaining how to get to the vineyard.

I don't understand. Owen wasn't in Italy. I place the iPad down with trembling fingers. Then I hear the crunch of feet on my gravel path and the doorbell rings. Owen is here.

Chapter 43
Andrew

Andrew gazed unseeing at the spectacular scenery as Liz negotiated the twists and turns of the mountainous road to the vineyard, his phone like an unexploded bomb in his pocket. He couldn't believe Owen was here in Italy. What the hell was he thinking? He'd thought Owen was doing better with the whole divorce thing. It had been six months, for God's sake. He tapped out a reply.

What are you doing here? Where are you now?

The response was immediate.

I don't know, mate. Moment of madness. I'm just down the road from the villa.

Andrew wondered for a second how Owen knew where it was, but then remembered with a sinking feeling that it was his fault. It was Owen's kids, Milo and Ben, who had initially alerted Owen to the fact of the trip. They were excited about spending the weekend with their grandparents who had promised to take them to a theme park and when Owen asked them why, they had no reason not to tell him. He'd asked Andrew about it, and he'd shown Owen the villa – but he'd done it in solidarity, in a *look at the house this flash twat has rented* way. He'd wanted to reassure Owen that Todd couldn't buy his support, that he would never take Andrew away from Owen. It didn't cross his mind for a second that Owen would show up here.

Owen wanted to see Andrew, but Andrew told him they were off to a wine tasting and that he'd try and get away later. As the morning wore on, Andrew's tolerance for Todd and his posturing ebbed lower and lower. His poor best friend had been brought so low, almost to the brink of madness, by this man's actions that he'd flown here on some as yet unexplained but ultimately futile mission. Andrew couldn't bear to spend another minute in his company, so when lunch was served, he made an excuse and went to the car park to call Owen.

'Hi.' Owen sounded low and flat.

'Mate, what's going on?'

'I don't honestly know myself. Have you finished your wine tasting?'

'The others are having lunch here but I've had enough. I presume you've got a car? Can you come and pick me up? I'll text you the details.'

Andrew walked down to the end of the drive to wait for Owen. Dust puffed up under his feet from the track, bordered on either side with flower beds bursting with sweet-scented jasmine, and beyond them neat rows of vines that stretched to the horizon. At the end of the drive, he rounded the corner so he couldn't be seen from the car park and sat on the grey stone wall to wait. His phone rang. Liz calling. He let it ring out. Ahead, the vista rolled down to the sea and above it the sky, deep blue with a single wisp of fluffy cloud. The air was still, so he heard the car long before it appeared, Owen haggard and wan at the wheel. He climbed in, folding his legs with difficulty into the passenger footwell. Owen had evidently hired the smallest, cheapest car available. The men exchanged an awkward hug over the handbrake.

'Can we get straight out of here?' Owen threw a nervous look up the drive. 'I don't want anyone to see me.'

'With pleasure. I've had enough of the lot of them.'

Owen had been about to pull off, but he stopped at this and turned to Andrew.

'Not including Liz?'

'Things aren't great between us either to be honest.'

'Why, what's up?'

'I'll tell you later. Let's go.'

Owen reversed into the drive and headed back the way he came, stopping a few minutes later at a small roadside trattoria Andrew hadn't noticed on the way. At the rear of the building was a veranda with views of the sea and they took a seat at a rough wooden table. They attempted to decipher the menu with the help of Google Translate. What a rarefied world he'd inhabited so far this weekend, thanks to Todd and Saffie. He'd only encountered

Italians who spoke fluent English, or the minions doing their bidding. He hadn't had to give any thought to what he wanted to eat or drink, or to lift a finger to do anything for himself. He smugly internally congratulated himself on finally seeing the 'real' Italy.

After some back and forth with the waiter, and a lot of pointing and gesturing, they ordered what they hoped were two dishes of seafood pasta and a bottle of local red wine. Whilst they waited for the wine to arrive they engaged in what was – under the circumstances – some rather ludicrous chitchat about work and kids, but once the first glasses had been poured, Andrew leaned forward on his elbows and asked Owen what was really going on.

'I can hardly explain it to myself,' Owen said. 'Ever since I found out about the weekend, I haven't been able to stop thinking about it.' He took a sip of wine. 'This is going to sound mad, and I wouldn't say it to anyone except you, but the thought of you all here, my best friends – or the people I thought were my best friends – celebrating with the man who stole my wife, I couldn't bear it. I know, I know, it's madness. He couldn't have stolen her if she didn't want to be stolen, and I don't seriously . . . I can't expect you guys to shun Saff because of what she did, but it grates. It hurts. It's like you've all chosen her over me. I kept going over and over it, and before I knew it I found myself online booking a flight and a cheap hotel. Even on my way to the airport I kept expecting to turn the car around, snap out of it, but it never happened.'

'What did you plan to do once you got here?'

'I don't know specifically, but I thought I'd storm up to the villa, make a scene. I wanted to punish you all, make you understand what you've done to me. I know, it's crazy. I'm sorry, I'm so sorry.'

'Oh, mate.' It was crazy, but Andrew couldn't help but feel sorry for him. He'd obviously seen the error of his ways, otherwise he wouldn't have called. 'What changed your mind?'

'I drove to the villa last night. I crept up to the dining-room window. You all looked so happy. I saw the way Saffie was looking at Todd. She never looked at me like that. We weren't right for each other – I'm not sure we ever were. She needs someone Alpha and that was never going to be me. You're all getting on with your lives, and I've been stuck. Making a scene wasn't going to make me feel better. In fact, it would have made me feel a hundred times worse. I took a long hard look at myself and realised I've been an absolute bloody fool.'

'Why did you call me today?'

'I almost didn't. I was going to stay in my horrible, dingy hotel room and catch my flight home tomorrow with my tail between my legs. But I don't want to lose you and Liz. The others I can live without, to be honest, but you two are true friends. I needed to be honest with you, otherwise I couldn't have continued spending time with you.'

'You won't lose me, mate.' Andrew was incredibly moved, and gladder than ever that he hadn't fallen under Todd's spell like the others. 'I didn't want to come on this weekend in the first place, and so far it's been an utter nightmare. It may have looked like happy families from the outside, but believe me, that's far from the truth.'

'What d'you mean?'

'As I've said to you before, I can't accept Saffie and Todd's relationship. You're my best mate, and I know how much it's hurt you. There's been times over the last couple of days where I haven't been able to . . . keep that in, you might say. It's made things difficult for everyone, especially Liz.'

'I appreciate that, I really do.'

'Thanks. But there's a few other things going on as well.'

The pasta arrived, announced in a gabble of Italian by the waiter. They nodded their thanks and Andrew steadied himself to share the burden of his new, unwanted knowledge.

'Do you remember when I met Liz?'

'Exeter. Your twenty-first birthday party.'

'Right. So there was this one night about a month after we met when Trina came over, and . . . '

'I know, mate,' Owen said.

'You know?'

'I had the room next to yours.' Owen laughed in a strangely brittle way.

'Oh. I didn't think you were in. Why didn't you ever say anything?'

'I thought you'd tell me if you wanted to.'

'Right. OK. The thing is, Trina got pregnant that night.'

305

'What?'

So he didn't know everything. 'She told me she'd had an abortion. But last night she confessed that she didn't. She had the baby, and had it adopted.'

'Jesus.' Owen put his fork down.

'I know. The daughter, Olivia her name is, has been in touch with her and wants to meet, and to meet me. Trina doesn't want to see her, and she doesn't want me to either. She thinks Julian's going to do his nut when he finds out we slept together when she and Julian were together. But how can I reject her, if she comes to find me? She's my daughter.'

'What about Liz? She'll be devastated.'

'Yes, I know that. That's what I'm worried about.'

'Sounded like you were more worried about Trina and this Olivia, a girl you don't even know.'

'What? No, of course I'm most worried about Liz.'

'Sorry, mate,' Owen said. 'I'm knackered and stressed out and wishing I wasn't here.'

Andrew's phone rang. They must have finished at the vineyard. He didn't pick up.

'It's Liz,' he said. 'I should go back. I didn't tell anyone where I was going.'

'OK. I'll take you.'

'What time's your flight tomorrow?'

'Early. What a bloody stupid waste of money.'

'Ah OK, I don't think I'll have a chance to see you again, then. We've got this big dinner tonight for the birthday boy. Let's have a drink this week, though, at home.'

'Definitely, mate. Call me when you get back.'

In the car, Andrew closed his eyes and rested his head against the window, hot from the afternoon sun. He just had to get through the rest of the weekend, and then he could figure out how to tell Liz. He had to make her understand. Things had been rocky lately, but Andrew couldn't live without her.

Chapter 44

Liz

'Hi.'

Owen smiles, his eyes creasing at the corners in a way I've come to look forward to.

'Hi,' I say, not moving, unsure what to do with this recent knowledge that makes no sense at all.

'Can I come in?' he says, confused.

'Right, OK.'

He takes off his jacket and hangs it on a peg, and I lead the way to the kitchen, my heart hammering in my chest. I automatically flick the kettle on and scoop coffee into the cafetière.

'Are you OK, Liz?'

I used to be good at hiding my emotions, but since being widowed it's like I've had a layer of skin flayed off. Owen in particular is skilled at seeing behind the front I've constructed. He knows me so well.

'Yes. No. I'm not sure.' I keep my back to him, ostensibly waiting for the kettle to boil.

He moves up behind me, so close I can feel his breath on the back of my neck.

'What is it?' he says. 'I know when you're not OK, Liz. I know you.'

'Why didn't you tell me you were in Italy?' I say, turning round to face him, the kitchen worktop digging into the base of my spine.

'Oh.' He takes a step away from me. 'How did you find out?'

The last shred of ridiculous hope I had that there was another explanation for those messages fades away.

'I found Andrew's iPad.' I point towards the table. 'It's got his messages on it. Why didn't you tell me?'

'I suppose I was ashamed. Ashamed I behaved so childishly, when you've been going through this awful thing, losing Andrew.'

'But what were you doing there?'

'I don't know. Losing my mind a bit? The thought of you all there, my best friends, without me. I felt excluded. It's always upset me that Saffie got to keep you all, as a gang, and I was left out in the cold, even though she was the one who left me. I had a few too many drinks and found myself booking a flight.'

'What did you plan to do?' I can't believe he was there. Was he watching us, spying on us? And Andrew knew. He knew and didn't tell me.

'I don't know. I came up to the house on the Friday night with some idea of making a scene. I know, I know, it's so stupid. I feel like such an idiot.'

He sounds so pathetic I can't help but feel a pang of sympathy. We all do stupid things sometimes, don't we?

'I even came to the house and looked through the window. I saw you all having dinner.'

'Oh! I saw you. Well, I saw something, a movement.'

'You were all so happy. In that moment, it hit me, how ridiculous I was being. I crept back to the car and returned to the hotel to lick my wounds. I vowed that this would be my rock bottom, that I'd move on with my life, seek out new friends, try to be happy. The next morning, I texted Andrew to let him know I was there. Later, he called and asked me to pick him up from the vineyard. He was having a rough time. We had lunch together, he calmed me down.'

'Did you . . . ' I can't believe I'm having to ask this. My skin tingles all over. 'Did you see him again after that?'

'No! God, no, Liz.'

I have to believe him. This is Owen. Andrew's best friend. One of my best friends too.

'Did he say anything about what had been going on at the villa?'

'A bit. I know how he felt about seeing Saffie with Todd. And although I was grateful for his support, I told him he should try to let it go. Partly for his own sake but also to make things easier for the rest of you. You in particular.'

His eyes are suddenly very blue, very intense.

'What do you mean, me in particular?' It's quiet in here, the only sounds the hum of the fridge and a lawn-mower whining in the distance.

'OK.' He takes a deep breath. 'I hope this isn't the wrong thing to say.'

My fists are clenched, nails digging into my palms.

'You and I have always been close, but since Andrew died ... and this sounds very weird, given the circumstances ... I've really enjoyed spending time with you.'

'Me too. You've been such a great support.' This is the safe thing to say. He can agree that he's been supporting me in my grief and we can move on.

'I'm glad about that, but ... to me, it feels like more than that. Like there might be ... something between us.'

I open my mouth to reply but nothing comes out. My face is flaming and my heart is bursting out of my throat.

'I'm sorry, I shouldn't have said anything. It's too soon. I mean, maybe it's not that, maybe I'm barking up the wrong tree entirely. I'm sorry. I'm so sorry.'

'No.' The air around us is thin, like at the top of a mountain.

'No?' he says hopefully.

'I feel it too.' I had thought the words would stick in my throat if I ever tried to get them out – but there's something right about them. 'It's OK. I feel it too,' I repeat.

'Thank God for that,' he says. We both laugh, a welcome release.

'But you're right, it is very soon for me,' I say. 'Everything's still so raw.'

'Of course. The last thing I want is to rush you.'

Our eyes meet and a blush blooms all over my body. The silence lengthens. My breathing isn't working in its normal way and I can't believe he can't hear my heart pounding. He leans forward and then stops, an unspoken question hovering in the space between us. I answer it by moving closer still and placing my lips on his. His kiss is soft and tender and as he slides his hands up the sides of my neck, running his fingers through my hair, I let out a soft exhalation of pleasure. It's so good to be touched after so long without physical contact with anyone except my children, who are only ever wanting comfort instead of giving it. I allow myself to sink into his kiss, inhabiting my body for the first time in months, allowing my mind to be still and blank.

When we pull apart, he smiles and strokes my cheek.

'God, I've been wanting to do that for twenty-four years.'

'What?' I draw back, confused. 'I thought ... what d'you mean?'

'Forget it.' Owen shakes his head as if trying to shrug off what he's said. 'Sorry, I didn't mean that. I just meant I've been wanting to do that for a while. In fact, I'd like to do it again as soon as possible.' He leans in again but I shrink away.

'You've been wanting to kiss me since ... ever since we met? Since Andrew's twenty-first party?'

'You must remember. You and I were talking when you first got there. I liked you then. I liked you first. But I never said anything once you were with Andrew. I would never have tried to ruin things between you because I thought – I mean, I knew he loved you. If I'm honest, the hardest thing about the break-up wasn't losing Saffie, it was losing you. That's not too weird, is it?'

'I suppose not.' But it is. I run over all the times he and I have spent together over the years, alone or with Saffie and Andrew. Was he looking at me then? Did he want to kiss me, touch me? I get up and fuss around the kitchen, putting the milk away and wiping imaginary crumbs off the side.

'Did Andrew know? That you ... liked me?'

'No. I never told him. I could see that you loved him and I wanted you to be happy. But since he died, I've loved spending more time with you. I feel like I've got you back. You said yourself earlier that I've been a support to you, that there's something between us that's more than friends. You can feel that, can't you?'

'Yes.' I can't really say anything else as I've just kissed him, but I'm beginning to suspect I've made a horrible mistake. I've lost my husband, I'm lonely and although I hate to admit it, I'm vulnerable.

'I'm sorry, Owen, but would you mind leaving? I need time to think, to process all this.'

'Of course,' he says. 'I'll give you a call later.'

I follow him to the hallway, weak with relief. He opens the door and turns to say goodbye.

'Don't forget your jacket.' I grab it from the peg and hold it out towards him. He reaches out, but when I see it properly, it slips from my grasp, my hand limp and lifeless. Owen bends to retrieve it, but when he straightens up he sees the look on my face.

'What's the matter, Liz? Are you OK?'

'Did you . . . ' I clear my throat and try again. 'Did you have that jacket with you in Italy?'

'Yes. I wasn't sure if I'd need a coat, but I was glad of it in the evening.'

He slips his arms into it, the material flattening and smoothing as he does, displaying, on each sleeve, three fluorescent, yellow stripes. It wasn't Julian that Trina saw heading down to the cove with Andrew. It was Owen.

Chapter 45

Andrew

SATURDAY NIGHT, VILLA ROSA

Andrew sat on the wall at the end of the garden to wait for Owen. It was deathly quiet and everything was cast in an unearthly light by the large, bright moon and the stars that sprinkled the night sky. His head spun. It wasn't that late but he'd been drinking fast and angrily, as if alcohol could neutralise the acid that curdled inside him.

Eventually, he heard the grumble of a distant engine, and saw two pinpricks of light that appeared and disappeared as Owen made his way towards him through the rolling hills. The engine stopped, and a few minutes later he heard Owen's footsteps.

'Thank God,' Andrew said. 'I've been dying to talk to you all night.'

'I've left the car in a layby down on the lane – is that OK? Do you want to walk back with me and we can go for a drive?'

'Not really.' Andrew feared the motion would make the head spinning morph into full-blown nausea. 'Shall we walk down to the beach? The steps are not far.'

Andrew went first. Owen had to reach out and steady him a couple of times before they reached the bottom.

'Wow, the tide's far in,' Owen said, the curling breakers just visible in the starlight, ten or so metres from the cliff face.

'Yeah, apparently the owners said it comes all the way in at high tide, there's no beach at all.'

'We'd better be careful,' Owen said. 'I'll keep an eye out.'

'We'll be fine,' Andrew said with the confidence of the hammered. 'Let's sit here by these rocks, and then we're not far from the steps if we need to make a quick exit.'

'What happened tonight?' Owen said once they were sitting on the sand facing the sea, the rock face digging into their backs.

'It was an absolute shitshow, mate. I probably had a bit too much to drink.'

'I hope you haven't made yourself unpopular on my account. I don't need you to fight my battles for me. Coming out here has brought it home to me that I need to move on.'

'I always have, though, haven't I, mate? Back at school, I always looked out for you when the other boys were taking the piss out of your accent and your clothes and all that. All I've done this weekend is tell a few home truths. It's not my fault if people didn't want to hear them.'

'What, not about Trina?'

'No, no. I didn't give away any secrets ... I don't think.' Andrew's memory of the confrontation around the table was hazy.

'What about Liz? Did you tell her about Trina?'

'No.'

'You're going to have to, you know.'

'All right, all right! I know I am. Jesus.'

'It's not fair on her otherwise.'

'I know, Owen! She's my wife, not yours.'

'What's that supposed to mean?' Owen sounded defensive, upset.

'I know you liked her, that first night we met her.'

'Yes, I did. But so what? She chose you.'

'I may have given her a bit of help with that.' Andrew had a sense that he shouldn't be saying this, that he should stop, but he'd never had an argument with Owen before and he didn't know the rules.

'What?'

If Andrew hadn't been so drunk, he would have heard the note of danger.

'I might have given her a little nudge in my direction, that's all. But it's water under the bridge now, isn't it?'

'What did you say to her?'

Owen got to his feet, his voice rising.

'Calm down, mate.' Andrew stood up too, staggering. 'What's your problem?'

'What did you say to her?' Owen repeated.

'I told her you had a girlfriend back home, and that

317

you'd cheated on her while you were at uni. Look, mate, it's not a big deal. It was years ago. I could see she kind of liked us both. I just wanted to give myself a chance. Let the best man win, and all that.'

'No big deal? But you lied to her. I was never in the race. Of course you were going to win. You always do. You were brought up to win. With the money and education and confidence your background gives you, there's no way you can fail. You're so fucking privileged and you can't even see it.'

'Don't give me that. We're talking about getting off with a girl almost twenty-five years ago, not getting a job because of the old boy network. It's got nothing to do with your bloody council estate.'

'It does. Everything does. You couldn't let me have that one thing, could you? If you hadn't lied to her, she could have ended up with me instead.'

'So what? You ended up with Saffie.'

'Yeah, and look how that turned out. I should never have married her in the first place. She was never the one for me.'

'What, and Liz was?' Andrew can't hide his incredulity.

'Yes! I only stepped back because I thought she'd chosen you, and you were my best mate. And I thought, well, if they stay together, at least I still get to see her all the time. But now Saffie's left me, I've been left behind. You've all chosen her and Todd over me and I'm going to be frozen out. I'll never get to see Liz again.'

'Jesus Christ! We're not going to be able to see you after

this anyway. I can't believe you've been … creeping on Liz all these years. She'll be disgusted when she finds out.'

'Will she? There's nothing disgusting about it. I love her. But I've kept that a secret because I wanted her to be happy. Will she really be disgusted by that? Or will she be disgusted that you cheated on her, that your marriage is based on a lie? That you have a daughter who was conceived while her and you were together?'

'I can't believe this! She's my wife! How can you compare what we feel for each other with your weird crush? Do you seriously think she would have ended up with you if I hadn't said anything? You're kidding yourself!'

'She liked me.' Owen's eyes glittered. 'At that party, before she met you, she liked me. We've got much more in common than you and her. I know she did. So yes, I do think she could have ended up with me. Or with someone else who wasn't my best friend. She's much too good for you. I've always known it. This has just confirmed it.'

'Fuck you.' Andrew took a drunken swing at Owen, his fist connecting with his cheekbone. Andrew clasped his hand. It bloody hurt. He'd never hit anyone before in his life. Owen held his face, looking at Andrew in disbelief.

'Are you serious?' he said.

'Deadly,' Andrew said. 'You're a joke. You're pathetic. If I hadn't let you hang around with me at school you would have spent seven years being bullied. You should be on your knees thanking me. Even your own wife didn't want you. She came on to me before she met Todd.'

'What the hell are you talking about?'

'It was that night I came round for dinner, about … ooh … eight months ago? You were held up at work. Saffie tried to kiss me. It wasn't the first time either. She tried it once before, at my twenty-first birthday party – the same night I met Liz. So don't try and tell me you're better than me, because nobody will ever prefer you over me. What did you think you were doing, turning up here? How fucking sad is that? Liz would never look at you in a million years. Not if you were the last man on earth.' He couldn't stop the bile spewing from his mouth, things he half thought but had never intended to say. 'You'll never see either of us again after this.'

'We'll see about that.' Owen was pale and determined in the starlight as he drew his fist back and smashed it into Andrew's face. Already unsteady from drinking, Andrew's legs went from under him and he fell backwards, a terrifying crack ringing out as his skull connected with the sharp edge of the rocky outcrop that spidered out from the base of the cliff. Pain exploded from the point of impact, scissoring through him. The sand was damp and grainy against his cheek, and he fought to stay awake, knowing he mustn't slip under.

Owen stood over him, his eyes wide with shock.

'Please … help me,' Andrew spoke as loudly as he could but he was drowned out by the sound of the sea.

Owen looked wildly around, up and down the beach and towards the house. Andrew couldn't tell if he was searching for help or for confirmation that no one had seen what happened.

'Sorry,' Andrew managed to get the word out. It was imperative to get Owen back on his side. He wanted to explain that he hadn't meant all of the things he'd said in the heat of the moment. The weekend had left him tired and angry and unsettled, and he'd taken it out on the one person he thought he was safe with. He tried to say all this but the pain was too much. Darkness seeped into his vision.

Owen took hold of his ankles and for one blissful moment Andrew thought he was going to try and carry him to the villa, but incomprehension morphed into terror as it dawned on him that they were going the wrong way. Owen was dragging Andrew towards the sea, not taking any care, bumping him over the rocks in his path, ripping Andrew's skin. When he got to the water's edge, Owen gave him a final heave into the shallows, his breath coming in short, panicked gasps.

Andrew tried to form words, but no sound came out. He willed his eyes to stay open, to remain fixed on Owen. Owen grimaced in pain, let out one choking cry and turned to walk away.

'Help me!' Andrew used every ounce of strength he had left and this time his voice rang out, audible above the sound of the waves. Owen paused for a second, and strode on without looking back.

The water that the others had insisted was so inviting earlier that morning lapped hungrily around him, cold and black. Andrew felt his life ebbing from him. He closed his eyes.

Chapter 46

Liz

'Your jacket. You were there.' The words are out of my mouth before I have a chance to think them through.

'What? Where?' he says, concerned, taking a step towards me.

'Your jacket,' I repeat stupidly, my tongue thick. It feels like all the moisture has left my mouth. 'On the beach. That night. You were there. With Andrew. Trina saw your jacket. She thought it was Julian. But it was you.'

'No,' he says, but the colour has drained from him. He knows that I know he's lying.

'The police don't know you were in Italy. Why haven't you told them?' I can't believe this wasn't the first thing I asked him.

'I was scared,' he says. 'I know it's stupid but I worried they wouldn't believe me.'

'I don't believe you,' I say, my words almost swallowed by the fear that is rising inside me.

'You have to,' he says urgently. 'I don't want there to

322

be any secrets between us, not now I know how you feel about me.'

'But I don't ... I'm not ... Owen, I shouldn't have kissed you, it was ...'

'It was an accident,' he says, his eyes burning.

'The kiss?' I say, but it hits me with a sinking sensation that's not what he means.

'No, Liz.' He steps closer. I can feel the heat of his body and I suppress a shudder. I can't get any further away, my back against the wall, pressed up against my children's coats on their pegs. 'Andrew. It was an accident.' The air settles around his words. They sit there in the space between us like a gaping wound. 'You believe me, don't you?'

'I don't understand.' My voice is little more than a whisper.

'It's always been you, Liz. Saffie was never anything but a second choice for me. When we split up, it was losing you that scared me the most. I can't bear the thought of it. I wasn't thinking straight.'

'Do you ... know what happened to Andrew?'

'It was an accident,' he repeats.

'You need to go to the police.'

'No. It's too late. They won't believe me. All that matters is that you believe me. You do, don't you?'

There's a strange intensity about him that ties my stomach in a knot. I don't understand how things have changed so quickly.

'Liz, you have to believe me. You have to forgive me.'

'What did you do, Owen?' I don't think I really want to know, but it's too late now.

'I didn't hurt him.'

He's so close to me I can smell his sweat, see the pulse ticking in his neck.

'It was an accident,' he says again. 'He was drunk, and he fell and hit his head on a rock. I checked his pulse but there was nothing. He was dead. There was nothing I could do. But I knew if I called the police, they'd say I'd hurt him. So I . . . left him there. But I swear to God there was nothing I could have done. Nothing that would have helped him – it was too late.'

I want to believe him. I can't bear to conceive of a world where Andrew's best friend hurt him or meant to kill him. But if it was an accident, why didn't he raise the alarm, call an ambulance?

'You have to tell the police,' I say again.

'You don't understand! They'll say I did it deliberately. If we keep quiet, this will all blow over. And then . . . we can be together.'

'I . . . don't know about that . . . ' Every fibre of my being screams out against it. The scales have been lifted from my eyes and it's suddenly so clear that anything I thought I felt for Owen recently was no more than a desire to be loved, wanted, thought of – a place to put my love for Andrew, now that it has nowhere to go. 'It's too soon. I'm not ready.'

'What? But just now you said . . . You said you feel it too. You know we've always been close, Liz. We're the same, you and me. We didn't grow up like the others with everything handed to us on a silver plate. We understand each other better than anyone else does. We always have. Andrew didn't love you like I do. I've been waiting all this time.'

'Andrew loved me.' I need to hold onto that.

'Not like I do,' he repeats. 'We've got something special, something different. Something you never had with Andrew.'

'What do you know about what I had with Andrew?' Despite the fear that's building in me, anger flares. 'We were happy. We loved each other.' There's a release in saying it out loud, having spent so much time mistrusting him after I found the condom in his bag.

'He only loved himself.' Owen almost spits the words.

'No.' I need to hold on to what I know to be true about Andrew. 'He loved me.'

'Do you really believe that? He didn't even tell you when he found out Trina had his daughter!'

'You . . . you knew about that?' I say, bewildered.

'He told me in Italy. I kept it from you because it wasn't my place to tell you, and because I didn't want to hurt you any further. That's how much I care about you.'

'Owen, you need to leave.' I can't take any more of this.

'No! You need me, Liz. You always have. Do you know, when I walked away from Andrew, he wasn't thinking about you? He was thinking about himself, like always – the last words he called after me weren't even about you.'

'What?' My body contracts, every nerve tingling. 'You said he was dead when you left him.'

A sheen of sweat coats Owen's face, beading on his upper lip. There's a twitch in his jaw.

'No, I said ... he was ... he assaulted me.'

'But you said ... he fell ...'

'He did, he fell. There was a struggle. I was just defending myself.'

'You said he was dead when you left him,' I repeat. My God. 'You said there was nothing you could do. But now you're saying he called after you.'

Owen's shoulders drop in defeat and he moves away from me. I take a gulp of air.

'I just wanted you and me to be together.'

'I'm sorry, Owen.' I reach out a tentative hand to him. If I can placate him, make him believe that I'm truly sympathetic, maybe I can get him out of the house. His hand snakes up and grabs my wrist, biting into it.

'I didn't mean to hurt him.'

'I know,' I say, trying to control the tremble in my voice. 'Of course you didn't. It's OK.'

He relinquishes his grip on my wrist and takes a half-step back. I lean against the wall to steady myself.

'I won't tell anyone,' I say, attempting to sound as if I mean it. I need to get him out of here.

'You will.' His eyes brim with tears. 'I thought I could trust you, but I can't.'

'You can,' I say hopelessly.

He cups my face, looking down at me with unbearable

sorrow and tenderness. I keep my neck rigid, not wanting or able to relax under his touch. The atmosphere is charged, heavy with the threat of what is about to happen.

My brain is frozen but my body knows it is in danger. Almost without thinking, I duck and swoop to my left in one fluid movement, heading towards the front door and freedom. I'm halfway there when from behind Owen grabs hold of me, pinning my arms to my sides. There have been so many times since Andrew died when I've welcomed his embrace – when it has been a place of safety. Of home. Now, suddenly, it's a prison. The scales have tipped and neither of us can pretend any longer that Owen hasn't done something monstrous, the enormity of which I can hardly comprehend.

He drags me backwards away from the door and into the kitchen. I strain, my legs kicking ineffectually, but I'm nowhere near strong enough. Holding me tightly with one arm, he twists me around to face him and slams me against the wall. Before I know it, his hands are around my throat. Any energy I might have had to fight back drains from my limbs.

'I'm sorry,' he says. 'I never wanted you to know.'

I try to speak but I can't get the air in, can't move. Can't breathe. Spots float into my vision and all I can think of is my boys, my darling boys who have already lost so much.

'I can't go to prison. I can't let that happen,' I hear him say through the haze. 'I'd never survive it. And then there's Seb and Milo . . . it's not fair on them.'

Then the doorbell rings. He freezes. We stand for

twenty seconds or so, as if suspended in time. It rings again, and we hear a voice through the letter box.

'Liz! Are you home? It's me.' Oh God, it's Poppy.

Owen releases my neck and slams his hand across my mouth, his eyes fixed on mine. I get the message. If I call out, ask for help, and she forces her way in somehow, he will hurt her too.

'Liz! Please let me in. I'm sorry. I'm so sorry.'

Tears run down my face. If I get out of this – and the fact that it's an 'if' chills me to the bone – the first thing I will do is tell her I forgive her. I know her as well as I know myself; she would never have done what she did if she hadn't been truly desperate. I should have known that all along. The flap of the letter box clinks shut and another scrap of hope dies. Owen leans against me more heavily, pinning me to the wall, his hands slipping back up to my neck.

'Liz, I'm sorry. I didn't want it to be like this,' he says. I claw uselessly at his chest. Adrenaline is pumping through me, giving me strength, but he's taller and heavier and stronger and I don't stand a chance of fighting him off. His fingers dig further and further in, pressing into my flesh. I try helplessly to suck in air but it won't come. The blackness creeps ever closer and I have no choice but to give in, my body going limp.

Then there's a crash. The pressure on my neck vanishes. The kitchen inches slowly into focus, and when my vision sharpens I see Poppy standing inside the glass bifold garden doors like an avenging angel, shattered glass scattered around her like confetti, a decorative stone owl in her grasp. I open my mouth but what comes out is nothing more than a rasp.

'Leave her alone,' she says.

He pushes me roughly aside, correctly assuming I'm no threat in my current condition, and strides towards Poppy. I slide down to the floor, legs splayed out in front of me. He reaches for her, blind with fury. She opens her mouth and screams one word that reverberates around the house.

'No!'

As if in a dream, I watch her arm fly back and with all her strength she swings the owl towards the side of his head where it connects with a sickening crack.

There is silence. Poppy stands red-faced and panting. With every breath, my chest heaves, my throat stinging with the pin-sharp blades of a thousand razors. We stare at each other in horror, in relief. It is over.

Chapter 47

Liz

'He's going to be OK. Severe concussion, but nothing worse.'

The police have been very supportive, keeping me informed about Owen's condition. I know the doctors were worried he would have suffered a traumatic brain injury, but it seems he's escaped that, although whether he'll escape prosecution for Andrew's murder is another story.

'Oh, thank God.' Poppy puts her cup down with a trembling hand. 'I haven't been able to stop thinking about what would happen to me if he was dead.'

'Surely it would have been a clear-cut case of self-defence?'

'We know that, but who knows how a lawyer would have tried to twist it?'

It's so good to have Poppy back in my kitchen – back in my life. She continues to apologise approximately a million times a day for lying to me about the business, despite my assurances that I've forgiven her. I understand that she was terrifyingly in debt and couldn't see another way out – apart from the one Todd was offering, and thank God she didn't take him up on that. I also – more than anyone – understand how her worries about Scarlet clouded her judgement. Being a single parent now myself, I have a better understanding of the weight she has carried all these years. It's not only all the things you physically have to do yourself – cook every single meal, wash every item of clothing, clean every toilet, floor and surface. It's not even that every single time your child has to go somewhere – be that school, club, social activity – it's you that has to take them. Those things are hard, but more than that, it's the mental load. Every time there's a decision to make, there's no one to talk it over with. Your friends are not invested in your child the way another parent would be, and they will never love them as a parent would. As a single parent, you carry every worry, sadness and fear your child has as if it were your own. Even the triumphs and joys lose something when there's no one to share them with.

I'd never properly appreciated what Poppy had to do until I was widowed, but now I understand the part her fears for Scarlet played in what she did. Scarlet's now going from strength to strength back at uni, and is continuing to seek help for her mental health. I'm looking forward too – we're even talking about me going into the business with Poppy, as I suggested before, but there's a lot to figure out.

'How are things between you and Trina?' Poppy asks.

'Much better. We sat down together and talked it through. What happened between her and Andrew was so long ago. Holding onto my anger about it is only going to hurt me – and her. And after everything I've been through, I need my friends more than ever.'

'What about Olivia?' Poppy asks.

'Trina and I are going to meet with her.'

'That's brilliant, Liz! I do think that's the right thing.'

'I do too. She's Andrew's flesh and blood. That's what he would have wanted. And it's nice for me to have another connection with him.'

'What about Julian? Do you know how he is with it?'

'Trina said he's getting there. I think they'll be OK. I spoke to Kitty too.'

'Wow, how is she?'

'Not great. Todd's still not speaking to her – neither is Saffie, for that matter. But she wanted me to know that Andrew had nothing to do with hiring the escorts for that meeting. It was the guy from DOSH who had arranged the whole thing, She said Andrew seemed really shocked and unhappy with it.'

'That was decent of her,' Poppy says. 'What about Saffie? Have you heard any more from her?'

'No, not a word.'

I confronted Saffie about the messages I found on Andrew's phone. She blamed her actions on being drunk, but that didn't wash with me. I've been able to forgive Trina for sleeping with Andrew, partly because it was so long ago but also because she didn't know me then, and Andrew had told her things were uncertain between him and I, which was true. But Saffie came on to Andrew less than a year ago. She cared more about propping up her fragile ego the only way she's ever known how than she did about our twenty-plus years of friendship. That I cannot forgive. What's more, Saffie is standing by Todd, still maintaining that Poppy is lying about Todd's horrendous offer of 'help'. I don't know if she is blinded by love, or frightened of Todd, or merely unwilling to give up the privileged lifestyle he can offer her. I try not to, but sometimes I can't resist checking out her Instagram feed. To her followers her life looks as amazing as ever, but I know it's rotten at its core.

'And how are the boys?' Poppy asks now.

'Good. Better. Getting there.'

Their lives will forever be divided into before and after this period, but I know they'll be OK. They have shown themselves to be extraordinarily resilient, and I've got them in to see a therapist so they're getting the help and support they need. Telling them what Owen did was incredibly tough, but Poppy has been there every step of the way to support me and help glue the pieces of their shattered world back together.

After Poppy has gone, I pick up Andrew's iPad, which the police have returned to me having taken everything they need. I scroll down the messages, not knowing what I'm looking for, wanting to find something, anything that will make me feel connected to Andrew. There's nothing. I close the messages and on a whim, open his Notes app. The top entry, dated the Saturday we were in Italy, is headed *Dear Liz*. It's a letter to me. I don't know whether this is a draft version of a message he planned to actually send to me, or if he was working out his feelings and I was never meant to see it. With my heart in my mouth, I tap on it.

Dear Liz

You feel so far away at the moment. I don't know if it's my fault or yours – no, scrap that, it's my fault. I've been keeping you at arm's length recently due to various things, and I want so much to talk to you about them. There are things in my past that I wish I could change, but I can't. I can only change the future and I'm going to make sure our future is amazing. You and the boys, our family, is the only thing that matters to me. I want

He either got interrupted or didn't know quite what he wanted to say, but the intention is clear. I'm assailed by memories – good ones, the ones that have refused to come over the last few months, having been overridden by the painful questions I was left with in the wake of his death. How he would spend hours on the floor with the boys when they were little, letting them climb all over him and inventing endless silly games that made them hysterical with laughter; his expression as I walked up the aisle on our wedding day – happy and proud and overwhelmed at his luck at marrying me, barely able to get his vows out through the tears; the nights we spent talking when we first got together, when we were so open and made ourselves so vulnerable. It felt like there'd never be enough time to say everything we had to say to each other.

I'm overcome by juddering sobs so violent I'm almost sick. Every ounce of grief I've stuffed down since I found the condom, every occasion where I've been ambushed by one of Andrew's possessions and put it aside with nothing more than a tightening of my lips, every time I've smiled when a friend has said how well I'm doing not falling apart – it all comes pouring out in an unstoppable wave of sorrow. I weep and weep for a man who wasn't perfect but who was doing his best. A man who loved me and our children beyond measure. A man with whom I had a lifetime of experiences that no one else will ever understand, and with whom I inhabited a shared world that no longer exists without him in it.

In the end, I am glad. Glad I made a life with him, despite the difficulties, despite the tragic way it ended. The only anger I have now is directed at Owen. Andrew loved him, and he repaid that love with nothing but violence. From the moment they met at school, Andrew took Owen, the scholarship boy with no friends, under his wing. Owen should have valued that more highly.

I'll never take my friends for granted, especially Poppy,

who has been with me through thick and thin. I could have lost her if I hadn't been able to forgive her, but I know I've made the right decision. She'll never hurt me or lie to me again.

Chapter 48

Poppy

'Can't sleep?'

Poppy knows who it is before she turns, and her heart sinks. Ever since Todd cornered her on Friday night, she hasn't been able to get his proposal out of her head. Her skin crawls at the repulsive prospect, but she can't let go of the idea that she could do it. She could close her eyes and get it over with – God knows she's done it before, as every woman has. She's done it to please a man, or to make him like her, or to keep him quiet, or out of a kind of dysfunctional politeness. Once or twice she's done it because she was scared not to. This wouldn't be so different, and afterwards she could replace the money into the agency's bank account with Andrew none the wiser, pay off her debts and have a secure home for Scarlet.

She gathers her robe tighter around her, wishing her ancient vest top did a better job of covering her cleavage.

337

Todd, amused, lets his eyes roam lazily over her breasts and lower, to where her robe has fallen open a little over her thighs.

'No. Thought I might as well get up rather than tossing and turning in bed.' As soon as the word 'tossing' is out of her mouth, she regrets it.

'Tossing and turning. Sounds interesting.'

He raises his eyebrows and Poppy smiles, conflicted. She wants to tell him to sod off, stop being such a disgusting perv, but she can't deny the fact that she's considering doing what he wants. She can't afford to piss him off completely.

'Have you thought any more about my offer?' he says.

'No.' She can't, won't look at him.

'Don't wait too long.' His tone has shifted, not teasing any more. 'I might change my mind.'

He walks over to the table where Poppy is sitting and lightly draws his index finger down the side of her face. She shudders. He lets it drift further, down the side of her neck and across her shoulder. She fights the urge to jerk away.

'Just a little preview,' Todd says. 'You may even find you enjoy it.' He brings his hand back up to cup her chin, forcing her to meet his gaze. 'Think about it and let me know.'

He goes back inside, but Poppy can still smell his cologne – citrus and sandalwood – and an earthier scent that emanates from the man himself. She scrubs at her cheek as if to wipe him off.

The moon is full and bright, the sky huge and sprinkled with stars that cast an unearthly glow over the lawn. The air is pleasantly cool compared to the heat of the day. In the silence, an owl hoots, and Poppy hears a rustling at the far end of the garden. She squints in the darkness, and sees a figure emerging up from the path that leads down to the cove. She assumes whoever it is will come on up to the house but they turn immediately left and head towards the driveway that leads to the lane outside. A minute or two later, a car engine springs into life, roaring away with a screech of tyres.

Intrigued, Poppy wanders down the lawn towards the cliff path, the grass damp and cool under her bare feet. Standing at the top of the steps that lead down to the beach, everything is silent apart from the rhythmic ebb and flow of the tide. It's almost all the way in, just a triangle of sand at the bottom of the steps. In the light of the moon, Poppy can make out a dark shape at the shoreline, breakers frothing over and over it. She makes her way down the steps. About halfway down, she understands what she's seeing and quickens her pace, but it's not until she's standing over the body, waves lapping at her feet, the hems of her pyjama legs sodden and clinging to her ankles, that she realises it's Andrew. One side of his head is swollen and bleeding. His eyes are closed and for a moment Poppy assumes he's dead, but then a rasp escapes his lips and his eyelids flicker. He's alive.

Poppy's breath is coming in short, frantic bursts. She looks towards the villa as if for help, but of course there's no one there. He must have stumbled down here drunk and hit his head – but no, the figure in the garden, the car screeching off into the night. What in God's name has happened here? She gets out her phone but there's no signal – it says emergency calls only but she has no idea what the number is in Italy. A large wave crashes into her, almost knocking her off her feet. Soon the tide will be all the way in. If she goes up to the house for help, Andrew could have been washed out to sea by the time they get back.

She reaches down, puts her hands under his armpits and tugs as hard as she can, but there's no way she's strong enough to move him on her own. In the dim light, and with the crashing of the waves, and the panic that courses through her, she can't even be sure he's still alive. For a second, she imagines what life would be like if he isn't. If he was dead, he would never have to find out about the money she has taken from the company. She knows they have partnership protection insurance that would mean she could buy the business and own it outright – she organised it herself. She could pay off her debts and stop dreading every knock on the door. She could provide the security for Scarlet she's always yearned for. The heaviness that has dogged her for the past few months would be lifted.

No. This is absurd. Andrew is not only her business partner, he's her friend. He's married to her best friend in the world. She must try and pull him further up the beach, away from the hungry waves, and run for help as

340

fast as she can. Then she remembers Todd running his finger down the side of her face. She thinks about where else he would want to touch her if she agrees to his proposal. What else he will do to her. If Andrew dies, she'll be able to throw Todd's loathsome offer back at him with all the contempt it deserves.

She looks down at Andrew's battered visage. She puts her fingers to his neck to try and feel for a pulse, but the waves keep throwing her off balance. The longer she prevaricates here, the further in the tide will be. Perhaps he is already dead. Poppy didn't do this to him, somebody else did. It's not her fault. If she leaves him here, she hasn't actually done anything bad. She has simply done nothing. Even if he isn't dead now, surely he soon will be, no matter what Poppy does.

The horror of what she is considering creeps into her bones, colder than the sea water around her knees. Could she live with herself if she did nothing, went back to bed, considered this episode a bad dream, a nightmare that never happened? Could she look herself in the eye? Could she look Liz in the eye? It would be hard, but not as hard as having to tell Scarlet their home has been repossessed, or that she's going to prison. Not as hard as getting into bed with Todd Blake, having to perform whatever degrading acts he has planned for her. She knows the kind of man he is. Just having sex with her will not be enough. He will want her to do things that will shame and humiliate her to the maximum possible degree.

341

She will not touch Andrew or look at him again, in case she sees him move or feels the blood pumping around his body. Andrew is dead. There is nothing to be done except support Liz in her time of need. She turns and makes her way back up the beach, her feet icy-cold and sand-gritty. Her nightclothes are soaked from the thighs down. If she hangs them over the bath and turns off the air conditioning, they'll be dry by morning. No one will ever know she was here.

Acknowledgements

Thanks as ever go to my fabulous agent, Felicity Blunt, and my brilliant publishing team especially editors extraordinaire Lucy Malagoni, Tilda MacDonald and Rosanna Forte.

To Roz Watkins for her insights into partnership protection insurance and how one partner might attempt to defraud another. Any mistakes are, as ever, my own.

To Tom Starks for providing some very helpful and comprehensive information on climbing, which eventually helped me decide that no one would die in a climbing accident in this book. Turns out climbing is a lot safer than you think.

To Graham Bartlett for his invaluable advice on police matters.

To all my writing friends, especially the Ladykillers. I'm often asked if writing is a cut-throat, competitive industry but in my experience it's the complete opposite. One of the best things about my mid-life career change to being an author is the friends I've made in the crime writing community, and the support we give each other.

To my friends, especially my first readers, Claire and Natasha. And my girls – Jane, Naomi and Rachel, and our darling Hattie, always remembered and loved.

To Michael, my late husband, who was such a huge supporter of my writing. This book is not about me, or you, but some of my experiences of young widowhood and single parenthood have seeped in. I miss you.

To my boys Charlie and Arthur, the best sons I could ever have wished for and in fact, two of the best people to have ever walked the earth.

And to Jon, who probably thought going out with a writer would be all glamorous parties and award ceremonies. I hope it hasn't been too much of a disappointment that it's mainly sitting around in a hoodie eating biscuits and moaning about plot holes. I love you.